WYOMING
WILD

WYOMING WILD

PROPER ROMANCE

SARAH M. EDEN

SHADOW
MOUNTAIN
PUBLISHING

Visit us at shadowmountain.com

PROPER ROMANCE is a registered trademark.

Library of Congress Cataloging-in-Publication Data
CIP on file
ISBN 978-1-63993-092-0

Printed in the United States of America
Lake Book Manufacturing, Inc., Melrose Park, IL

10 9 8 7 6 5 4 3 2 1

To the word "ain't,"
which doesn't usually get to appear in my writing
but, to my delight, peppered itself all over this story

Chapter 1

Wyoming Territory, 1876

Every day the Wild West grew a little less wild. At least in John Hawking's corner of it. Hawk, as he was known, was the US Marshal in Wyoming and for small parts of the surrounding territories. He'd cleaned up the area, overseen the running of it, and made it safer for those who called it home. He was focused and determined, dedicated to his work, and, according to a saloon owner in Cheyenne, possessed a heart of stone. He'd thanked the man for that assessment and worn the label with pride ever since.

Soft hearts didn't save lives.

He rode alongside two of his deputies, Ensio Cooper and Paisley O'Brien, into the town of Sunset, a tiny place not far from Laramie. Word had reached him that two men, wanted for a long string of bank robberies, had gone into hiding in this small hamlet. The lawbreakers in Wyoming Territory could do themselves a favor if they learned a simple truth: no one hid from Hawk for long.

"I have it on good authority that the criminal element hibernates in the winter," Ensio said. "Seems to me we could avoid the misery of a cold-weather roundup if we remembered that."

"You have it on *Hawk's* authority that these two are in Sunset," Paisley said.

"Hawk's getting old. We have to wonder if he's . . ." Ensio pulled a face meant to imply that Hawk had been dropped on his head a few times.

Hawk and his entire team of deputies knew Ensio well enough to take his ridiculousness in stride. He was a fine deputy, reliable in a pinch, and smart as a whip, which made his near-constant joking more endurable.

"Stop your bawling," Hawk said. "It's never too cold to clean up the territory."

"Maybe not for the two of us, but Paisley, here, is riding in a dress. That's gotta be one devil of a breeze."

"And yet," Paisley said, "I ain't the one complaining."

She was the only woman among Hawk's deputies and, as far as he knew, the only woman "officially" part of the US Marshal's program. He knew of a handful of ladies who acted in a law enforcement capacity, either by necessity or choice, and most of them received no credit for what they did.

"You don't suppose these no-good bums would agree to be apprehended somewhere near a roaring fire and a pot of hot coffee?" Ensio wasn't actually a featherweight; he just enjoyed talking more than any deputy marshal should.

"Bring 'em in," Hawk said, "and I'm sure Sheriff Jones'll give you all the coffee and blankets and bed warmers you could want. Might even invite you to stay permanently so you can round up criminals any time he needs you to."

"I wouldn't mind hanging my hat here." Ensio adjusted his coat collar, keeping one hand on his horse's reins. "Near enough to Laramie for a bit of a lark."

"Hawk's deputies don't have larks," Paisley said. "Or if they do, they don't tell him about them."

Hawk tended toward somberness when faced with a dangerous undertaking, but he smiled despite the looming mission ahead. "Are you calling me a tyrant?"

"Are you claiming you ain't one?" Ensio tossed back. "The preacher'd have something to say about you casually tossing around a fib of that size."

"Shut your flapper, Ensio," Paisley said. "Hawk will knock your teeth out if you don't."

Ensio shook his head. "Hawk likes me. He'll leave these pearlies right where they are."

They kept their badges hidden beneath their coats as they rode into the outskirts of Sunset. No point tipping their hand. They hitched their horses down the boardwalk from the jail. Hawk had been in Sunset a few times during the previous sheriff's time in charge. He knew the layout.

The walk toward the jail gave them time to study their surroundings, something he didn't even have to tell his deputies to do. He recruited the best he could find, then improved on their training. His team ran as well as a fine-tuned watch. He wouldn't abide anything less.

Sheriff Jones was watching for them. He ushered them in quickly, closing the door behind them.

"Marshal Hawking," the sheriff greeted.

Hawk nodded. "Have you been keeping an eye on our criminals?"

Jones nodded. "They're in the saloon. Went in about ten minutes ago and haven't left." He gave Hawk a wanted poster with the faces of two men sketched on it. "This is them."

Hawk knew who they'd come for, and he'd studied their poster enough to be fully aware of what they looked like. He eyed his deputies. "Either of you need a reminder glance?"

They shook their heads. Neither was the type to have arrived unprepared. Hawk returned the poster. "Ensio, you go in now. Get the lay of the place. Badge hidden. Position yourself to cover any vulnerabilities. Jones and I will follow in a few minutes."

Ensio gave a quick nod and sauntered out. He had the rough-and-tumble look of the West and a knack for assuming whatever demeanor suited the situation, blending in as easily on a cattle ranch as he did in a seedy watering hole.

Hawk turned to Paisley. "Did you spy a good lookout spot? You'll need an unimpeded view of the front of the saloon. Ensio won't let them escape out the back."

"If you don't let them escape out the front, I'll have a nice leisurely afternoon."

"You ain't as much a fan of leisure as you're making yourself out to be." Hawk re-pinned his badge on his chest where it would be visible. Unlike Ensio, he needed his authority to be known the minute he walked into the saloon with the sheriff.

Jones stepped up directly beside him and lowered his voice. "You've brought a woman?"

"That woman is a Deputy US Marshal," he said. "And she can outshoot Cade O'Brien."

Jones's mouth dropped open. "No one outshoots Cade O'Brien. The man's a legend."

"I've seen her do it," Hawk said. "She's here as our sharpshooter. If you don't want her help because she's female, I'll fetch my other deputy, and we'll be on our way."

Jones shook his head quickly, a bit of worry entering his eyes. "I ain't complaining, only surprised."

Paisley took it in stride; it certainly wasn't the first time this had happened. She slipped the strap of her Springfield rifle off her shoulder and flipped open the trapdoor breechblock, checking to make certain her weapon was properly loaded. She had it closed up again and slung back in place in a flash.

"I'll assume my position," she said. "Consider the front of the saloon secured." She nodded to Hawk and slipped out.

Hawk leaned his shoulder against the front window frame, eyeing the street beyond. It was quiet. That would help.

"Should we be heading to the saloon?" Jones asked.

"Patience, Jones. Most of a battle's won or lost before it starts."

Hawk watched Paisley casually cross the wide street, unlikely to draw much attention even with her gun slung across her back. She positioned herself against a porch post across the street from the saloon. An excellent spot for her role in all this. Ensio should be in place by now as well, with a full understanding of the situation inside.

Jones needed to calm himself a bit, so Hawk chose to wait a few extra minutes. The man wasn't a bad sheriff, but he was inexperienced.

"How soon until you hire a deputy?" Hawk asked. "You're too close to Laramie for the law in this town to be lax."

"I have a couple of people in mind."

"After we get the ruffians locked up, tell me who your candidates are. We'll have it sorted before I go." He wasn't about to leave while Sunset was a liability. His territory would be safe. It was his most specific and unwavering goal. A man didn't dedicate himself to a cause unless he was willing to put in all his effort.

Hawk adjusted his gun belt, making certain his matching pistols sat in the optimum spot for drawing quickly and accurately. "We'll walk into the saloon together, but with you one step ahead of me. This town needs to see that their sheriff demands attention and exudes authority. My team and I need to look like the helpers not the doers."

"I'm not incompetent," Jones insisted.

"I know you ain't. You're just outgunned."

The sheriff gave a quick nod of acknowledgment. "But not for long."

"Let's do this." Hawk pointed him out the door.

They walked down the boardwalk. Hawk kept only the smallest bit behind Jones. A show of solidarity would go far.

The sun was blazing, but the air was cold. Winter would be on them soon enough. In another six weeks, give or take a few, the snow would be permanent until spring. It would make their job more difficult; Ensio was right on that score.

The familiar twank of a poorly tuned piano floated out through the saloon's swinging doors—the siren song of drinking establishments in the West. Hawk's work took him to enough that he knew the sounds and smells of them well.

Jones threw open the doors and walked inside without hesitation, head high, shoulders squared. The man's courage was impressive and reassuring. He'd do fine once he had the help he needed.

A hush fell over the saloon, the piano ending on a clash of notes. All eyes turned to them. Hawk moved to stand beside Jones, presenting a unified front. He swept open his coat to reveal his six-shooters and offer an even better view of his US Marshal's badge.

"Rod Carlisle. Hepp Minor," Jones said. "You're coming with us."

The two men, bearing a close resemblance to the images on the wanted poster, sat beside each other at a nearby table. They both rose, eyes on Hawk and Jones.

"Marshal Hawking." Hawk introduced himself with an upward twitch of his chin. "You've likely heard of me, which means you know I'd still outdraw you on my deathbed. So, come peaceably."

"I ain't going to jail," Hepp said.

"Jail or the graveyard," Jones tossed back. "You can pick."

The other occupants of the saloon backed swiftly away, clear of what might soon be flying bullets.

"There are two of us and two of you," Hepp said. "Not bad odds."

"Correction, chum," Ensio said, flipping his coat back to flash his badge. "There are three of us."

"And more outside," Hawk added. "Trust me, compadre, the odds ain't in your favor at all. And, personally, I prefer you take the graveyard option. Keeps life interesting. Well, *my* life, anyway."

Rod eyed his partner, then the three law officers. "We choose jail." He spoke firmly, calmly, no hint of apprehension. "It's not a bad option."

Hawk nodded. Rod, then, was the leader of the duo, while Hepp was the hothead. Both would bear watching.

No matter that he'd said otherwise, Hawk preferred bringing people in without bloodshed. But the smugness in Rod's face and tone didn't sit well. A man surrounded by lawmen and facing the noose wouldn't look that content if he didn't have something up his sleeve.

"Weapons on the table," Jones said. "Then back away with your hands on your heads."

"And remember, you've one gun already drawn and aimed at your backs," Hawk said. "And you're about to have one at your front as well. No sudden moves, no tricks."

They complied, and Jones and Ensio had the men firmly in hand a moment later. Hawk gathered the bank robbers' six-shooters and followed them all out of the saloon.

"We've a sharpshooter trained on the both of you," Jones warned. "Best shot in the West, I'm told. You'd do well not to test that, as learning the answer would be fatal."

The miscreants were dragged back to the jail and tossed behind bars. An easier feat than Hawk had expected. Far too easy, in fact. Rod looked pleased as a skunk in moonlight. Hepp grumbled a great deal but had made no attempt at resistance. These men hadn't been peaceable during their robberies. That they'd simply turn themselves over didn't make any sense.

"Ensio, you stay here in Sunset until these louts get dragged to Laramie," Hawk said. "They look about as disappointed as a flea in a doghouse."

He nodded. "They *are* a touch too comfortable with it all."

Hawk took a seat near the potbelly stove across the room. Jones sat at a desk nearby. With Ensio at the front window and Paisley still patrolling the street, things were likely to remain calm for a while.

"Tell me about your candidates for deputy sheriff." Hawk spoke to Jones but never stopped studying the prisoners. They were entirely at their ease in that cell.

Jones told him of two different men in town. Both seemed qualified and, he said, had expressed some interest in the position.

"Does the town have money enough for two deputies?"

"Might. Might."

"See if you can hire them both," Hawk said. "If not, pick the one you work best with, the one you'd trust most to have your back in a tight situation. Good with a gun, gritty, and fast on his feet are only part of the qualifications for the job. You have to work effortlessly with each other. And you have to trust each other entirely. If you don't, the whole thing falls apart."

"Is that your secret to keeping this territory together, Marshal?" Jones asked. "I'd say you're doing a shockingly good job of it."

"I don't abide yellowbellies, double-crossers, or second-guessers. A flawless network of deputies and sheriffs, anyone involved in keeping the peace, is the only thing that'll keep order out West. Otherwise, it's lawlessness and anarchy."

Across the room, Rod laughed low.

"You findin' something amusing, there, prisoner?" Hawk asked.

"You don't know your 'flawless network' as well as you think you do, Marshal."

Hawk sat up straighter, eyeing the man. He looked as sincere as he did amused. "You've spied a weak link in my chain?"

"A sheriff who's a . . . Well, let's just say he's a good friend of *my* flawless network."

That had Ensio's attention as well.

"What sheriff?" Hawk asked.

Rod smiled crookedly. "I ain't a snitch."

"You'd be amazed how many jailbirds sing when they're eyeing a noose," Hawk observed dryly.

Rod kept his mouth shut after that, refusing to say a word. Hepp's comments were limited to his certainty he would have come out champion in the gun battle Rod had denied him.

As Jones made final preparations to hire his deputies and Ensio saw himself settled for his extended stay, Hawk mulled over Rod's words. A sheriff Hawk didn't know well. One who put the lie to his insistence the territory was well managed. A liability. A weak link.

As he and Paisley rode from Sunset, heading in the general direction of Savage Wells, the town they both called home, he couldn't shake the blaring of intuition in his brain. "Have you heard whispers of any inept or corrupt sheriffs?"

"I ain't," she said. "Have you?"

"Not until today."

She watched him, brows drawn. "Cade hasn't mentioned any either, and he's got a lot of ears to the ground."

Cade O'Brien, the legendary lawman, was sheriff of the town Hawk called home. He was also Paisley's husband.

"Ask him when we get back. I'll send around a few telegrams."

She nodded. "You really think there's a double-crosser in the territory?"

"Might be. Might not be," he said. "But one thing's for certain: if there's a snake in the grass out there somewhere, then I won't rest until I have myself a new pair of snakeskin boots."

Chapter 2

Sand Creek, Wyoming Territory

For twenty-three years, Liesl Hodges had barely resisted the temptation to spit in her father's food. Her forbearance ought to have been chronicled in history books and guides to saintliness. She would have settled for a cash reward, but her father would simply have confiscated it to spend on drinks at the saloon or gambled it away. Saintliness was not *his* area of expertise.

"You're running close to the line, Liesl." Mother cast worried eyes at the mantel clock.

"I see the time," she said. "I won't be late."

It was lunchtime, and Liesl had been required to bring her father his midday meal ever since he'd become sheriff. As it was Thursday, his cronies would be at the jailhouse for their weekly poker game and would all be expecting to be fed.

"He'll be in a rage if you aren't on time." Mother didn't actually need to tell Liesl that; they were both well acquainted with her father's temper.

"But his rages are so educational," Liesl said. "I learn a great many new and exciting words."

Her mother sometimes joined in Liesl's lightheartedness, but not when Father was the topic of discussion. Humor was Liesl's escape. Mother, it seemed, didn't have one.

With her arm hooked through the handle of the lunch hamper, Liesl moved toward the door of their small and increasingly shabby house. "Wish me luck with the Charming Chaps."

"I'll do better than that. I'll pray."

"Ooh. If you discover heaven is accepting requests, I would be very appreciative of a team of elves to finish putting up the preserves. I am woefully behind schedule."

Mother shook her head, but she also smiled. Liesl preferred when Mother was smiling. That was a rare thing.

She stepped out of the house, walking jauntily and whistling to match. Anyone who didn't know her destination might actually believe she was happy to be making this particular delivery. In addition to being in complete control of her spit, she was a remarkably good actress. Though everyone in Sand Creek knew her father could be vicious, she made a show of everything being perfectly fine in her life. Some people had tried protecting her and Mother in the past, but it had only made things worse.

The little Harper boy flew past her, running at his usual breakneck speed. His mother chased after him.

"He went that way." Liesl pointed at the boy's back.

"That child's going to be the death of me," Mrs. Harper tossed back as she continued her pursuit.

Liesl shouted after her, "You'll catch him one of these days."

As she passed the carpentry shop, Mr. Moore nodded to her. "Headed to the jail?"

"I am going to turn myself in. My guilty conscience has finally gotten the best of me."

He laughed and waved her on. "No one would ever believe you guilty of a thing, Miss Liesl."

"If I don't quicken my step, our autocratic sheriff will find me guilty of being late with his lunch. That's likely a hanging offense in this town."

"Best not risk it," Mr. Moore said.

When she had been a little girl, Liesl had cowered anytime she had to be in her father's presence. She'd actually felt some relief five years earlier when he'd taken the job as sheriff. Not because she thought he'd be a better man for having taken the position or because he would be good for the town, but because he'd be gone most of the time.

She hadn't, however, realized how often she would be required to be part of his days. Still, she no longer hesitated when she reached the door of the jailhouse. She'd learned to do what was required of her, quickly and quietly, and move on, none the worse for the experience.

Not one of the four men in Father's Thursday crowd acknowledged her arrival. They never did, but it was best that way. While her father was the most volatile of the group Liesl referred to as the "Charming Chaps," none of them would ever be deemed harmless.

She moved a smaller table closer to where their game was being played. Once settled, she placed the basket on top. This had long ago become a memorized routine. Four plates set out. Food placed on each one.

More meat on Father's than anyone else's, otherwise he flew off the handle. More cobbler on Mr. Kirkpatrick's, otherwise he turned nasty—or rather, *nastier*. The same was true if she didn't spread a generous slab of butter on Mr. Dana's roll, or if she placed mustard, peaches, or string beans on Mr. Yarrow's plate.

The game continued without the slightest pause, the men talking over the dealing and drawing of cards.

"They're being taken to the prison in Laramie," Mr. Kirkpatrick said. "Near as I've been able to find out, they ain't squealed."

Father had his hand in any number of shady things. Liesl was never shocked by what she heard the men discuss: bank and train robberies, prison breaks, bribery, stealing, killing.

"How'd they get themselves caught, anyway?" Mr. Yarrow asked. "Thought they'd hidden out in a quiet spot with a turnip for a sheriff."

"US Marshal rode into town," Father grumbled. "He and his deputies surrounded the saloon. A regular ambush."

"Sure was a fine time before Marshal Hawking ruined it all." Mr. Dana snatched a plate off the table. Fortunately, Liesl had finished with it, and it wasn't the plate meant for Mr. Kirkpatrick or Father.

"Territory'd be far better off if he weren't meddling in everything." Father's glare settled on her. "Quit dawdling, girl."

She knew better than to respond. Without a glance, a smile, or a word of apology, she added a chicken leg to Father's plate, then set it beside him on the card table.

"Maybe Marshal Hawking'll do us a favor and come riding into town." Bits of potato flew from Mr. Dana's mouth as he spoke. "We could rid the world of a scourge."

Threatening fellow lawmen wasn't entirely unheard of from this group, but it wasn't usually spoken of so boldly and bitterly. Liesl tried to make it seem as though she wasn't hearing anything out of the ordinary as she set the last two plates beside their recipients, but worry was settling heavy in her chest.

"He ain't likely to come to Sand Creek," Mr. Kirkpatrick said. "Nothing of interest here. Anyone wanting to knock his hat off would have more opportunity in Savage Wells; he's there most of the time."

Father shook his head before the suggestion was done being spoken. "Cade O'Brien's sheriff there. He'd have a bullet in every one of us before we took a single breath."

"The marshal helped nab Rod and Hepp," Mr. Yarrow said. "He might go to Laramie for the sentencing."

Mr. Kirkpatrick scratched at his stubbled chin. "I ain't been to Laramie in ages. Might make a trip down."

Liesl quietly moved the serving table back to its place, but her ears remained pricked to their conversation.

"Do you know what Marshal Hawking looks like?" Mr. Yarrow asked.

"Someone there will," Mr. Kirkpatrick said. "He shouldn't be difficult to identify." He looked to Father. "What about you, Irwin? Wanna make a hunting trip?"

A hunting trip. Liesl's heart dropped to her toes.

Father shook his head. "Sand Creek needs a firm hand. I'll stay here. Between the three of you, someone ought to manage to pick the man off."

"The three of us?" Mr. Kirkpatrick shook his head. "We ain't limited to that."

"But do we bring in bird dogs or another gun?" Father wondered aloud.

As the men discussed their hunting trip, Liesl realized they were planning, in earnest, to assassinate a US Marshal. It was possible the talk was nothing but hot air, but she doubted it. A man's life was in danger. Yes, it was a man she'd never met and never heard of, but it was still a human life, and that made it worth saving. On that point, she and her father had differing views. Yet another firm argument against him acquiring sainthood, as if more reasons were needed.

"I'll be back for your plates," she said, moving toward the door.

"Don't interrupt, girl," Father snapped. "Keep your mouth shut."

She slipped out without another word. Normally, while the Charming Chaps ate their meal and planned any number of crimes, Liesl would take the opportunity to walk around town, greet a few people, and enjoy the last bit of warmth before winter settled in. But the felonious foursome were planning a murder. She tried not to think too hard on the fact that she knew with painful clarity that it wasn't their first.

I can't simply pretend I don't know. She'd be little better than they were if she did. And if they began killing lawmen who actually had integrity, there'd not be a single safe corner in all of Wyoming.

Father would beat her bloody if he had any idea what she was contemplating.

Mr. Yarrow was the telegraph operator in town. Mr. Dana ran the post office. Together, they controlled every communication in and out of town. But both were filling their mouths and flapping their gums in the jailhouse at that moment. If she were very fast, she could get a telegram out before returning to fetch their plates. Liesl had taught herself how to send and read telegrams when she was young and too naïve to realize she would never be permitted to send word of the true state of things in Sand Creek. She'd once tried slipping in to the telegraph office to send out a plea on behalf of her brother, but as soon as Mr. Yarrow had realized the contents of her telegram, he'd knocked her to the ground, away from the telegraph, and handed her over to her Father. She'd not tried again.

Until now.

If I get myself killed over this, my efforts had better receive their own chapter in that saintliness guide.

She moved casually down the street, waving to the people she knew but not pausing for conversations as she usually did. The roundabout way deposited her at the back of the telegraph office with no one the wiser. Father's tendency to lock her in rooms had necessitated her acquisition of both the tools and the skills to pick any lock presented to her. She had herself inside the office quick as a match strike.

Since the office was closed for lunch, the window coverings were pulled. No one would see her inside, which was a boon, but she also wouldn't see anyone approaching, which could invite danger. She needed to be fast.

She would direct the message to Savage Wells, the town where Marshal Hawking had his headquarters. She tapped the direction in, then began her message.

WARNING FOR MARSHAL HAWKING |STOP|
ASSASSINATION PLANNED IN LARAMIE |STOP|
HAWKING THE TARGET |STOP|
DO NOT REPLY OR ACKNOWLEDGE |STOP|
INFORMANT IN DANGER |STOP|

That should be enough to warn the marshal and to prevent Mr. Yarrow from realizing she'd sent a wire. Though, should word come back to Sand Creek, she could certainly be identified as the informant, having been present while the men were planning Hawking's fate and the Charming Chaps being aware that she knew how to send a telegram.

Father might literally kill her for sending this message, and he wouldn't have to arrange a "hunting trip" to do it.

Liesl made absolutely certain she'd not displaced anything or left footprints. She moved quickly and quietly to the back door where she'd let herself in. With her tools, she locked the door behind her. Mr. Yarrow would know something had happened if he sauntered back to work and the door simply opened.

She stood a moment at the now-secured door and breathed a sigh of relief. It all might yet go as bad as a trapdoor in a canoe, but she'd done her bit. Her hasty warning might keep the marshal on the right side of the ground.

With her eyes heavenward, she offered a quick plea. "It'd be more than my life's worth if any of the Charming Chaps sorts this out. A miracle or two'd be much appreciated."

Miracles were few and far between in Sand Creek. She'd learned it was best to do all she could to not need them.

She moved swiftly along the back of a few buildings so she'd re-emerge on the street somewhere other than directly beside the telegraph office. Slowing her steps so she'd not look to be in a hurry, she made her way back toward the jail. She'd not quite reached it when her father stepped out.

He eyed the street with a hard, narrowed glare, hand hovering near his gun. The few people milling about grew very still, eyes on him. He knew they were as scared of him as they'd be standing bare-foot in a nest of rattlers.

In a flash of hair and flying limbs, little Jamie Harper ran past. Liesl didn't have a chance to grab hold of him. Her father spied him in time to stick his boot out and trip him up, sending the boy sprawling onto the boardwalk.

Liesl bit back a gasp of shock and worry. Showing any measure of concern for those her father hurt always made things worse. She kept an eye on his gun hand. It didn't twitch. If Jamie had been a grown man rather than a six-year-old boy, he'd likely have been shot. Father had pulled his weapon on plenty of people for lesser things.

Jamie scrambled to his feet, wide eyes locked on the sheriff. The knees of the boy's pants were scuffed up. His hands were likely cut as well.

"Don't come runnin' past here again, y'hear?" Father growled at him.

"I won't, Sheriff." Jamie's voice shook. "Promise I won't." His eyes flicked to Liesl, standing on the other side of the sheriff from him. She made a tiny motion, urging him to slip off and get himself clean away.

Bless the heavens, the boy understood. He walked backward a few steps, before spinning around and ducking behind a building. Jamie had managed not to antagonize her father further. Maybe that was the miracle the heavens meant to send. They never sent more than one.

With quiet steps, Liesl slid into the jail. She was expected to clear the lunch things without disturbing anyone. She saw to the task, making every effort to convince herself it was like any other day.

"Should've whipped that boy," Mr. Dana said, standing near the window. "Gotta teach 'em young to respect the law."

Should've whipped that boy. Father often deputized the Charming Chaps, giving them authority and power. The men who should be upstanding citizens of the town instead plotted assassinations, terrorized the townsfolk, and delighted in violence against children. Liesl tried to soften the blows they delivered, but she was only one person, and she wasn't exactly safe from them herself.

She needed a miracle, but she'd have happily settled for some friendly help.

Chapter 3

Savage Wells

Hawk had been back in his current hometown less than two days, hardly enough time to enjoy even a moment's relaxation, when he saw Mayor Brimble rushing across the street from the telegraph office. The mayor wasn't one for physical exertion, so something had the man in a panic. Hawk's instincts told him the man was bringing a matter *to him.*

Sure enough, his lumbering footsteps sounded on the staircase outside. Brimble was not one for stealth. None of Hawk's deputies would have made a lick as much noise. They'd not have dared.

Despite the frantic knock at the door, Hawk moved unhurriedly across the room. He pulled the door open.

"Just. Came. In." Mayor Brimble struggled to speak through his breathlessness.

Hawk took the telegram, flipping the paper over to read it.

SAVAGE WELLS, WYOMING TERR |STOP|
WARNING FOR MARSHAL HAWKING |STOP|
ASSASSINATION PLANNED IN LARAMIE |STOP|
HAWKING THE TARGET |STOP|
DO NOT REPLY OR ACKNOWLEDGE |STOP|
INFORMANT IN DANGER |STOP|

Someone was planning to kill him. Again. Being tipped off by telegram wasn't new either. But this was the first time the message had arrived with specific instructions not to respond.

"Do you know where the telegram came from?"

"I know it came in on the north line. Transmitted through Barnard."

"But it didn't begin there?"

Brimble shook his head.

"Can you ask Barnard if they know which direction it came from?"

"I can."

Hawk folded the telegram and put it in his pocket. "Don't send word back to the original sender, in case there's any truth to the snitch being in danger."

Mayor Brimble nodded and hurried back out. Conversations with him didn't usually wrap up so quickly. Perhaps Hawk and Cade had finally gotten through to him about the importance of speed when dealing with pressing matters.

Hawk locked up his office before going downstairs to the jailhouse. Cade and Paisley would be there. The two of them had a knack for strategy and planning. Bouncing thoughts off them had saved his hide more than once.

Sure enough, they were there. Cade stood behind Paisley with his arms around her waist.

Hawk eyed them. "Ain't exactly all-business in here, is it?"

"You took my wife away for more than a week," Cade said. "I'm owed a bit of sparkin'."

"Pull yourselves together a minute. I have something important."

"Don't you think romance counts as 'important'?" Paisley asked.

"Romance requires a heart, and I've been told often enough that I don't have one."

Paisley laughed, pulling free of Cade's embrace.

Cade tossed him a look of annoyance. "You owe me."

"I'm not sparkin' with you no matter how put out you are."

"Ain't what I meant." Cade sauntered back to his desk and dropped into the chair, propping his feet on the desk, crossing his boots at the ankles. "What's your matter of importance?"

"Someone's decided to kill me."

"Again?" Cade and Paisley asked in unison.

Hawk was unrattled and unamused. "I received this." He pulled the telegram from his pocket and held it out to Paisley.

She took it and crossed to Cade, setting the paper on the desk so they both could read it.

After a moment, she looked at Hawk. "Do you know where it originated?"

"Brimble is trying to discover that without word getting back to the original station."

Cade scratched the back of his neck. "Likely a town with more than one telegraph operator. The one who sent it don't want the other one to intercept a reply."

"Meaning the other one would be part of the assassination plot?" Paisley asked.

"Or the sender don't want to risk his colleague asking questions that spill into the wrong ears," Cade said.

"Too many unknowns." Hawk shook his head in frustration. "I don't like it."

Paisley sat on the edge of Cade's desk. "The warning was specific to Laramie. Maybe the telegram came from there."

"Brimble said it came in on the north line. Laramie's south of here."

"There ain't much north of here," Cade said. "Isolated towns, is all."

"Gideon travels north quite often," Paisley said. "He might have some ideas."

The town doctor was the only man of medicine in a hundred-mile radius. He knew the territory almost as well as Hawk did. Occasionally, though, he had information Hawk didn't. "Worth asking him."

Paisley left to fetch him.

Cade leaned back in his chair once more. "You've had threats on your life before. Why is this one stuck in your craw?"

Hawk paced in front of the cells, thinking through everything he knew. "Sending the telegram was a risk, so the threat can't be dismissed as idle. And the sender must think the would-be assassin is capable of managing the thing without being caught, else he'd not have put himself in that kind of danger. The sender can't be anyone I know, or he'd have identified himself. That'll make it harder to sort out who the culprit is."

"You think they'll get you?"

Hawk shook his head. "No, but I don't like finding out there's even more corners of this territory needing cleaning up. I pride myself on how well it's running, how safe it's becoming. I don't like this."

"Paisley told me you're sniffing out the scent of a rogue sheriff somewhere."

Hawk took a tense breath. "I'll pinch out that flame as well, just as soon as I corner it." He hooked his thumbs around his gun belt. "It's a big territory. Washington hasn't given me all the deputies I need."

The mayor returned, stepping inside the jailhouse. Hawk watched him, waiting.

"Upline of Barnard is Porterville, Kaper, and Sand Creek," he said. "Barnard doesn't know which of them the telegram came from."

"Fine." Hawk turned back to Cade. "Thoughts?"

"Porterville's near enough that a messenger could have ridden here. Less likely to have risked a telegram."

There was wisdom in that. Hawk addressed the mayor again.

"Do you know how many telegraph operators Kaper and Sand Creek each have?"

"One apiece."

That didn't help. "Let me know if any other cryptic messages come through."

"I will." With that, he left the jailhouse, just as Paisley and Gideon arrived.

Hawk didn't waste any breath on greetings. "What do you know of Kaper and Sand Creek?"

Gideon wasn't the least daunted by the sudden interrogation. "I don't make regular trips there. They have telegraphs, so they can send for me if needed."

"How big are they?"

"Kaper isn't really a town. Mostly ranches, spread out in all directions. The 'town' boasts a telegraph and post office, and a small trading post, though it's seldom open."

"Peaceful?" Hawk asked.

The doctor nodded.

"And Sand Creek?"

Gideon gave it a moment's thought. "It's smaller than Savage Wells, but not insignificant. The people tend to keep to themselves. That's another reason I don't travel there often; they aren't likely to drop in during 'office hours.' But if they've sent for me, they'll let me help them."

"How far north is the town?"

"It's nearly in Montana Territory," Gideon said. "There's not much nearby, but the road in and out is a busy one. The town exports some things, brings in quite a bit. The people are doing relatively well for themselves."

An isolated, reclusive sort of town but with easy access. The doctor didn't visit it often, and Hawk, himself, had never been there, but he'd wager every last penny he had that Sand Creek was the source of the telegram.

"How much of a stir do you think a new arrival in town would cause?" he asked.

"Not too much. There's a great deal of land surrounding the town. Someone coming in to try their hand at living off the land or hoping to open an establishment would be noted, but it wouldn't be entirely unheard of."

"A US Marshal arriving would, though," Paisley jumped in. "Especially one someone there knows is under the thick cloud of a death threat."

He took in a nostril-flaring breath. "I hadn't meant to go in badges blazing. Just a simple man and his sister looking to start a new life."

"Sister?" Paisley never could entirely hide her excitement at taking on a new mission. There was a reason he'd nabbed her for the deputy marshal's job.

"You just got back," Cade objected. "Two days ago, Pais. Two days."

"You think I can't read a calendar, Fergus?"

Hawk had never heard anyone else call Cade by his actual given name. And Paisley only ever did, as far as he knew, when she was a bit put out with her husband.

She set her hands defiantly on her hips. "If someone's looking to off the marshal, it won't be long before he goes after the deputies as well. I'm not sitting here twiddling my thumbs waiting to be top on the list. We're going to pinch this flame out now."

Cade turned hard eyes on Hawk, a familiar expression.

"I know," Hawk said. "If she gets killed, you'll murder me. Get in line."

Cade missed his wife when she was away, and, though Paisley enjoyed her work, it was obvious she felt the same way. No one missed Hawk; not in that way, at least.

He'd accomplished more than most in his line of work, and he'd done it efficiently. But the price had been his youth and his levity.

A person had to be cold and calculating to turn the tide of the lawless West. He'd saved this territory and made it safer. He had given up too much in the pursuit of that goal to not keep protecting the people in his charge.

If that meant doing so without a warm embrace to return home to, without the deep connections most people enjoyed . . . so be it.

So be it.

Chapter 4

Three days had passed since Liesl had sent the telegram. The sky hadn't fallen, so she felt certain she'd managed the thing without getting caught. Though whether she'd done a bit of good, she didn't know. There were other troubles to contend with as it was.

She rushed into her family home, her arms laden with the remainder of that day's jailhouse lunch and her mind in a state of near panic. She set the dishes in the washbasin without scraping any of the food bits into the slop bucket.

"What has you so frantic?" Mother asked, crossing the room to her. "What did your father do?"

"It's not what he *did*, but what he's *about* to do." She tied her bonnet more firmly on her head. "I'm taking the pony cart to the Harper farm."

"What's he going to do out—" Worried realization filled Mother's face. "Their taxes are due."

Liesl nodded. "And I know they can't pay."

"Quickly."

She didn't need to be told twice. Whichever of the Charming Chaps Father deputized for this tax collection would ride out with him as soon as they finished their poker game.

She hurried through the hitching up of the pony and set the cart in motion. The poor animal likely had forgotten what it felt like to not be set to a frantic run. Liesl seldom left home when she wasn't in a desperate race against pending doom for some poor soul or another.

Jamie was in front of the house when she arrived. He waved and smiled. She pulled around the side and headed to the back of the house. If her father got there faster than she anticipated, it wouldn't do for him to spot his own cart out front.

Mrs. Harper was crossing from the kitchen garden to the back door. She, like her son, smiled in greeting. "Liesl, what brings you 'round?"

"Nothing good, I'm afraid. Tax collectors are coming your way."

Mrs. Harper paled on the instant. "Oh, mercy. We thought we had a few weeks yet."

"He comes when it suits him, not when the calendar dictates." Liesl suspected this early visit was retaliation for little Jamie running past the courthouse the other day. The boy's family was to be punished because the sheriff didn't care for children and had been annoyed by one acting perfectly normal for a boy his age.

Mrs. Harper waved her husband over from the open barn door.

"Can you pay?" Liesl asked while they waited for Mr. Harper to join them.

"Not all of it. He collected so much last time, we're still behind."

She had been afraid of that. "I can't help you make up the difference this time." Every penny Liesl had scrounged together in the years since she'd learned of her father's taxes had gone to saving the people of Sand Creek from the consequences of delinquency.

"Good afternoon, Liesl," Mr. Harper said.

"My father and one of his cronies are coming. They've declared it your tax day."

For a moment, Mr. Harper didn't move. His wife clutched his arm, her wide eyes filled with worry.

"I know you can't pay in full," she said. "I think it'd be safest if you weren't at home when they arrive."

"How long do we have?" Mr. Harper asked.

"Likely not more than thirty minutes."

Mrs. Harper's expression took on an edge of desperate determination. "I'll fetch blankets and food. We should likely take the puppy with us."

Liesl wished she could be certain her father and the Charming Chaps wouldn't take their anger out on a puppy, but she'd seen the injuries their tempers had inflicted on far too many innocent people to think anyone or anything was safe when they felt disrespected or thwarted or denied what they felt was their due.

To Mr. Harper, Liesl said, "I'll help you hitch up your wagon. The sooner you can leave, the safer you'll be."

He didn't hesitate, didn't insist he could do it all himself. The Harpers had lived in Sand Creek long enough to know the consequences of upsetting the sheriff.

"How long do you suppose we'll have to be gone?" Mr. Harper asked as they worked quickly and anxiously. "The cow'll need milking, and the pigs and chickens fed. I can't afford to lose animals."

"I'd suggest not returning until tomorrow afternoon, at the earliest. I don't know how long your home will be watched."

Mr. Harper nodded. "If it stretches much longer, maybe Beatty'll come tend to the animals. He'd be willing to say we'd left town to visit family or something."

"I can take word to him." She adjusted the collar on the bay gelding, making certain it wouldn't rub the poor animal. "We can tuck you away at the old Reynoldses' place. My father's never thought to look there."

"Can't." Mr. Harper adjusted the blinders on the calico mare. "Reynoldses' place ain't empty anymore."

"They're back?" Happiness warred with worry. She liked Mr. and

Mrs. Reynolds, but she hated the thought of them being imprisoned in this town again when they had managed to escape. So few did.

"New family," Mr. Harper said. "Just moved in yesterday. Brother and sister."

"Elderly?" She hoped not. If they weren't physically able to grow enough crops or keep a sufficient number of animals to pay their taxes, the consequences would be dire. The Charming Chaps preferred their victims vulnerable and fragile.

"No. Young. Fit. They'll survive."

She and Mr. Harper finished hitching the team. Neither spoke, but she suspected his mind was a whirl of worries. "I had probably better see if I can convince these newcomers to go. If they haven't put money on the land yet, they might be persuaded."

"I hope they can be." Mr. Harper rubbed the calico mare's nose as he passed. "I think I'll head over to Newell Lake. We can make camp on the banks and stay a day or two."

"Good plan." Liesl buckled the crupper under the tail of the bay gelding. "I'll talk to Mr. Beatty about looking after your animals."

"Thank you."

He slipped into the barn just as Mrs. Harper came out of the house, blankets tucked under one arm and a large sack under the other. She set the things in the wagon bed and returned quickly to the house.

Little Jamie came around the corner of the house, holding the hand of his even littler sister, Margaret. "Mama says we're leaving," he said.

"You're going for a little adventure." Liesl slipped the lines through the harness rings. "Where's your puppy?"

"Mama says she's fetching him," Jamie said. "He's coming with us."

Mr. Harper returned and set a canvas bundle and tent poles in the wagon bed. "C'mon, children. Let's get you up."

He lifted Margaret into the wagon, setting her on a blanket, then followed with Jamie. Mrs. Harper came out again, another large bag under her arm, tugging a tiny puppy alongside her on a lead.

"Give me your keys," Liesl said. "I'll lock your house while you finish putting everything in the wagon. The sooner you're on your way the better."

Mr. Harper fished a brass key from his pocket and tossed it to her. She caught it and rushed inside, leaving him to make a final check of the harnesses and buckles. She put the heavy wood plank across the inside of the back door, effectively locking it from the inside. The small house was easily crossed. She stepped through the front door and closed it behind her. Her hand shook a little as she tried to lock the door.

She hadn't the first doubt they were running out of time. If her father arrived while the Harpers were still at home and found them unable to make their tax payment, they'd pay dearly. If he found *her* there aiding the family . . .

She held back a shudder, forcing herself to focus on her task. At last, she managed to lock the door. Not content to walk, she ran around to the back of the house and returned Mr. Harper's key.

"Make like a twister and be quick. Can't be much time remainin'," she said.

"You took a mighty risk coming to warn us," Mrs. Harper said. "You risk so much for the whole town."

"It's my kin hurting the lot of you. If I can't stop him, I'll at least slow him up as much as I can." She climbed into her pony cart. "Vamoose. I can't do a blasted thing for you if you're caught here."

Mr. Harper flicked the lines, and the wagon rumbled away.

Oh, please let them be fast enough. She'd seen the results of her father's taxation visits. They made the cuts and bruises she'd received at his hands seem like nothing at all. He'd not beaten anyone else's children, but he'd subjected them to the terror of their homes being ransacked and their fathers injured.

She needed to warn the new arrivals. If Lady Luck meant to play kindly, this brother and sister would not yet have purchased the land they were living on. They'd not ever get that money back, and having only just made the purchase, they likely have nothing to live on if they scampered. If they were going to have to stay, she would make certain they received a friendly welcome and knew she could be trusted.

She made for the Reynoldses' one-time home, moving swiftly so she could turn off the road as soon as possible. Being seen by her father anywhere near the Harpers' farm would raise his suspicions when he found them missing. If he thought they'd just happened to be away from home, he'd be more likely to leave peaceably and come back later—hopefully long enough for the family to gather what they needed to pay him.

None of the Charming Chaps had come within sight before she guided her cart off the road. Her heart slowed. Her breaths came more easily. Every time she rode out ahead of the monster she lived with, she did so shaking in her boots. Someday, she knew her luck would run short.

Her nerves had almost entirely settled by the time she came to a stop in front of the weathered and dusty farmhouse. The Reynoldses had kept it up beautifully while they'd lived there, and everyone had assumed they'd resigned themselves to living out their lives in Sand Creek no matter the tyrant running the place. If these new arrivals did in fact stay, Liesl hoped they meant to restore the house to its former loveliness.

She tied the pony to a front-porch post, then knocked at the door. These "welcome to town" visits were always difficult. She liked meeting new people; she certainly wasn't shy. But she knew all too well the kind of town they'd come to, and by the time she met them, it was usually too late for them to escape. It felt rather like welcoming people to a nightmare, one her own father had created.

A woman opened the door. She was likely about Liesl's age. Her dark hair sat in a messy knot at the nape of her neck. She was tall and slender and showed not the slightest sign of bashfulness. "Hey."

An unexpected greeting, but not an unfriendly one.

"I'm Liesl Hodges. The Harpers told me you'd moved in."

"Mary Butler," the woman said. "Word of our arrival has made its way through the town quickly, I see. It seems there aren't many secrets in Sand Creek."

Oh, there were far more than anyone other than Liesl realized. Still, she offered a smile and kept her tone light and friendly. "We're a small town. Everyone knows everyone."

"Come in." Mary motioned her through the door.

Liesl accepted the invitation. The house was fairly sparse. A few unpacked crates sat around the room. The furniture would serve its purpose, but that was all that could really be said for it. There was still the possibility that they weren't committed to staying long-term.

"Things are still a bit slapdash," Mary said. "We have a lot of unpacking yet to do."

"Settling in takes time."

That appeared to put her hostess at ease. "And we only purchased the farm two days ago. I should be more patient with myself."

Purchased. They'd bought the land. This family wouldn't be in a position to up and leave. Liesl's approach in these cases was to make clear she was a friend and an ally, so when the reality of their new situation became unavoidable, they would be willing to let her help them.

"Where have you moved here from?" she asked as she sat in one of the spindly chairs.

"Montana Territory, most recently. My brother and I are eager to put roots down somewhere. Our parents were never ones for biding in any place for long."

This got worse and worse. Not only had they bought the land, they were meaning to stay. "Why did you choose Sand Creek?"

Mary looked past her. "Why'd you choose it, John?"

"Land came cheap."

Liesl turned at the sound of a rich, rumbling voice.

Standing behind her—his gray-striped shirt fitting trim across his broad shoulders, suspenders hanging from his trousers, and deep-brown hair tousled in a way that, oddly enough, made it a little difficult to breathe—was a man handsome as sin.

"Have you made a new friend, Mary?" He smiled a little as he spoke.

This stranger was managing to do very odd things to Liesl's heart, making it flip about and tie itself in knots. Her head was not usually so easily turned.

"This is Liesl Hodges," Mary said. "She's come to welcome us to Sand Creek."

He crossed toward them, head tipped in thought. "Hodges. I think I've heard that name since arriving."

A weight dropped heavy in her stomach. She only hoped she kept her distaste and misery hidden. "My father is Sheriff Hodges. Perhaps you've met him."

The siblings shook their heads. That was a relief. They could form their opinion of her without her father tainting it.

"I'm certain he'll introduce himself. He insists on knowing everyone's comings and goings."

"That sounds . . . cozy." John's dry tone was surprisingly comforting.

"Oh, it's delightful. We're an entire town of peas in a very confining pod." Her wry tone brought a laughing smile to his face. "We've made quite a competition out of seeing who can keep their deepest secrets hidden the longest."

"Who's winning?" he asked.

"Everyone's losing."

"Except the sheriff, I'd imagine." He didn't seem intimidated or bothered by any of this. Of course, she was making more light of it than was warranted.

"Our sheriff don't care to lose. I learned long ago to pretend I'm bumbling at horseshoes, and everyone in town gives him a wide berth when he's looking for someone to join a poker game."

"How does Sheriff Hodges feel about hide-and-seek?"

"Territorial champion," she said as if entirely serious. "And quite proud of it. I think if sheriffing hadn't proven so much to his liking, he would have attempted to obtain international distinction in hide-and-seek."

John sat in the chair nearest hers. He slouched to one side, but nothing in his posture spoke of indolence or laziness.

Mary had crossed to the table and begun mixing something in a bowl. This visit, it seemed, was to be with John. Despite his being a stranger, Liesl didn't mind. He seemed to enjoy her odd sense of humor.

"Does the town approve of your father's nosiness?" he asked

"Not particularly." She had come with the hope of warning them off. Knowing they meant to stay, dropping a word in their ears wouldn't be a bad thing. "He will know anything and everything about you both soon enough. And, like I said, he don't care to 'lose,' in any sense. Life in Sand Creek ain't always comfortable."

"You sound as though you've come here issuing a warning." The observation felt more teasing than accusing. She appreciated that.

"I am, I suppose. If your secrets are deep and precious enough, you might not want to stay."

His smile was warm and made her feel slightly dizzy. "Do you think I have secrets, Miss Hodges?"

"Please, call me Liesl," she said. "And, yes. Everyone has secrets of one sort or another."

"But not in Sand Creek," he said, almost like a question.

"Not for long."

His smile bloomed more fully, setting her heart skipping about like a frog on a hot rock. This man had snagged her attention right quick and didn't seem likely to let go. A dangerous but highly enjoyable turn of events. She would enjoy getting to know him. But it would hurt that much more when he came to realize a monster resided in her family. Though the townsfolk insisted they didn't blame her for her father's iron fist, they still kept a distance.

"I don't mean to keep you from the work of unpacking and settling in," she said. "I wanted only to introduce myself. We live in town. I hope you'll call when you're there."

He rose as she did and dipped his head. "I'd be honored to do so, Liesl."

She ignored the heat touching her cheeks. She bid farewell to Mary, who offered a brief but friendly wave of her own. John walked Liesl to the door. He stood in the threshold, leaning an upturned arm against one side of the doorframe, watching as she climbed into her pony cart. He smiled and nodded as she set the cart in motion.

The Butlers seemed like good people. It was a shame they'd chosen Sand Creek. This town destroyed good people.

Chapter 5

Hawk stood in the doorway of his and Paisley's "family home," watching Liesl Hodges drive away in her pony cart. The woman was a boon he'd not anticipated. She was personable, friendly, and with that breath-catching smile and eyes as pretty as a sunrise.

"You enjoyed that," Paisley said from the table.

"Just gathering information." He stepped back inside and closed the door. "That woman, I'd wager, knows everything in this town. Maybe more than she realizes. We'll get good leads through her if we can win her trust."

"And the flirting was a trust-building scheme, was it?" Paisley never was one to let him off any hook easily.

"You know my motto: Flirt 'Til They Blurt." He pulled his suspenders over his shoulders. "Nearly worked with Miriam."

"Miriam came nowhere near spilling her secrets in your ear. Took a full investigation and a tender-hearted physician to solve that mystery." Paisley tossed him an apple. "Peel that."

He dropped onto a chair at the table and pulled out his pocketknife. "This intrusive sheriff's worth keeping an eye on." He pressed the edge of the blade against the apple and made slow turns, removing the skin. "Between him and his daughter, we'll learn about every person in Sand Creek."

"Any chance the sheriff is our secretive informant?" Paisley pushed the small pile of apples over to him. "He'd be likely to hear about something like that."

"He's the law here. If he knew of an assassination plot, why not arrest the culprit himself?"

"Maybe he's outgunned. Or a coward. Or being targeted himself."

"Hmm." Hawk finished peeling the first apple, the dark-red skin dropping to the table in one long twist. "We need to meet him, get the lay of that particular land."

"You could always shower Liesl with a few more melting smiles. Then you can make her father's acquaintance while the two of you scrape her swooning form off the ground." Paisley took his peeled apple and sliced it.

"I wasn't flirting *that* much." He peeled the next apple as they talked.

"You tell yourself whatever you want, Hawk. I know what I saw."

He *had* been flirting. Truth be told, he'd enjoyed it. Smiles from a beautiful woman were never a terrible thing, and she'd bantered like an expert.

"What was your impression of the Harpers?" he asked.

"Ordinary family. Quiet. Neither of them struck me as having gumption enough to send a telegram that'd risk their lives." She kept slicing.

"My thoughts as well." He took up another apple. "We'll have to meet more of the folks hereabout. One of 'em's our tipster. Find him, and we'll find the would-be assassin."

"Oh, is that why we've come?" Paisley made a show of being surprised. "Here I was thinking we were just wandering about, hoping to find an empty house to make apple fritters in."

She knew well enough that he regularly repeated the goals of the missions they were on. It was his way of staying focused. Talking it through, however often, didn't usually aggravate her.

"What's stuck in your craw?" He pushed another peeled apple in her direction.

"I don't know." She sliced her knife through an apple with a thwack. "I miss home, I guess."

"You miss Cade, you mean."

She sent him a look, daring him to poke fun at her sentimentality. "Cade and my father. I only got to see 'em for a couple of days this time. I'm feeling a little cheated." She pointed her knife at him. "And I have every right to."

"Family's important," he said. "I wouldn't pull you away from yours so soon if any of the other deputies could've played this role."

She set back to her apple slicing. "I know. And having a woman here will make it easier to get information from the other women in town. It's still a misery to be away."

There were few things Hawk appreciated about not having a family of his own. The freedom to do his job without his mind and heart being distracted by the pull of home was one of them.

A knock sounded at the door.

Paisley looked up from her apple slicing. "Three visitors in one day. Friendly town."

"Liesl did warn us." He rose, intending to answer the knock.

"Was it just me, or did you feel like there was something more she was hinting at? Something other than the sheriff's nosiness?"

"She made a lot of talk about there being no secrets in Sand Creek, but she's hiding something. I've no doubt about that." But what the secret might be, he didn't know.

He reached for the door handle, reminding himself to tone down his aura of authority; he was playing the role of a farmer, not a lawman. Liesl had managed to pull him a little out of that. He couldn't let that happen again.

Two large and imposing men stood on the other side of the door. Confidence dripped from them like rain down a gutter. The taller of the two visitors boasted a sheriff's badge on his vest.

"Welcome." Hawk assumed a less forceful tone than he otherwise would have by default. "What can we do for you?"

"I heard you'd recently moved in and wanted to come introduce myself." The sheriff appeared to be speaking for his partner as well, though he hadn't said "we."

As Hawk motioned them inside, Paisley set down her knife—a good thing; she could be unintentionally menacing—and crossed to them.

"Miss." The second man eyed her appreciatively.

She demurred, something she'd had to practice. Paisley was made of steel. He'd known from the first moment he met her that she'd make a blasted fine deputy marshal, and she'd proven him correct time and again.

The men were invited to sit, and they wasted no time launching into relatively prying questions. Between Hawk and Paisley, they managed to get in a few questions of their own and discovered this was, indeed, Sheriff Hodges, and his companion was Mr. Yarrow, the telegraph operator who was sometimes deputized. That was an interesting development.

In return, Hodges and Yarrow received an entirely fictitious story about the Butler siblings and their decision to put down roots and start a farm. They learned their ages, birthplaces, where they'd last lived, that they were both unwed with no prospects, and that they hadn't yet paid—indeed hadn't even heard of—their land taxes. Hodges assured them that there was plenty of time remaining to get that done.

"We dropped in on your neighbors, but they weren't home," Sheriff Hodges said. "You don't happen to know where they went, do you?"

"The Harpers?" Paisley asked.

The sheriff nodded.

"We met them briefly," Paisley said, "but ain't visited with them since."

"When did they call on you?" Hodges pressed.

Hawk had been duly warned the sheriff was nosy, and he didn't intend to make his nosiness fruitful. "Not long after we moved in. A little while back." In truth, it had been that very morning, but Sheriff Curiosity didn't need to know that.

The two men nodded. The visit, oddly enough, wound down quickly after that. They had, it seemed, come to find out what they could about the new arrivals but also to learn what they could about the Harpers.

There are no secrets in this town.

The men offered farewells. Mr. Yarrow's departure took longer. He lingered over his goodbye to Paisley, holding her hand overly long, assessing her pointedly and with a sly smile of approval. If only he realized how little his approach would work with a woman like her, and not only because she was already married.

Paisley closed the door behind them, then tossed Hawk a look of absolute annoyance. "Are you certain I ain't allowed to shoot him?"

"As much as I believe the man's a snake in the grass, he's the telegraph operator. He might very well be our informant. He won't do us a lick of good if he's dead."

She returned to the table and took up her knife once more. "Why is it we never seem to get this sort of helpful information from decent people?"

"Because the chances of overhearing dastardly plots ain't very high if a person don't spend time with dastardly folks."

Paisley nodded her acknowledgment. "If he is our mystery telegram sender, why not tell the sheriff? They're clearly friends."

"Probably because the sheriff can't keep his blasted mouth shut."

She laughed. "Liesl wasn't wrong about that, was she?"

"I've half a mind to find out what else she isn't wrong about."

Paisley cut into another apple. "Still thinking about her, are you?"

"Don't read too much into it." Hawk tapped his chest above his heart. "Cold as stone, and just as soft."

She didn't look the least convinced. "We'll see."

Yes, she would. She would see that Hawk was as calculating and heartless as everyone said. He didn't mind people . . . at a safe distance. Those who got too close to him got hurt. He couldn't let that happen again.

Chapter 6

Most people who knew Hawk would be surprised that he hadn't needed to do any research before taking on the role of a farmer. He knew precisely how he ought to pretend to be spending his days, knew what he needed to purchase at the mercantile. Paisley mostly kept to the house and the familiar work there. It'd be what was expected so no one would look sideways at them.

Their third day as John and Mary they went into town together under the guise of making purchases, but with the real purpose of doing a little digging.

Hawk held the mercantile door open for her.

"I'll jaw with the proprietress," Paisley said under her breath as she passed inside.

He nodded, and they parted ways. A group of men sat near the front window, two bent over a checkerboard. Two others stood over them, gabbing and watching.

Hawk pulled his hat off and approached. "Howdy. John Butler. I'm new in town."

"Bought the Reynolds place, I heard," the man working the red pieces said.

"You live there with your sister," the man over his shoulder added.

Hawk allowed a little laugh. "Liesl wasn't making grand of it when she said there were no secrets in Sand Creek."

The group grew very quiet, eyes darting between them all. For a town with no secrets, they were acting very secretive. The townsfolk might not be as forthcoming as he'd hoped.

"Seems a right friendly town," he said with an easy and personable smile.

"Amos Kirkpatrick," the red-checker player motioned to himself. He hooked his thumb over his shoulder. "Frank Porter." He pointed to his opponent. "Burt Caper." He motioned to the last of their group, standing with a shoulder against the wall. "Roger Dana."

"Pleasure." Hawk dipped his head as he took their measure in order. Kirkpatrick: cold-eyed. Porter: friendly. Caper: harmless. Dana: watching Hawk a little too closely. "We've come too late for planting our fields this season." Hawk tucked his hand in his pocket, his other still holding his hat. "Any advice for preparing my fields for next year?"

Dana and Kirkpatrick offered no advice; no one seemed to expect them to. They were, he would wager, town folk and not farmers. Being in town 'round the clock increased the number of people they'd pass each day and the number of conversations they'd overhear. Those two would bear watching.

Hawk chatted with the others, asking questions about the land, rainfall, crops, any number of things a farmer would want and need to know. In the middle of it all, Liesl Hodges came inside. She walked arm-in-arm with a woman who looked too much like her to not be kin. Hawk'd guess she was Liesl's mother.

As the two passed fully into the mercantile, Paisley struck up a conversation with them. Hawk's deputies didn't need coddling. They knew what to do when the situation changed.

"Have you seen the Harpers about lately?" Mr. Dana asked Hawk. "They live out near you. No one's seen 'em in a couple of days."

Though he'd only known the man a few minutes, Hawk trusted him about as much as he would a steer in a stampede. "Ain't seen the Harpers since we first moved in. Days ago."

"Did they say anything about being gone or where they were going?" Mr. Dana didn't seem likely to let the topic go. Why did it matter so much to him? Was it just the legendary Sand Creek curiosity?

"All they said was 'howdy' and 'we live just up the road,'" Hawk answered. "Didn't feel like I needed to know more than that."

"You don't care about your neighbors?" Mr. Kirkpatrick asked.

"I care enough not to press my nose in their business if they haven't invited me to."

That answer didn't seem to satisfy Kirkpatrick or Dana, though it clearly shocked Porter and Caper. The sheriff, apparently, wasn't the only meddlesome person in town.

Hawk dipped his head. "A pleasure to meet you, men."

On that note, he crossed the mercantile to where Paisley stood, still in conversation with the Hodges women.

"John. You remember Liesl." Paisley gave the perfect impression of a sister greeting an older brother; no one would guess he was her boss.

"I most certainly do." He offered a smile and quick nod.

"This is her mother—Mrs. Hodges." Paisley made the introduction Hawk hadn't truly needed. "They were just telling me there's a town social at the end of the week. We're invited."

He cringed. "I'm not expected to dance, am I?"

Liesl smiled at him, her eyes sparkling with amusement. "Do you not dance, John?"

"With about as much grace as a one-legged squirrel." That wasn't actually true, but the right kind of shortcomings put people at ease. "Do your town socials have room for wallflowers?"

"The bachelors far outnumber the unattached women," Liesl said. "We have an entire garden of wallflowers."

"Perfect. I'll plant myself there."

To his surprise, Liesl looked a little disappointed. "You won't even try to dance?"

"I'll spare you the painful display," he said.

"You can't be as bad as all that."

Paisley took up her role with perfection. "There have been complaints. His dancing is considered a crime in three territories and southern Canada."

That brought laughter to Liesl's green eyes. "That must be a terrible embarrassment to your family."

"We don't care to talk about it," Paisley said. "We've even considered changing our name."

"Remind me again why I brought you to Sand Creek with me." Hawk pretended to ponder.

"*I* brought *you*," Paisley tossed back. "Older brothers are good to have around in case something heavy needs to be lifted or when I find myself longing to watch some truly awful dancing."

Hawk met Liesl's eye with a look of dry annoyance. "Little sisters ought to be trial enough for older brothers to be guaranteed a spot in heaven."

"That is certainly where my older brother is, though I think that has more to do with his saintliness than my trial-ness."

A piece in her puzzle, that.

"I am sorry to hear you lost a brother," he said. Looking to her mother, he added, "And a son. Losing people we love ain't ever easy."

But Mrs. Hodges wasn't paying much heed to their conversation. She watched the windows and the street outside almost frantically. "We have to get lunch to the jailhouse, Liesl. We'll be late."

"We have time," Liesl said.

"There's less than an hour."

Liesl turned to her mother and, lowering her voice, said, "Mr.

Dana and Mr. Kirkpatrick are still *here*. Lunch won't be expected until well after they make the trek over. We have time."

"It ain't worth the risk, Liesl." There was more than punctuality in Mrs. Hodges's voice. She sounded genuinely afraid.

Paisley's posture stiffened almost imperceptibly. She'd noticed as well.

"I'd like to grab a few things so we can begin baking for the social. There's plenty of time for putting together lunch."

Mrs. Hodges's eyes darted to the checkerboard. "We can fetch the social supplies after lunch, Liesl. Please."

"I suppose I could come after the men have finished eating." She gave Hawk and Paisley apologetic looks. "It was nice to see you both again. I hope you'll come to the social."

"We'll be there," Paisley said. "Be sure to warn the rest of the town."

"Warn?" Liesl repeated with a laugh.

"About John's dancing. I'd hate to frighten the children."

Hawk shook his head, making a show of being annoyed. Liesl sent him another of her sparkling smiles. She hooked her arm with her mother's, then turned and made for the door.

Mr. Dana watched them as they left, the same studying gaze he'd set on Hawk earlier.

"That man with the black hair bears watching," Paisley said out the side of her mouth.

"I've a hunch he lives in town," Hawk said quietly, though no one was near enough to overhear.

Paisley's hand hovered near her hip where her gun would have hung. "And I've an inkling that lunch at the jailhouse is a dangerous proposition."

Hawk's instincts were piqued. "For a town without secrets, this one has plenty."

By the time the town social rolled around, Paisley had met nearly all the women on the east side of town, and Hawk had made the acquaintance of a good number of the men. From that, they'd assembled a list of possible informants, a list they hoped to narrow down after the social.

"Bill Yarrow is the only telegraph operator, so he has to be considered. Charles Dana is the postmaster, which puts him next door to the telegraph office every day."

Hawk rattled off the list as they approached town. The social was going to be held in a field behind the schoolhouse. It'd be too cold for outdoor gatherings in a few weeks, so he and Paisley needed to take advantage while they could.

"Mr. and Mrs. Harper disappeared for days on end without explanation. That bears considering," he added.

"Sheriff Hodges is a shady character," Paisley said. "But I don't peg him as the sort to do anything bordering on heroic if he wasn't going to get credit for it."

"What about his family?"

"His wife is more mouse than alley cat," Paisley said. "I spent a full thirty minutes with her yesterday, and she hesitated to ask questions as harmless as whether or not I'd like a slice of bread."

That matched Hawk's impression of her. "What about Liesl?"

"She knows what everyone's about, so if anyone were to hear about a clandestine plot, she would."

"But is she brassy enough to send a telegram that might put her in danger?"

Paisley glanced at him. "You've spent more time chatting with her than I have. You tell me."

"You were at the Hodgeses' house just yesterday."

She shook her head. "Liesl wasn't there. She was taking lunch to the jailhouse."

"And did she return in one piece? That seemed in question at the mercantile."

"We'll find out tonight, won't we?"

They arrived at the social, stopping their wagon alongside dozens of others. Mr. Harper was there, and Hawk made the man his first stop.

"Good to see you again," he said. "Thank you for warning me about the leak in the roof of the barn. I've had a chance to mend it."

Mr. Harper nodded. "We have to look out for each other around here."

"If you jaunt off again in the future, I'd be happy to look out for your place while you're away," Hawk said. "I know what it is to worry over the land. When you put so much into making it yours, losing it feels like losing a limb."

"The land here is never ours." Mr. Harper watched the gathering with the look of a cornered fox.

"Did you not purchase yours?"

Their eyes met for a brief, pointed moment. "That is the question around here, ain't it?"

"Is it?"

Mr. Harper tucked his hands in his trouser pockets and walked away. He knew something Hawk didn't. More secrets. More troubles. If any town in the territory were to hatch an assassination plot reported secretly by an anonymous eavesdropper, Sand Creek would.

Hawk dropped himself among the men standing along the edge of the gathering, leaning against the back wall of the schoolhouse. He could watch the comings and goings from there without drawing any notice. Mr. Harper joined his wife out amongst the townsfolk. They sat beside each other, a child on each lap, watching the gathering without even a hint of a smile. Whatever business had taken them away from home, it didn't appear to have been pleasant.

From among the crowd, Liesl moved toward the line of bachelors, drawing everyone's attention. She walked all the way to where he stood. "You've decided to dance after all."

He shook his head. "I'm willing to attend, but I ain't gonna dance."

"Even if I asked you to?"

Oh, that was a coquettish look if he'd ever seen one. This woman was trouble, the kind he rather enjoyed sorting out.

"I'm sparing you from agony, lamb. My dancing would be considered torture to most."

"'Lamb'?" He couldn't tell if she was more amused or shocked at the pet name he'd pulled out for her.

He shrugged. "'To the slaughter' and all that. You were looking to toss yourself right in the thick of it."

"Oh, but now I'm far too intrigued not to dance with you. A one-legged squirrel is something my curiosity cain't resist."

He'd do best to stand around gabbing with her, asking the questions he needed answered along with a few extra to hide his trail. But *his* curiosity couldn't resist the temptation either. He stood upright and took a single step away from the wall.

"Don't say you weren't warned, lamb."

She laughed, the sound tinkling like a bell in a breeze. "I sincerely hope you are every bit as terrible as you claim to be."

"You're an odd sort, you know," he said. "I ain't got the first idea what to make of you."

The smile she tossed his way was full to the brim with mischief. "That's the way I prefer it."

"I don't doubt that in the least."

They took their places in the square, standing kitty-corner to each other. She smiled at him, and he threw back a grin with just a hint of a troublemaker in it.

The music started up, and the caller set them in motion. Hawk listened closely enough to follow instructions but not execute them well—he had an image to maintain. Liesl patiently pointed him in the right direction when he made a wrong move. For a time, at least.

After several bumps and collisions, she finally gave up, shaking her head and laughing as they abandoned the dancing.

"That was terrible," she said.

"Did you think I was lying?"

"Yes." She made the declaration so bluntly and unapologetically. "I'll tell you something, I still ain't convinced you weren't making a show of being bad at it. If I could think of a reason why you would pretend to be a terrible dancer, then I'd say my first instinct was right. But what reason could you have?"

She had seen through his mask a little. *Very* few people ever managed that.

Playing along was usually the best means of throwing someone off a scent. "Maybe I hate to dance, and it's a good way to get out of doing it?"

She shook her head. "That ain't it."

"Then, maybe I'm trying to make everyone else feel better about their own dancing?"

"By colliding with them so often they couldn't manage the steps?" she tossed back dryly.

"I was raised in a house where dancing was considered scandalous, and I feel so guilty when I do it that I'm miserable at it?"

She laughed. "If that were true, your sister would likely not be dancing with Mr. Kersey."

Kersey. That was a name they'd not yet investigated. *Good work, Paisley.*

"That look." She pointed at him. "You wear that look now and then, and I can't for the life of me identify it."

"What look?" He laughed off her observation. This woman saw too blasted much.

"Your eyes get sharp, and your forehead wrinkles in a way that says, 'I'm pondering something very serious' even though your mouth still has an 'everything's coming up roses' turn to it."

Tarnation. But he just laughed again, and when she joined in without hesitation, he took it as a good sign.

"I saw the Harpers are back," he said. "It's nice to have neighbors again. Gets a mite lonesome out there."

"I'm glad they weren't gone too long," she said. "I'd have missed seeing Jamie running all over town like he tends to do. More bounce than a jackrabbit, that one."

"Mr. Harper seemed heavy, though. Muttering something about people not purchasing the land they bought." Hawk let his confusion show. "I can't sort that bit out to save me."

Her expression sobered. She took hold of his hand and tugged him a few steps away from the gathering, but not so far as to draw attention.

"Something happens to the land deeds," she whispered. "People buy land here, but when they check the deeds, someone else owns it."

"I don't understand."

"You've purchased the farm you're living on now?" she asked.

He nodded.

"Drop in at the land office next chance you get," she said, "and ask for a copy of your deed. It won't have your name on it."

"But *I* bought it. I filed the deed."

She shook her head. "That won't make a difference. Everyone here has bought their land and followed all the rules. But no one here owns a bit of it."

Someone was stealing people's farms. "Why doesn't everyone turn this thief in?"

"It's not that simple. The name on the deed isn't one anyone knows. The prevalent theory is it's an assumed name. How does a person go about 'turning in' someone who don't exist?"

His blood started to heat. "So every person in Sand Creek has been swindled—including me, now—and there's not a blasted thing to be done about it?"

She shook her head. "And with everyone's money spent on land they don't own, no one can afford to leave."

"And even a few seasons' crop yield ain't enough for them to afford to start again?"

"The sheriff hasn't visited you yet."

She called her father "the sheriff." Odd. "He did—right after you visited a few days ago."

Her brow pulled in confusion. "Did he tell you when your tax day will be?"

"Tax day?"

"The day you have to pay taxes on your land," she said.

"The land I might not actually own?" The heat turned to a boil.

She sighed. "No one ever escapes Sand Creek, John. There's never money enough. Never freedom enough."

"The townspeople are prisoners?"

She nodded. "For all intents and purposes. Only the Reynoldses ever escaped, but no one knows how. We're all stuck, John. And I'm afraid you are now, too. You and Mary both."

"And if I'm not content to be happily imprisoned?"

She took a step back, pale and clearly unnerved. "Don't kick beehives. Around here, they do more than sting."

"What do the Sand Creek bees do, Liesl?"

She shook her head and moved away quickly. He'd not known Liesl long, but he felt in his bones she was not usually upended. That she'd been shaken by this topic didn't bode well.

He'd been searching out corruption in his territory. It seemed he'd stumbled on an entire valley of it.

Chapter 7

John Butler was going to get himself killed.

Liesl had dedicated her life to saving people from the monster in her family, but she couldn't do a blasted thing for John if he insisted on being a dolt. She needed to get a thought or two through that thick head of his.

With that aim in mind, she'd convinced her mother to go with her to the Butlers' farm two days after the town social, saying they were just being neighborly. Mother was not usually at ease with people—new or otherwise—but, apparently, Mary Butler had been kind to her, and she felt safe enough to spend an afternoon in the woman's company.

Mary greeted them warmly, though with the distance Liesl had come to suspect was typical for her. Where her brother was all warm glances and flirtatious banter, Mary was self-contained and standoffish. Liesl wouldn't have guessed that their new neighbor's sometimes-gruff manners would have put her mother so entirely at ease.

"You won't be offended if I work while we visit?" Mary asked after ushering them in.

"Not at all." Mother sat at the table with a sigh of contentment.

"What are you working on?" Liesl asked. "I'd be happy to help."

"One of the shelves near the stove is loose." Mary grabbed a hammer off the chair set over by the shelves and stood on the seat. She popped a couple of nails between her teeth and set to work.

"This house was empty for some time," Liesl said, looking around. "There are likely a few things in need of repair."

"Plenty enough." Even with her lips holding nails in place, Mary could be understood. "John's up to his eyes."

"The Reynoldses took such good care of their home and land," Mother said. "And they've been gone only six months. Has it fallen to bits so quickly?"

"Mother Nature stakes her claim quickly," Liesl said.

After pounding in a nail, Mary offered her thoughts. "Not all of the problems have been from a house sitting idle. There were wall boards broken in the barn that had to've been shattered by some kind of blow. And John said the window in the bedroom was broken from the inside; he found glass in the dirt outside."

"So, not likely a tree branch blown by the wind or something like that." Liesl had been telling herself in the months since the Reynoldses had departed that they'd left peacefully. Sometimes that was hard to believe. Signs of violence didn't at all give her peace of mind.

Mary pounded in her last remaining nail, then tested the sturdiness of the shelf. Apparently satisfied, she climbed down.

"The floorboards were pulled up in some places," she said. "Makes me wonder if someone had hidden something there and fetched it out later, or if someone *thought* something was hidden and went looking for it."

Liesl knew the Charming Chaps sometimes ransacked houses when townspeople didn't pay their taxes. Might've been her father and his cronies pilfering after the Reynoldses left. Or the Reynoldses, themselves, might've torn up the floor in order to retrieve something they'd tucked away.

Mary returned the chair to the table. "My brother'd likely sell his soul for an apple tart," she said. "I try to make them regularly so he'll not be tempted if Old Scratch comes along offering one. I was planning to make some just now. Do you mind—"

"We didn't come to disrupt your day," Liesl assured her. "We'll help if we can and leave when you need us to."

She shook her head. "You don't need to go. I like having company."

Liesl and her mother took up the task of peeling apples, which Mary then sliced.

"Does Mr. Butler demand apple tarts often?" Mother asked.

"Demand?" Mary smiled as she repeated the word. "I cain't imagine John 'demanding' anything. He's a bit rough around the edges, and I'd not care to be at odds with him, but he's a good sort, treats people well."

"But as the man of the house," Mother pressed. "Not getting his way'll make him madder than a hornet in a jar. I'd not want you to have any difficulty on account of us."

Mary looked at her more closely. "By 'difficulty' do you mean 'danger'?"

Mother kept at her peeling, the short, quick strokes with the paring knife made with more earnestness than grace. "Men aren't the sort that ought to be crossed."

"Not all men are horrible when they're angry," Mary said.

Mother looked entirely unconvinced.

"Otto was a gentle soul," Liesl reminded her. "You cain't deny that." To Mary's confused expression, Liesl said, "My brother."

Mary nodded.

Mother turned miserable eyes on Liesl. "Do you suppose poor Mr. Butler will end the same as Otto did, being a gentle soul and all?"

"I said he was a good sort," Mary said, quick to correct. "I didn't say he was a 'gentle soul.'"

Now that was an interesting clarification.

"Is he violent?" Mother asked quietly.

Mary, who'd seemed a little thick-skinned, reached over and patted Mother's hand. "John is, I suspect, nothing at all like . . . the man you're comparing him to. He is forceful and fearsome when he needs to be, and his past ain't exactly pristine, but he's a man of principle and honor. I ain't never been afraid of him, and you don't need to be either."

John Butler grew more intriguing by the moment.

"If you're late with his meals, he don't hurt you?" Mother pressed, her eyes darting to Liesl.

"Not ever," Mary said.

That earned Liesl a quick, pointed look from her mother. They both knew not all men were so forgiving of delays. What would it be like to have a man in her life who she didn't have to be afraid of, whose whims and hunger and pride didn't pose a constant and changing threat?

Liesl said very little as they continued helping Mary prepare her tart. She wasn't feeling pensive; she simply didn't have a chance. It was such an odd thing to hear her mother talking at length with anyone, let alone someone new. Though Liesl hated the idea of the Butlers being trapped in a place as miserable as Sand Creek, her heart was grateful that her mother had managed to make a friend.

They'd nearly finished their work when the door flew open, and John stormed inside, his jaw tight and his hands curled in fists. Mother tensed and pulled back in her chair.

"What has you in such a taking?" Mary asked her brother in a tone that contained not the tiniest bit of worry.

He held up a piece of paper, crumpled by the white-knuckle hold he had on it. "*This* was nailed to the barn door."

"I'm going to assume it weren't a love letter," Mary said.

He flipped it around and read out loud. "You are hereby under notice that your municipal taxes are scheduled to be collected in five days."

Liesl's heart dropped.

"Municipal taxes?" Mary rose and crossed to him, looking down at the paper he held. "The land agent didn't say anything about additional taxes."

"That blasted land agent also didn't say that our deed wouldn't be filed in our name."

"What?" Mary shot him a wide-eyed look.

"Liesl, here, suggested I take a peek at our deed, so I dropped in to the land office this morning. Our land is recorded as belonging to some fella named Harry Bendtkirk with the two of us listed as 'tenants.'"

"Tenants, my eye," Mary snapped. "We bought this land."

"Not according to the territorial government. Dressen, the land clerk, claims he don't know how this happens. Swore up and down that he files the deeds just like he's supposed to and never touches 'em again, but when people come look at 'em, they've been changed so all the land belongs to this same Harry Bendtkirk."

"If the papers are only changed here, that don't change the ownership officially," Mary said.

"Asked him that. He said he's looked into it, and the deeds *are* filed with the territorial government in Bendtkirk's name. *Officially.*"

Mary didn't say anything, but there was no mistaking she was angry.

"And that ain't all." He held up the paper once more. "We get to pay taxes for the privilege of living here on this land that's been stolen from us."

Mother sat tense and terrified, watching this mountain of a man rage at the reality of life in this isolated corner of the world. Though Liesl didn't know John well yet, she felt certain Mary had been honest about her brother's character. Even angry, he didn't seem to be a danger to any of them in the house.

He looked to Liesl. "Is this your father's doing?" He waved the paper.

"He enforces the taxation," she said.

"But didn't implement it?"

She shrugged. "I don't know how it started. Been happening for as long as I can remember, even before he became sheriff."

"Well, it stops now." He wadded up the paper and tossed it in the empty fireplace. "I ain't paying these blame cursed taxes."

"Oh, Mary," Mother pleaded. "You have to convince him. You have to, please. It's dangerous."

Mary's eyes darted from John to Mother and back a few times, clearly unsure which crisis to address first.

Liesl rose. "I'll try to explain to him, Mother. Don't fret. I've managed it before."

Mary took Liesl's unspoken cue and returned to the table, speaking quietly and calmly to Mother while Liesl crossed to the fireplace.

"Is this the beehive you told me not to kick?" John grumbled.

"I told you no one has money enough to leave this place. This is why. What they pay for their land disappears. What they make from their land is taken from them in taxes."

"The taxes are a swindle, then?"

"Oh, no. They're very real. As are the consequences of refusing to pay them."

That brought his eyes to hers. What she saw there sent her back a step. She didn't feel threatened, but there was no denying the hardness she saw in his expression. This was a man who had known battle, who had put down threats, who had—as Mary said—a less-than-pristine past.

This was no mere farmer.

"And what if I don't have the money for these taxes?" He spoke through tight teeth.

"It can be paid in kind."

He shook his head. "I don't have anything of value."

Lands, this was not a good turn of events. "You must have something."

"Not even a gold tooth."

Liesl rubbed at her temple. "The Harpers know of a place out by Newell Lake where you could make camp for a few days. It'd grant you a little extra time to think of something."

He glanced in the direction of the Harper farm. "That's where they were those few days they disappeared."

She nodded. "I don't know what they paid with in the end, but being away for a time saved them a lot of misery."

"Except they are still poorer for it."

"Everyone is poor here, John."

"And trapped." He paced away. "And, I suspect, in danger."

"I do my best to help," she said. "I warn people when I can. I help them sort out ways to pay their taxes or barter for more time. I show them they're not alone in all this."

"But you don't help them escape?"

She held up her hands, helpless. "What can I do? I'm as much a prisoner as they are. More so, in many ways."

His pacing brought him back to her. Eyes holding hers, he asked, softly, "Are you afraid of your father, Liesl?"

"Anyone with any sense is afraid of him," she answered.

"He's outnumbered, though."

She shook her head. "Not as much as you think."

Understanding dawned in his dark eyes. "He don't work alone."

She set her hand on his arm, pleading with him. "Find a way to pay the tax bill, John. I'm beggin' you."

He set his hand on top of hers. "What happens to people who don't?"

"People who kick the beehive?" Regret broke in her voice. "I can't always save them from the stings."

"You said the bees in Sand Creek do *more* than just sting."

So many faces flipped through her memory: the Reynoldses, Otto, Mr. Jones, old widow Bloom. "Please don't shake things, John. Keep the hive calm. It's safer if you do."

His hand gently cupped her jaw. "Is this how you spend your days, lamb? Saving people?"

"I try." The two-syllable response was all she could manage. The brush of his hand on her face had tied her in surprisingly enjoyable knots and tossed her thoughts into commotion.

John leaned close and whispered, "You let yourself rest on the matter of John Butler's safety, Liesl. I've faced fiercer lions than the ones that roam these parts."

She wanted to tell him not to underestimate the threat. She wanted to warn him that the lions grew rabid when crossed. But her heart pounded too hard for words, silencing her as she stood there, a mere breath separating them.

A quiet but rapid knock echoed off the door. They all looked in that direction, but it was Mary who moved first.

She pulled it open and little Jamie Harper rushed inside. "You have to help me, Mr. But—" His eyes fell on Liesl, and he immediately changed course, crossing to her instead. "Miss Hodges." He snagged her dress in his fist, pulling her toward the door. "Please help. You have to help Papa."

"What happened to your papa?" she asked as he dragged her forward.

"He didn't have the taxes."

Mercy. "The men who came to collect—are they still there?" She needed to know how much danger she would be in when she arrived.

"They took our things." He'd pulled her out of the house and was well on his way to reaching the road. "Mama and Margaret and me, we hid."

"Are they gone now?" she pressed.

He looked up at her with tears covering his lashes and pooling in the corners of his eyes. "They're gone, but Papa's in a bad way."

She pried his fingers from her dress and took his hand in hers, moving at as fast a clip as his short legs could keep up. The Harpers were the nearest neighbors, but it was still a fair pace to their house.

At the sound of wheels rolling up behind them, she tugged Jamie off the road to let it pass, praying it wasn't her father or any of the Charming Chaps coming to inflict more consequences on the Harper family.

It was John, driving her pony cart.

"Hop up." It was not a suggestion. "This'll be faster."

"My mother—"

"Mary'll drive her home in our wagon. She'll be fine." He motioned them up once more. "We need to see to Mr. Harper."

Liesl lifted Jamie to the wagon bench, then climbed up herself. John set the cart in motion, and Jamie clung to her, clearly unsure of this near-stranger taking charge of the effort.

They reached the Harper place quickly. Liesl rushed in first with Jamie quick on her heels. John, she had no doubt, would join them as soon as he could secure the pony.

The inside of the home was even worse than she'd feared. It had been left in chaos. Furniture was broken and overturned. Floorboards were pulled up. The damage was still too fresh for her to be able to tell if anything had been taken.

In the midst of it all, Mrs. Harper knelt on the ground beside her husband, pressing a damp cloth to his forehead. She looked up as Liesl approached. All the color had drained from her face. Absolute terror still shone in her eyes.

"They wouldn't accept a partial payment." Her voice quivered.

"I didn't know they were coming." Liesl knelt on the other side of Mr. Harper. "I'd have warned you if they'd let even a hint slip. They usually talk at length during lunch about their plans for the day."

Mr. Harper was conscious and alert, which was a good sign, but he'd been beaten. Liesl hoped he wasn't bleeding inside. The nearest doctor was in Savage Wells, too far for emergencies.

"I wish I could stop this," she said to them both. "Heaven knows I've tried. We did better when Otto was—" She couldn't finish the sentence.

Mrs. Harper continued cleaning the blood from her husband's face while Liesl checked for broken bones. They'd need to splint any before moving him. The Harper children stood nearby, too scared to even whimper.

My family has done this. My father. The guilt of that never fully left her shoulders. It weighed her down every day of her life. Nothing she did would ever make right the wrongs committed by her father.

If John's heavy, confident footsteps hadn't given him away, his low rumbling voice muttering a coarse word Liesl had learned in the jailhouse would have.

"Oh, Mr. Butler." Mrs. Harper's voice warbled. "Look what they've done to our house, and after you helped us fix the damage from last time."

"I hadn't realized that damage was done by tax collectors." John didn't cross to the prostrate form on the ground but directly to the trembling children. He took one in each arm and held them firmly, closely, comfortingly.

"We thought they might accept some of our seed for next year as payment, but they refused," Mrs. Harper said.

"Without your seed, you wouldn't have a crop." John patted Jamie's back, and Margaret tucked herself tighter into his arms.

Tears spilled from Mrs. Harper's eyes. "We don't have anything else."

John brought the children over but kept them turned away from the sight of their father. "Take the little ones away from here for a few minutes." He spoke gently, but firmly. "Liesl and I will see to your husband."

"Don't let him die," Mrs. Harper pleaded.

"He ain't gonna."

She took her children and walked with slow steps out the back door.

John took her spot on the floor. He looked at Liesl. "Did I just lie to that woman? Is her husband aiming for the grave?"

"I don't think so." She met Mr. Harper's eye. "You ain't dying, are you?"

"Wish I were," he answered in an anguished whisper.

"None of that kind of talk," Liesl said. "You're hurting now, but you'll be grateful to still be alive once the pain has ebbed." She motioned with her head for John to take up the efforts Mrs. Harper had abandoned. "Do you have any pain powders in the house?"

"Shelf." Mr. Harper breathed out the word. "By the basin."

She rose, speaking to John as she crossed the room. "I think his right arm's broken. We'll need to splint it."

John reached across the man to check the bones in his forearm. "We'll have to straighten it first. Won't do him a lick of good to have it heal like this."

"I'm not strong enough to put a bone back in place." Liesl'd had plenty of chances to try.

"I am," John assured her. "I've done it more than once."

This man had a past, no denying it. But what exactly that past was, she didn't know. She was almost afraid to ask. She would simply cling to Mary's reassurances that he was a good man even if he weren't a saintly one.

They worked in tandem for more than an hour. Mr. Harper was cleaned and tended. His bone was set, the experience excruciating for him. John splinted Mr. Harper's arm. Liesl stitched up a nasty gash in his shoulder. Finally, John carried the bruised and broken man to his bed.

They then set themselves the task of putting the house to rights, but some things couldn't be fixed without tools and supplies. John promised his neighbor he'd come by and make those repairs as soon as he was able.

By the time Mrs. Harper returned with the children, she looked calmer, and the house was once more livable.

"I am sorry," Liesl said as they were making their farewells. "I am sorry my father does this. I'm sorry he hurts people."

"It ain't your fault, Liesl," Mrs. Harper said. "Without you, he'd hurt a lot more."

It was cold comfort, but it was all she had. She'd described Sand Creek as a beehive, as a prison, a trap. But, more than anything, it was hell.

Chapter 8

Hawk knew the lay of the land everywhere he went and in every situation. But Sand Creek had him befuddled, and he didn't like it.

Sheriff Hodges was the driving force behind the violent collection of taxes. But was that his only area of corruption? Hawk knew there was a no-good sheriff somewhere in his jurisdiction. Was Hodges the one Rod Carlisle had been referring to, or was there *another* weak link in the chain? Someone in Sand Creek was plotting to assassinate Hawk; could that someone be the sheriff? And who had sent the telegram warning him? And what had happened to the Reynoldses? Who else had disappeared under shady circumstances? And who the blazes was Harry Bendtkirk, the man who laid claim to everyone's land in the area? And was the land clerk, Dressen, really innocent in the whole thing?

Too many questions with no answers. No. He didn't like it at all.

"I did try to warn you." Liesl's voice broke into his spinning thoughts.

He was driving her back to her house in town, but she'd been so quiet, he'd nearly forgotten she was there.

"More mercy is shown with first payments than later ones," she said. "If you can pay even a portion of it, you aren't likely to be torn up like Mr. Harper."

Hawk shook his head. "I ain't paying a single cent."

"You saw what they did, John. You might think yourself able to defend against an attack on you, but Mary might not be so fortunate."

He looked away from the road just long enough to evaluate how serious she was. *Fully and completely.* "They'd attack a woman?"

"There's a reason Mrs. Harper and the children were hiding too."

Whether this was the rogue sheriff that Hawk was searching out or not, Hodges needed to be brought down.

Liesl had said her father didn't do his dirty work alone.

"How many people are part of these tax collecting efforts?" They'd reached the edges of the small town, so Hawk kept his voice low.

"There are four of them in his core group, but there are others in his pocket as well." She spoke low and fast as well.

"Is Dressen at the land office one of them others?"

"Strangely enough, I don't think so. But I suppose he could be." She shook her head. "No one's able to say for certain who the others might be. Even when people in town start to trust each other, there's always a question. There's always a chance they oughtn't be trusted."

Hawk pulled the pony cart along the back of Liesl's home. "And there ain't no stopping what can't be identified."

"I've tried, John. My father's a dangerous man." Her gaze remained firm and her posture determined, but real fear had entered her eyes. "And he knows a great many dangerous people."

"Why ain't you told this to the territorial government? Or the US Marshals?"

"And tell 'em what? That my father's extorting people and having them beaten if they try to resist, but that I can't prove it because he denies it and his victims are too terrified to testify against him?" She held her hands out in a show of frustration. "Without evidence, he'd saunter right out of any courtroom free as a jaybird, and he'd be bolder and meaner, and all of Sand Creek would pay dearly for it."

"Even *you*? His own daughter?"

She tossed him a look that told him in no uncertain terms that, if he didn't know the answer to his own question, then he wasn't terribly bright.

"I'll walk in with you, then. Make certain all's well."

Caution entered her expression. "Don't confront him, John. It'll only make things worse."

He could appreciate that. "I'll keep to a different room. I do need to fetch Mary, though. And it'd set my mind at ease to know she and your mother arrived safely."

"We can slip in the door of the lean-to and through the kitchen," Liesl said. "My father's never in the kitchen, but it's where my mother's most likely to be."

They did precisely that, but instead of finding Mrs. Hodges, Paisley sat in a chair near the woodstove, watching them as they emerged from the lean-to.

"Wondered if that was you," she said, her voice quiet. "You're missing quite a conversation."

Hawk perked his ears. Voices floated in from just beyond the room.

"That's my father," Liesl said quietly.

Paisley nodded. "And Mr. Dana. They've been discussing . . . taxes."

Hawk eyed her with a small inquisitive raise of one brow. She gave the tiniest, almost imperceptible shake of her head. It seemed neither man had managed to reveal anything useful during the over-heard conversation.

"Your mother went up to her room," Paisley told Liesl. "But your father managed to toss a few complaints her way before she escaped."

"He always does." Liesl set her shoulders. "I'll go check on my mother. Thank you both for your help today."

Hawk dipped his head. "Our pleasure, Miss Liesl."

She slipped from the kitchen, and Hawk turned to address Paisley, but she shushed him, motioning with her head toward the door Liesl had just stepped through.

In the next instant, Sheriff Hodges's voice carried back to them. "I'll not abide dillydallying, girl."

"I wasn't lazing about," Liesl said from the next room. "Mr. Harper was in a bad way, and I was being neighborly."

"The man probably got drunk, busted up his house, and got himself hurt in the process." Sheriff Hodges made the accusation with just enough jeering in his voice to turn the stomach of anyone who knew the true source of Harper's injuries. "You should've let him sort his own mess."

"I saw no evidence of drunkenness," Liesl said.

In a tone tight with anger, the sheriff replied, "Are you calling me a liar, girl?"

"Of course not." Her tone had turned cautious.

"Seems to me you are." Mr. Dana entered the conversation. "I've heard from a lot of people that Harper is a drunkard. All of Sand Creek knows it."

Hawk had heard absolutely nothing of the sort. He doubted anyone other than Dana and Hodges had ever insinuated any such thing.

"I'll leave you to your visit," Liesl said.

"And go where?" Hodges never seemed to make any comment without turning it into an accusation.

"Upstairs," Liesl said.

"We've not had our dinner. You'll not laze about the place while we're hungry."

"I'll hang my coat on its nail then hop straight to the stove."

"See to it you don't keep us waiting. You know I won't abide that."

A threat. It oughtn't to have been surprising.

"We should scoot," Paisley said. "Liesl will have enough to juggle without us adding to the tension."

Wise. "But is she safe here?"

"Is a woman ever safe in the home of a cur like that?"

Frustration bubbled inside Hawk. "We can't simply leave the ladies here where there's danger."

Paisley rose, eyeing him with obvious curiosity. "You're usually more levelheaded than this. Don't tell me the 'Marshal with a Heart of Stone' is having some tender feelings for a certain sheriff's daughter."

He'd have laughed if the suggestion were any less ridiculous. "I'm charged with keeping the entire territory safe. Not knowing about Sheriff Hodges's reign of terror has endangered lives here, including his daughter's. That's a failure I mean to make up for."

He made his way back through the lean-to, knowing Paisley would follow. They climbed into their wagon and set off in the direction of the home they'd paid for but, apparently, had no claim on.

Tender feelings? Ridiculous.

He was Marshal Hawking. The man who'd brought peace to a dangerous territory. The man who'd assembled a team of deputies who were equally feared and respected. The man who'd dedicated his life to saving others.

He had no tender feelings.

He couldn't afford them.

Chapter 9

Ain't no stopping what can't be identified.

John's words from the night before had echoed in Liesl's mind ever since. She'd been trying for years to protect the town against a threat she couldn't entirely identify. It had been a losing battle from the beginning.

She wasn't willing to give up, which left her with only one option: identify every member of her father's ruthless band and gather enough evidence to convict them all. And try to keep herself safe while doing it.

Her determination solidified quickly, but her nervousness remained. She'd somehow managed to get the telegram out to Marshal Hawking without being caught, though she wasn't certain it'd done any good. Her next bit of bravery might see her luck run out.

She'd failed her brother. She wouldn't fail Sand Creek too.

Her father had stayed up late, drinking and cussing and generally grumbling about the "ungrateful" people who didn't appreciate the need to pay their "fair share" in taxes. The more sauced he'd grown, the less useful his grumblings had been. She'd gone to bed, determined to eavesdrop, as usual, during lunch the next day.

With that goal in mind, she arrived at the jail with a tray of food for her father and the Charming Chaps. Meat for the sheriff. Cobbler for Mr. Kirkpatrick. No mustard, peaches, or string beans for Mr. Yarrow. Extra butter on the bread for Mr. Dana. She doled out their food without comment, but listening closely.

"Carlisle is still biding," Mr. Dana said. "Can't help with bird-watching if he's riding the calaboose."

Calaboose was jail. They were talking of someone behind bars. Another member of their criminal crew, no doubt.

Liesl silently repeated the name, committing it to memory. Should the man escape prison or be released and come to Sand Creek, he'd bear watching.

"Except there's those who're bird-watching in Laramie," her father said. "Carlisle can keep an ear perked from in the cage."

The territorial prison was in Laramie. Carlisle was not a half-bit criminal, then.

Liesl had set out all the plates. As quietly as she could, she moved her serving things out of the way, listening all the while.

"Porters ain't paid their taxes yet," Mr. Kirkpatrick said, tossing a coin into the ante. "Seems they're past due by now."

"Certainly are." Father eyed the gathered men and, with a smile a snake would be proud of, said, "Care for a late-afternoon stroll, chaps?"

Late afternoon. Taxes. Porters. Liesl needed to get a word of warning to them, which would prevent her from listening further. How was she to stop her father if her days were filled with rushing about saving people from him?

Just as she turned to step outside, John Butler stepped inside. The entire room went silent. No matter that he'd not said a word, no matter that he had no authority in Sand Creek, four of the most powerful men in the area grew instantly on alert at his arrival. He commanded a room that way, a farmer who was clearly a little dangerous. Sometimes Liesl didn't know what to make of him.

"Men," John said, his voice firm and demanding but still quiet. "A minute of your time." It wasn't a question.

"We're busy men." Father leaned back in his chair, adopting the air of one who was unimpressed with his company.

"If you've time enough for cards and meals, you've time enough for the townspeople you've taken an oath to serve."

Father sat straighter, eyeing John narrowly. "You calling me lazy?"

"Don't believe I said any such thing." John set his hat on a nail near the door. "I've a question on the matter of taxes."

"Ah." Father tossed his friends a smirk.

"Taxes are the duty of any citizen," Mr. Dana said. "You'd not wish to be a drain on the town, surely."

"I've come to ask for an accounting of them. What's being paid for with the taxes. A record of the laws passed that levied them. An audit of the town budget showing what the taxes are meant for and where they're going." John dipped his head to Mr. Dana. "I'd hate for my taxes to not be helping like they ought, making me a drain on the town rather than an asset."

"So it ain't that you're calling us lazy," Mr. Yarrow said. "You're saying you don't trust us."

"Us?" John repeated in a voice that wasn't entirely innocent. "Are all of you the town treasurer, collectively?"

"We're the town council. Sometimes we act as deputies to the sheriff, here," Mr. Dana said. "We run Sand Creek."

"A mighty big job for only four men."

"Not for the *right* four men." Mr. Yarrow couldn't have sounded more pompous if he'd tried.

John nodded. "I've come to the right men, then. I'll be obliged to you for them things I asked for. You know where to find me when you've gathered 'em."

"We know where to find you when your taxes come due," Father warned.

Unconcerned, John pulled his hat from the nail and plopped it on his head. "First things first, men. First things first."

On that, he left.

"He'll pay," Mr. Dana grumbled. "They always pay their taxes, one way or another."

That made two people Liesl needed to warn.

Trying not to draw too much attention, she slipped from the jailhouse in time to see John approaching his sister a bit up the street.

Liesl moved swiftly toward them. John said something to Mary, then met Liesl halfway.

"I know you told me not to kick the beehive," John said, "but shaking it is proving needful."

"They're going to be angry," Liesl said. "They're even more dangerous when their 'tax collecting' is personal."

"You've duly warned me. And I don't mean to press my luck overly much. Pointing out that there're ways to prove something ain't lawful is a good way to find out whether or not it is."

She didn't fully follow.

"The looks on their faces when I said I wanted to know which laws had been passed creating these taxes told me no laws were ever passed. That's a piece of the pie right there."

"And asking if they were *all* the town treasurers?" Liesl couldn't imagine that had been an idle question.

"Sorting out if they do, indeed, have others working for them."

"They didn't admit to anything," Liesl pointed out.

"Didn't have to. Yarrow's attempt at arrogance fell too short of the mark to have been anything but a shallow show. They've others, for sure and certain."

John had struck at the heart of the matter quickly and easily and without entirely playing his hand. He was precisely the sort of ally she could use. And trust. "One of those others is in jail in Laramie— they said as much."

"Laramie?" John seemed to know why that was significant. "Did they give a name for the prisoner?"

"Carlisle. I made sure to lock it in my brainbox."

"Maybe this fella'll prove a turncoat," John said. "How do we get word from here to Laramie? Might be there's someone down there who'll listen in."

"That'd be a risk."

His eyes narrowed. "The listening in or the getting word out."

"Both, I suppose," she said. "But for us, the 'getting word out' part. We've a telegraph office, but Mr. Yarrow runs it. And he's part of the trouble."

John rubbed the back of his neck. "Does anyone else work at the telegraph office? Anyone trustworthy?"

Thank heavens he'd not asked if anyone else knew how to send a telegram. She'd not have liked to lie to him, but admitting she knew how would tiptoe awfully close to giving away the fact that she'd done it before.

"He's the only operator we have."

John made a sound that was equal parts pondering and disappointment. "We'll have to think on that puzzle."

We. She'd not had anyone to help her thwart her father's reign of misery since losing her brother. She'd lost him *to* those efforts. Allowing others to take on the risk had been unthinkable. Yet, John had done so without hesitation, without quaking at the threat they faced.

"I've been fighting this fight for years without a 'we' to tackle it."

He met her eye, and something in his smile proved soothing, almost soft. John was clearly not a soft man, yet there was the tiniest bit of gentleness in his expression. "You've that now, Liesl. I'll help you. As will Mary. You're not doing this alone now."

"It is more dangerous than you likely know." She couldn't, in good conscience, let him proceed without at least trying to help him see how enormous the threat truly was. "People've been hurt, John. People have died."

"Then it's all the more important that we do what we can to stop the sheriff and his chums." Not even a moment's vacillation.

That set her mind a little at ease. A very little. "Would you or Mary be willing to drive me out to the Porter place after I clear out lunch at the jail? I need to issue a warning."

John nodded. "Another tax collection, I assume."

"Always."

He gave a quick nod. "Meet us back here once you've finished up at the jail. We'll be waiting."

Relief like Liesl hadn't known in ages spread through her. She had an ally, a friend. She had someone in this town she could trust.

Liesl's discussion with the Porters had been short and surprising. The Charming Chaps had declared the Porters late on their tax payment, but Mr. Porter swore up one side and down the other he never received a tax notice. He hadn't any idea his taxes were due. Was this her father's newest strategy, to attack without warning?

"You're pensive today," John said. She was sitting next to him on the wagon bench as they drove back to town. He'd dropped Mary off at their house on the way out to the Porters.

"I've never heard of the Charming Chaps declaring someone's taxes late before giving notice that they're due."

John glanced at her before returning his gaze to the road. "The Charming Chaps?"

She felt her lips tug to one side. "I started calling them that a few years back. It helped me not be so afraid of them."

"But you still are, aren't you?"

She nodded. "And I think they know it."

John pulled the wagon off the road and down a pace.

"Have you sniffed out some back way into town?" she asked.

He shook his head. "I thought the horses could use a rest. And I figured you might appreciate being able to breathe before having to go back into town."

How did he know that when she'd not said a word?

John stopped the wagon not far from the town's namesake creek. While he tended to his team, she settled herself in a spot on the banks of the creek, shaded by a scraggly tree. She didn't get many moments to herself; she was always either trying to keep her father happy or her mother safe or protecting the town from one danger or another.

Sometimes she forgot just how tired she was.

She picked up a flat-bottomed pebble and flicked out across the water, managing to get it to skip.

"Well done," John said. He sat next to her, his eyes on the creek. "Who taught you to skip rocks?"

She let the air empty from her lungs before answering. "My brother, Otto." Her heart ached every time she thought about him. He'd tried so hard to stop their father, and he'd paid so dearly for it.

John snatched a pebble himself and flicked it out toward the water just as she had, getting a skip of his own.

"Who taught *you* to skip rocks?" she asked him.

"My mother," he said.

She tossed another pebble. Still one skip. "Things were so much better when my brother was alive. My father was still a monster—that's been true of him probably all his life—but with Otto, there was another person helping rein in the monster."

"You must miss him something terrible." He skipped another pebble.

"Every day," she said. "My mother struggles to even talk about him. It's just as well. My father don't allow us to, anyhow."

"Does your father know how much you do to help Sand Creek survive him?"

She couldn't help the small shudder that echoed through her. "Criminy, no. He'd string me up, sure as you're sitting here."

"I assure you, lamb, if I were sitting beside you, he'd not be given a chance to string you up."

She looked at him, grinning. "You'd not care to see me dangling at the end of a rope?"

She meant it as a bit of light teasing. But that fierce crease between his eyes appeared, the one that warned a person he wasn't someone to be trifled with.

"I sure hope you ain't serious in asking that. How could you think I'd like for you to be killed?"

He made the declaration in frustration, but it tiptoed over her like the tenderest of compliments. "It's been a long time since someone cared what happened to me, John Butler. I ain't accustomed to it."

He flung another rock, this time getting two skips from it. "I'd wager your mother cares a great deal what happens to you. She's just so beaten down herself that she likely doesn't know what to do about it."

That was truer than the sky was blue. Liesl had watched, helplessly, as her mother changed over the years. With each passing day, week, month, her mother collapsed more and more into herself. It was little wonder Liesl felt so very alone.

"How are the Harpers doing?" she asked him. "I worry about them something fierce. My father was so angry that I helped Mr. Harper after his 'drunken episode'"—she uttered the last bit so dryly, no one would possibly have believed she was in earnest—"I've not dared make my way out there. I don't want to make things worse for them."

"Or for yourself," John added.

She smiled at him. "I'm beginning to suspect you're fond of me."

"Beginning to suspect?" He shook his head. "If you're only suspecting, you ain't paying much attention."

How was it he could say things that sounded frustrated when they hit her ears, but sounded lovely by the time they reached her heart?

She found another flat rock on the ground beside her. It was perfect for skipping. She tested it in her hand, finding the right angle. Careful as she could, she flicked it and counted the skips. One. Two. Three. It plunked and sank.

She turned to him, excitement filling her. She took hold of his arm. "Three! Did you see that, John? Three!"

He returned her smile with a dazzling one of his own. Land's sake, but that man could smile.

"I can see I've been bested for the day." He chuckled. "Well and truly bested."

It had been so long since she'd interacted with a man whose pride didn't make him angry at losing a simple game. John was something more than merely fair-minded. He was strong and firm, but also kind and thoughtful. He made her smile, made her laugh. Of all the people she'd known over the years, he seemed most likely to actually survive life in this soul-shattering place. If only he would be careful.

His smile slipped. "How is it you've gone from giddy to worried so quickly?" His dark eyes studied her face, seeming to linger just a moment on her mouth.

Her voice emerged, breathless. "Am I frowning?"

"You are a bit, lamb. I can't say I like seeing it."

His gaze remained on her downturned lips, and she couldn't help returning the scrutiny in kind. He did have a breath-snatching smile, but there was something else fascinating about the man's mouth, something that made her breath hitch up and made her heart dance about like that one-legged squirrel he'd talked about. It left her feeling warm all over, even on a day like today when the wind blew a bit chill. She never wanted to let go of his arm.

He reached over and brushed back a strand of hair the wind had blown across her face. Her hitched breath seemed to turn solid in an instant at his touch. She couldn't have spoken if she tried, and she certainly couldn't let go.

"For the record, Liesl Hodges, I do care what happens to you, and I worry about you."

Finding just enough presence of mind to whisper, she said, "That feeling is mutual, John Butler. Promise me you'll be careful. The Charming Chaps ain't charming in the least. They're dangerous, John."

She couldn't be certain, but she thought he moved closer. He was certainly *looking* more closely. She was entirely certain her heart was fixing to tear itself to bits, rattling around like it was in her chest.

"I've skinned fiercer cats than these, lamb. But I promise you I'll be careful."

"Are you fixin' to stay in Sand Creek, then?" She didn't know which answer she wanted to hear. Staying meant she might get to sit like this with him again. Might spend hours pondering why it was he couldn't seem to take his eyes off her lips for more than a moment at a time. She might find out if those mesmerizing lips of his were good for more than just smiling.

But staying also meant he'd be living under the tyranny of her father, trapped, frustrated, and angry. She couldn't abide the thought of him being unhappy.

"That's a complicated answer," he said. "But I can tell you that, for the moment, I intend to bide here awhile."

Even with the warmth of his tone and the nearness of his body and her heart pattering inside her, his answer was a much-needed splash of cold water. He didn't know if he'd be staying, and he hadn't said he was leaving on account of the tyranny here. He might simply up and go because it was what his family had always done. If her father drove him away, that'd hurt, but it wouldn't feel like he was leaving *her*. Moving on simply because Sand Creek was only a stop in his wanderings would feel far more personal.

Falling for John Butler would be a bad idea, indeed.

She pulled her arm away and flicked another rock. This time the rock only skipped once before sinking into the creek.

They spent time skipping rocks and talking pleasantly about little nothings. As he drove her back into town, she felt the energy between them growing warmer and more comfortable. And though her mind was following the course of their conversation, her heart was having another discussion entirely.

She'd told herself not to fall for John Butler. Her heart knew that was a fool's hope. Falling for him was no longer in question.

She'd fallen in love with him already.

Chapter 10

Sometimes a US Marshal needed to burst into a room. Sometimes he needed finesse.

Early in the morning, two days after learning of the Charming Chaps' connection to Rod Carlisle, Hawk employed a third approach: breaking into a place like a sneak thief.

He could pick locks with the best of them, but Paisley was faster. So he held the dark lantern, its shutters aiming light only to the precise place they needed it, while she swiftly fiddled with the lock of the telegraph office. Quick as anything, they were inside.

No words were needed between them as they got to work. They'd done this sort of thing often enough. Paisley took up the accounting book. Hawk set his sights on the indexing cabinet. He positioned the lantern so they had light enough to work by, but no one outside would have any idea anyone was inside.

Hawk started his search with the bottom drawers. Ink. Blank paper. Supplies. Nothing of much help.

"This telegram mentions Carlisle." Paisley held up a paper in the dim light from the lantern. "Incoming. One week ago."

The note was scrawled in rushed writing; Mr. Yarrow's, no doubt. He read it quickly.

CARLISLE STILL HELD |STOP|
BIRD-WATCHING HERE |STOP|
PLEASE ADVISE |STOP|

"Bird-watching?" Hawk repeated, tossing that around in his head. No prisoner was doing a lick of bird-watching. It had to mean something else.

"Wasn't the assassination plot you were warned of supposed to play out in Laramie?" Paisley asked.

He nodded. "Wouldn't put it past Carlisle to be part of it. Hodges, either."

"Or any of his conniving comrades." Paisley returned to her search.

Assassination plot. Bird-watching.

"Ah," he said as understanding dawned. "Bird-watching."

Paisley looked over at him, eyes curious.

"A hawk is a bird. They're watching for me in Laramie."

"Lands," Paisley muttered. "We've got to sort this out before bird-watching turns to hunting season."

"I'd prefer that." Hawk pulled open another drawer. "Liesl says no one in this town is likely to testify against the sheriff or his cronies. Coded messages won't be enough without witnesses."

"You say that a lot, you know."

He opened another drawer, finding nothing useful. "Say *what* a lot?"

"'Liesl says.' Can't tell you how many times those two words in that same order have spilled out of your mouth these last couple weeks."

"She's our source of information in Sand Creek. Stands to reason I'd mention her now and then."

"'Now and then,'" Paisley said with a scoff.

"We've haggled over this matter before, and I'll say what I always have. I like her well enough, but mine's a heart of stone. Always has been."

"That ain't true, and we both know it."

"This territory can be thankful for the lie, then." He pulled open another drawer, ignoring the fleeting twinge of regret he felt. He hadn't always been hard; the job had required it of him. He saved lives, even though in many ways it was costing him his own.

"A right shame we can't convince any of the folks in Sand Creek to testify against Hodges and his group," Paisley said. "Might be we couldn't bring him in for plotting to kill you, but snatching up property and beating people to a bloody pulp over illegal taxes would do just as well."

"Without us knowing everyone who is in his pocket, the man could still retaliate even if we tossed him behind bars." Hawk couldn't blame the townspeople for their scared silence, but it was blasted frustrating.

In a drawer about chest height, Hawk found a ledger, which was a far sight more useful than the paper and ink and other supplies he'd come across so far. They'd timed their break-in for the early-morning hours, after the saloon had emptied. That had afforded them more time and ease in their efforts, but not so much that they could dawdle.

Hawk hunched down in the lantern light, flipping through the ledger until he reached the last page that had been written on. The list of incoming and outgoing messages didn't reveal much. One telegram sent. One received. The telegraph operator's initials were listed as "B.Y." Mr. Yarrow, no doubt.

Hawk flipped back to the day he'd received the telegram in Savage Wells warning him of the assassination plot.

Telegram sent to Laramie, operator initials: BY

There were no other entries for that day. Hawk hadn't expected the anonymous messenger to have recorded his efforts, but he'd hoped for some kind of clue.

Yarrow was the only telegraph operator in Sand Creek. But had he always been the only one?

Hawk flipped through the pages backward, moving weeks and months into the past, watching for different initials. Page after page, every entry identified the operator by the initials "B.Y."

"This telegram came the day after we arrested Carlisle and Minor down in Sunset," Paisley said, holding up another paper she'd found. "No talk of bird-watching. Maybe the scheme wasn't hatched right away."

Hawk flipped further back in the ledger, beginning to wonder if they'd find anything at all helpful. And then his eyes fell on a telegraph entry from several years earlier with different initials.

Not "B.Y." But "L.H."

"Blazing buzzards," he muttered.

"What did you find?" Paisley asked.

"Sand Creek might have only one official telegraph operator, but they've two people who know how to work it."

"Who's the other one?" Paisley's tone made it clear she knew the answer would be important.

"Initials are L.H. I can think of only one person hereabouts who'd embroider those initials on her handkerchief."

"Liesl Hodges."

Hawk nodded. "Of all the people in this town, she's clearly the most likely to stand up to her father—the one who has come closest to it. She also knows how to send a telegram."

"*She* sent you the warning," Paisley said. "Which means she can testify about her father's plans to murder you."

"The trick being," Hawk said, "how do we convince her to? He's dangerous. She knows that better than anyone."

"If safety's her only reason for keeping mum, then we protect her," Paisley said. "Keep her safe until the sheriff and his accomplices are rounded up."

"She's said herself there's more of them than we know, more

than even she's been able to identify. We could search all of Sand Creek, all the surrounding area, and we wouldn't have the least idea who to protect her from."

Paisley hunched down beside him. "So we take her away from here, out of reach of her father."

"But to where?"

"Savage Wells," Paisley said. "The two of us'd be there, along with Cade and Tansy and Andrew. Miriam and Gideon'd keep an eye out for her. Enough deputy marshals pass through to make it a safe place for her."

It wasn't a terrible idea. "We'd have to tell her who we really are."

She eyed him sidelong. "You don't seem happy about that."

"She didn't ask to be lied to."

"Hasn't caused you hesitation before."

He knew where her line of questioning was leading. "Heart of stone, Paisley," he said, rising. "Don't try to read any softness into it."

Hawk snapped the ledger closed and returned it to its drawer, then took up the lantern. Paisley followed his lead, setting everything to rights that she'd thumbed through. They were out of the telegraph office a few minutes later, the lantern light extinguished, having left no trace of their presence.

They had a path forward and a witness to encourage to testify.

Hawk ought to have been pleased, but he wasn't. He wasn't at all.

Chapter 11

A note arrived at the house inviting Liesl to have lunch with the Butlers. Warmth wrapped around her heart. Mary treated her as a friend. John had proven himself something a little bit more. He talked to her kindly, told her he cared about what happened to her. He looked at her and smiled at her in a way no one else did. Seeing him again, she'd feel just like a cat that had found the cream pitcher.

Mother had suggested Liesl wear her Sunday dress. With heart lighter than it usually was, she arrived at the Butler house and was greeted by John. He tipped his hat to her, then reached up and helped her dismount.

"Thank you for inviting me for lunch," she said.

"Our pleasure, Liesl."

She walked beside John as he led her mare into the barn.

"Did the Porters scrounge up enough for their tax payment?" John asked.

"Enough to buy a bit of time." Liesl didn't know how much, but she hoped it had saved them from the worst.

"It'd do Sand Creek a world of good if the extortion could be stopped altogether." He led the horse into the only empty stall.

She nodded. "I've done my best to search the jailhouse for any kind of evidence. I ain't sure what I'm looking for, though."

"I suspect they cover their tracks well." Quickly and expertly, he removed the saddle, bridle, and other things from the horse. "Harper is doing better. Saw him this morning."

"I'm so glad to hear that." She leaned against the stall wall. "Have you heard any more about *your* tax bill?"

"Not a peep." A sly, subtle smile tugged at the corners of his mouth.

He was handsome when he smiled. Heavens, he was handsome even when he didn't smile.

And he looked after vulnerable people.

And wasn't afraid of her father.

And treated her with respect and confidence.

It was little wonder she'd fallen for him so fast. Liesl never had been one for calf love or falling to pieces whenever her heart grew partial to someone. Her wits were still intact even if her heart was misbehaving.

Liesl took up the task of brushing her horse while John set the saddle and other things safely aside.

"Are you enjoying Sand Creek?" she asked. "Aside from the taxes and threat of assault, of course."

Again, he allowed a little smile. His smiles came more easily than they had when she'd first met him. What would it take to get him to laugh?

"I enjoy the people in Sand Creek—other than the tax collectors and assault threateners, of course." He motioned her to the barn door. "Anytime I can eavesdrop with a pretty woman is a fine thing."

She shrugged a shoulder. "I am quite a talented eavesdropper."

"Apparently."

They crossed to the house. He held open the door and gestured for her to step inside ahead of him. He was rough around the edges—there was no denying that—but he was also considerate.

Mary nodded in welcome.

"Is there anything I can help with?" Liesl asked.

Mary shook her head, and with a quick flick of her thumb toward the pot simmering on the fire hook, said, "Everything's ready." She was nothing if not efficient.

Liesl took a seat at the table. So did the Butlers.

John rested his arms on the table and folded his hands together. "How long have you lived in Sand Creek?"

"Ten years now. Longer than almost anyone else." That decade felt more like a century. "My father's been sheriff for half that time, though he weren't exactly a model citizen before that."

"Were taxes being collected before he became sheriff?" John asked.

"He and the Chaps were the de facto law here before it was made official. Taxes have always been part of their schemes."

"When did Mr. Yarrow become the telegraph operator?" Mary asked.

It was an odd question, though not entirely so. Mr. Yarrow was one of the Charming Chaps, after all. Next, they'd likely ask her when Mr. Dana had taken charge of the post office and Mr. Kirkpatrick had joined their ranks. "Mr. Yarrow's been in Sand Creek for seven or eight years. He's run the telegraph ever since it came through here about five years ago."

John watched her more closely. "And has he taught anyone else in town how to operate the telegraph?"

Her breath caught in her throat. Before taking the risk to send a message to Marshal Hawking, her knowledge in that area wasn't anything she needed to keep hidden. "No, not as far as I know."

That didn't throw John off the scent at all. "Are there many people who know how but who weren't taught by him?" He watched her too pointedly for the question to be a casual one.

He knew.

But how?

"You've asked me about the telegraph before," she said.

"And you told me Mr. Yarrow was the only one who could operate it."

She shook her head. "You asked if anyone worked in the telegraph shop other than Mr. Yarrow. And no one else does."

"That's cracking the egg twice," John said dryly.

Mary took over the conversation, one that was inching too close to an interrogation for Liesl's peace of mind. "Is there a reason you tiptoed so carefully around your words? And why you're doing so again now?"

"Do you think *I* know how to send a telegram?"

John hadn't looked away. "Do you?" He seemed to know the answer already.

"Is this why you invited me here today?" She meant the question as a distraction, but as it emerged, her heart dropped to her toes. *Was* it the reason? Had it not, in fact, been an invitation issued because she was something special to them? Special to John? "Mr. Yarrow may be a terrible person, but he can send a telegram for you if you're needing to send one."

"Not if the telegram's about him," John said.

The calm calculation she'd admired in John was now proving more than a little disconcerting.

"I have thought about sending word to the territorial authorities about what's happening in Sand Creek." She could acknowledge that much.

"Does seem like a wise approach," John said.

"Not as wise as you think. There are consequences for attempting to rat out the Chaps."

"Someone has tried?"

"Someone needed to."

"Bow out, chum." Mary shook her head. "We need to have a conversation, not a verbal two-step."

John slouched in his chair but still managed to look alert and ready to move into action.

Mary took charge. "Several weeks ago, a telegram arrived in Savage Wells warning Marshal John Hawking of an assassination plot against him."

Liesl's lungs turned to stone.

"Though the telegram's origins weren't specified, it was traced here to Sand Creek. And though the sender was anonymous, you are the only one who could have sent it."

Panic. That was the only word she had for what was beginning to bubble inside. She didn't know all the people who worked for her father. Perhaps the Butlers were in his pockets too. And they knew what she'd done.

"How did you learn about the plot?" Mary asked.

Liesl kept her mouth firmly shut. This was a danger she hadn't anticipated, and she didn't have a plan.

"I think," John said to his sister, "we need to explain to her how *we* learned about the plot." He reached into his pocket.

Liesl glanced at the door. Ought she to try to run? It'd take time to saddle her mare, and Liesl'd be too slow on foot to outpace John.

John tossed something onto the table. It clanked. Light glinted off it as it spun to a stop in front of her.

A badge.

A US Marshal's badge.

"You're a marshal?" she asked, her voice a strangled whisper.

"I am."

Not a farmer. Not her new, heart-warming neighbor. Likely not even "John Butler."

Liesl looked at Mary, breathing through her worry and uncertainty. "Where do you fit in all this?"

She unbuttoned the cuff of her left sleeve and rolled it back, revealing another badge. "Deputy Marshal Paisley O'Brien."

They'd both been lying to her from the beginning. Using her to learn about this town, about her, about the telegram she'd begged to be kept secret. Liesl felt ready to leap out of her skin. She'd been in more danger than she'd realized.

"We came to Sand Creek looking to solve the mystery of who was plotting an assassination, and who'd sent the warning," Deputy O'Brien said. "We've sorted the last bit, but we'd appreciate your help sorting the rest."

"You lied to me, and now you're asking me to trust you?"

"That's the top and bottom of it," the deputy said. She, it seemed, would be keeping charge of the conversation. "We would have told you from the beginning, but we didn't know where the danger was coming from."

"You thought it might have been coming from me?"

The marshal answered. "No. But if you weren't the informant we were looking for, we didn't want to put you in more danger by pulling you into the mystery."

They'd been assessing her, getting close enough to sniff out whether she was a good source of information. Like a simpleton, she'd convinced herself they wanted to be her friend, that *John*—

Liesl pushed down the disappointment. Life in Sand Creek was about survival, not sunshine and flower-strewn paths. Foolish hopes had no place here. Even the birds didn't stay year-round, having sense enough to know they'd be happier in warmer climes.

"I overheard a conversation between the Charming Chaps," she said. "They often forget I'm nearby when I'm serving lunch, or perhaps they don't think I'd do anything about the things I hear them say." Liesl squared her shoulders. "Two associates of theirs, Rod and Hepp, are in the territorial prison in Laramie. The Chaps tossed away a few other ideas before realizing Marshal Hawking—" She stopped short, all her focus on "John," realizing something she should have the moment he'd tossed his badge on the table. "That's you, ain't it?"

He dipped his head.

"They realized that you might make an appearance when those two prisoners had their trials. That, they decided, would be a good opportunity to do you in."

"Did they write down their plan anywhere?" Marshal Hawking asked.

Liesl shook her head. "Not that I'm aware of."

The deputy and marshal exchanged a quick look.

"Have you overheard a great many plots from them?" Deputy O'Brien asked.

Liesl nodded. "Like I said, I'm insignificant to them. They forget I'm there."

The deputy set her arms on the table and leaned toward Liesl. "We have not been able to find written evidence of their plots, only vague references and what we suspect are coded messages. But, with your testimony, we could see them convicted. Sand Creek could be out from under the crushing thumb of the Charming Chaps."

Liesl shook her head. "I cain't speak to the details of the land scheme. They've not let much slip on that."

"Don't have to be that," Marshal Hawking said. "Plotting to kill a US Marshal would see them locked up for good. You can testify that they've done that."

Deputy O'Brien added, "And you can likely testify to a great many other crimes you *do* know the details of."

"I've seen 'em beat people to within an inch of their lives," Liesl admitted. "They've tossed families out into the deadly cold simply because they could. They killed—" She swallowed against the admission she'd never made aloud. The pain of the loss on that terrible, fear-filled day was still too fresh despite the passage of more than two years. "I know what they'd do to silence me if I so much as considered doing this."

Deputy O'Brien looked empathetic, but she showed no signs of abandoning the idea. "It wouldn't be without risk; we know that. But if it proved successful—"

"*If?*" Liesl shook her head firmly. "They're plotting to assassinate a lawman with a fearsome reputation, and they've associates enough to manage it. Do you think for a moment they or their comrades wouldn't kill me if they thought I meant to open my mouth?"

Marshal Hawking jumped into the discussion. "They can be arrested on the promise of your testimony. They couldn't do you harm while in jail."

Liesl met his eye, frustrated and afraid and angry at being misled. "You aren't listening to me. The Charming Chaps have partners—people I can't identify, people *no one* can identify. Some are in this town, but not all. And they are dangerous."

"You are absolutely certain that there are others?" he pressed.

How many times would she have to tell him the enormity of the threat? "When they were plotting to have you shot, Father suggested someone go with Mr. Kirkpatrick, that between the Chaps, they ought to be able to manage it. Mr. Kirkpatrick said they weren't limited to just themselves, that they had others. And they've made it clear they have a connection to those fellas in jail. And someone has to be helping them file land deeds in a false name."

Had she not made it clear enough to them the impossible situation the town was in, or how much danger her life was in? Did they simply not believe her? Not care? "You could jail the Chaps, but that wouldn't make me any safer, especially once my part in this is known."

"How safe are you now, *really?*" the marshal asked.

"Safe enough to watch over my mother. If the Chaps' accomplices don't come for *me*, they would come for *her*. I'll not toss her to the wolves."

"Your father would let them kill a member of his own family?" Both the marshal and his deputy seemed a little surprised by the idea.

Through tight teeth she said, "He 'let' them kill my brother. All of us are expendable to him." She stood, ignoring how Deputy

O'Brien's surprise turned to horror. "Their plan is for Laramie. You know who's behind it. And those fellas in jail are likely part of it too. You know what you came to learn; do what you need to with it."

She snatched her coat from where it hung on a nail beside the door. "A lawman," she muttered. "Of course."

"Why 'of course'?" the marshal asked from the table.

She looked over her shoulder as she stepped through the doorway. "Because lawmen lie."

Chapter 12

Lawmen lie.

That shouldn't've bothered Hawk so much. He'd been required to hide the truth now and then or twist it a bit to protect people and get information, but he didn't think of himself as a liar. He didn't lie simply to lie. He didn't deceive people without a good enough reason to justify it.

He also didn't give two shakes what people thought of him. Why, then, did Liesl's disapproval sting so blasted much?

In the days since their discussion about telegrams and true identities and dishonest lawmen, he'd offered a greeting every time they'd crossed paths. She'd answered with nothing more than a silent dip of her head.

"Ain't a pleasant thing to lose a friend," Paisley had said after one such encounter.

"I'm here to round up criminals, not make friends."

Friendship and fondness made a person soft. He hadn't the luxury of being anything but coldhearted.

Two days after Liesl's last visit, Hawk and Paisley were walking down the road to visit the Harpers. Paisley made a point of looking in on them regularly.

"Burt Caper has vanished," Paisley said. "No one knows where he's gone, but it was a widely known fact that he was deep in debt on account of unpaid taxes."

Hawk pushed out a breath. "We gotta bring down this ring one way or another."

"Without proof, nothing we toss at 'em will stick."

"And our 'proof' ain't willing to talk." Hawk shook his head. "Wish I knew how to convince her."

"And put herself and her mother in danger?" Paisley shook her head. "We cain't argue with her there. The Chaps killed her brother, and I suspect she saw them do it. She has every reason to believe they'd kill again."

"Convicting them of that murder, of plotting my murder, and of the assaults she can testify to would be enough to see them hung. They'd not be in a position to hurt her then."

"Charges of that nature would require a trial in front of the circuit judge, and he don't come this far north."

It was both a complication and a solution. "He travels to Savage Wells regularly. The trial can be held there, with plenty of eyes peeled for trouble and accomplices. She'd be safer there than she has been the last decade here."

"We have to get her there first," Paisley said. "Her father and the Chaps keep a close eye on the comings and goings in this town. I'd wager the people helping them do too. She can't simply pack up and walk out."

He kicked at a rock in the road. "This is beginning to feel impossible, and I don't like it one bit."

"Liesl told us many times people couldn't escape Sand Creek. Seems to me we ought to've listened to her."

You aren't listening to me. Liesl had snapped out that accusation with frustration during their last conversation. And Hawk had realized with frustration of his own that she was right.

"It'd take some doing," Paisley said, a look of contemplation on her face, "and there'd be no guarantees, but if we can manage to get Liesl and her mother out of Sand Creek and hide them in Savage Wells—and we kept their identity and location a secret until the Charming Chaps' trial—we might manage to see the criminals permanently thwarted, the Hodges ladies safe, and Sand Creek free from a tyrannical sheriff at the same time."

If only it were that simple. "The trick'll be getting Liesl to trust us enough to take the chance."

"We've walked this particular circle a few times the last couple of days," Paisley said. "Treading the path yet again ain't gonna get us any answers. It's past time we tried convincing her."

Liesl, of all people, stepped out the Harpers' door as they came in view of it. They'd a bit more ground to cover before crossing her path.

"You or me?" Paisley asked.

Hawk knew the unspoken bits of the question. "I'll talk to Liesl. The Harpers will benefit from your visit more than they would from mine."

"Yes, but Liesl and I are less likely to come to blows than the two of you are."

He tossed her a dry look. "I think she's far more likely to simply ignore me."

Annoyance touched Paisley's features. "If you think she has chilled to you on account of being indifferent, then you ain't the clever man I've always thought you to be."

That was a bit of ridiculousness. "Are you trying to convince me Liesl Hodges is swooning over me?"

Paisley groaned in frustration. "Why is it so many people think those are the only two options: indifference or desperate romantic love? She came to think of us as friends, then discovered we were lying to her. That's a painful thing. She's gone cold on you because you hurt her."

Even when he tried to help people, Hawk managed to push them away. Such was his lot, he supposed.

They met Liesl as she reached the end of the walk leading up to the Harpers' home.

"Could I have a minute, Liesl?" Hawk asked. "I wouldn't ask if it weren't important."

She nodded but without enthusiasm.

Paisley left them behind and made her way to the front door.

"We have an idea that might help you assist us in bringing down the Charming Chaps," Hawk said.

"Safely?" Doubt filled that single word.

He nodded and saw the tiniest spark of interest light her eyes.

"I headquarter in the town of Savage Wells, as does Deputy O'Brien. Her husband, Cade O'Brien, is—"

"A legend," Liesl finished for him.

"He's also the sheriff. He has a deputy who is, without question, the best lookout I've ever worked with. There's a woman in town, Tansy, who is absolutely fearless. She, along with the rest of the town, have protected people among them before." There was a reason Hawk had moved his operations there. "If you agree to testify, you and your mother can be kept safe in Savage Wells while your father and his conspirators are held in jail, awaiting trial."

She didn't immediately jump at the offer. What could she still be doubting?

"I don't shrivel under scrutiny, Liesl. Tell me what's making you doubt the plan."

"For one thing, I haven't the first idea how to get to Savage Wells. Wandering about lost with my mother is a terrible idea."

An easily solved difficulty. "Deputy O'Brien and I would accompany you there."

"And what is to stop the Charming Chaps' accomplices from simply springing them from jail while you and your deputy are driving us to safety? And how do you intend to round up the Chaps

when there are four of them and two of you? I don't want any innocent people hurt in the crossfire. And if I am hiding in Savage Wells,
and the two of you are no longer here, who will protect Sand Creek
from the members of the gang we cain't yet identify?"

"I will send for as many deputy marshals as I need to secure this
town. We will make no move against the sheriff until they are here
and in place." Hawk did not employ deputies he couldn't depend
on. Sand Creek would be in good hands, and Liesl and Mrs. Hodges
would be safely away in Savage Wells.

"And if someone follows us out of town?" Liesl had a sharp
mind, there was no doubting that. But she also had enough difficult
life experience to sort out the dangers of what was being proposed.

"You know Sheriff Cade O'Brien's reputation as a sharpshooter?"

Liesl nodded. "He's so legendary he has a gun named for him."

"And rightly so. I've only known one person who can consis-
tently outshoot him."

"You?" she asked, unimpressed.

"His wife." He let that declaration settle in. "There's a reason I
fought to get her as one of my deputies. She has a cool head in battle,
a mind for strategy, and she's one of the bravest people I know."

Liesl didn't say anything.

"If it'll give you confidence, I'll brag on myself, though I fear it'll
make you think even less of me. I have been offered prestigious posts
throughout the country because I'm trusted and valued and have
shown myself good at what I do. I hold this territory together. I've
saved lives. I've taken down crime rings far bigger than this one. And
while I'd lose to both O'Briens in a shooting match, it'd be a close
thing. You and your ma could not be safer than you'd be traveling
with us."

She didn't immediately say no. He knew enough to keep his
peace and let her think. If she felt he was pushing her, she might
simply push back.

"If you'd have so many deputies here and the Chaps were tucked behind bars, why would my mother and I need to go as far as Savage Wells? Why not hide ourselves somewhere closer to home?"

"The type of charges we'd be bringing—murder and a plot to assassinate a US Marshal—require trial by the circuit judge. Savage Wells is his nearest stop. You'd have to be there to testify."

Her gaze narrowed. "You can get your deputies here without my father or the Chaps learning of it?"

"Easily."

A bit of her doubt eased but didn't disappear. "And my mother would be safeguarded?"

"I swear to it."

"And Savage Wells is secure enough that suspicious new arrivals would be noticed and reported to you, seeing as they might be the Charming Chaps' conspirators from Laramie or elsewhere?"

"Like I said, Sheriff O'Brien's lookout is the most impressive I've ever known. And he ain't the only one we could depend on to keep a weather eye out."

She took a tight breath. "I can't let the Chaps keep hurting this town. If I am the only one who can prevent that, and this town you'd take us to can keep my mother safe, then I'll do it."

"Thank you."

Her expression hardened. "I ain't doing this for you." And, on that, she walked right past him and didn't look back.

Hawk and Paisley stepped into the telegraph office. Mr. Yarrow looked up at them as they approached his table.

"What can I do for you?" he asked.

"We wish to send a telegram," Hawk said, making certain to use his "John" voice and not the one that sent ne'er-do-wells cowering in a corner.

"Where to?" Yarrow pulled out his pad of paper and lead pencil.

"To our cousin Fergus Caden," Paisley said, managing to look unsuspiciously innocent. "He recently moved to a small town south of here. You might not have heard of it."

"If it's on the telegraph line, I've heard of it." Yarrow didn't want for confidence.

"It's called Savage Wells." Hawk spoke casually but watched the telegraph operator carefully for any signs of alarm. He saw none.

"Fergus Caden in Savage Wells." Mr. Yarrow repeated the information as he wrote it down.

"I don't know where in that town he lives," Paisley said, apologetically. "Do you suppose someone there will be able to find him?"

Yarrow nodded, the jerking motions oozing annoyance. "What's the message?"

Hawk knew precisely the language to use so Cade—whose actual given name was Fergus Caden O'Brien; though only Paisley, Hawk, Cade himself, and the man's late parents knew that—would understand that three deputies needed to be sent quietly to Sand Creek, and a safe place needed to be prepared in Savage Wells for people requiring protection.

"Good to have you nearby. Stop. Hope to see the three of you soon. Stop. Will try to come visit at Christmas. Stop."

Yarrow wrote it out, then calculated the cost. He showed not the tiniest suspicion. "Are you expecting a reply?"

"Cousin Fergus hasn't the money for sending telegrams," Paisley said as she paid for their coded message. "I'd be surprised if we heard from him."

"I'll let you know if he does." Mr. Yarrow dropped onto the chair at his table and began tapping out the telegram.

"Thank you," Paisley said.

Mr. Yarrow dipped his head to them but didn't reply aloud.

They slipped out of the telegraph office, tromped the boardwalk to where they'd tied the horse and wagon, and scrambled up onto the bench.

Only when they were well out of town did they turn their discussion to the most pressing matter.

"We likely have a week before Ensio and the deputies he selects arrive in Sand Creek. That's time enough for formulating our best way out of town without being caught by the Charming Chaps."

"I've been giving that some thought," Paisley said. "We don't know who hereabouts is in the employ of the sheriff, so we don't know who we can trust. We would do best not to take Liesl and her mother out of town together. It'd draw attention."

She wasn't wrong.

"It's no secret in town that Mrs. Hodges and I have a bit of a friendship. If I was seen driving out with her in our wagon under the guise of visiting someone, no one'd blink an eye. We could head south, seeing as there are townspeople in that direction, but we'd simply keep going, heading directly for Savage Wells."

"Leaving Liesl and me to formulate an excuse for being together, heading in a different direction."

Paisley offered him not the least sympathy. They both knew dangerous missions afforded no room for such things. "You've been known to call on the Harpers together. That'd take you west of town. It'd put you on a roundabout path to safety, but it wouldn't get people wondering."

"It's a few days' journey. Who's to say she won't kill me before it's over?"

Paisley shrugged. "We all have risks to take."

The journey he was anticipating would not be a pleasant one. "I suspect she's not going to like this idea."

"She's going to *hate* it. But she'll do it, because it'll keep her mother and her town safe."

"And the opportunity to do me in on the way?"

Paisley grinned unrepentantly. "A little bonus."

"Perfect," he muttered.

Chapter 13

Deputy O'Brien managed to let Liesl know in the midst of a seemingly otherwise unimportant conversation that she and her mother needed to be ready to depart Sand Creek on a moment's notice. Mother would go with Deputy O'Brien and Liesl with Marshal Hawking.

Liesl wasn't particularly happy about the arrangement, but she understood. Leaving at different times and heading in different directions would help keep them safe. Hiding out in Savage Wells would keep her alive long enough to swear to the circuit judge that her father and the Chaps were mangy, no-account, murderous scoundrels.

She could endure the discomfort of Marshal Hawking's company for a few days if it meant ending the Chaps' reign.

In the end, she'd decided it'd be best not to tell her mother about the plans until the very last possible moment. Mother would fret, and that might very well tip their hand.

While her father was at the jail, Liesl had spent a desperate few hours deciding which things were essential to take with them when they left, and which things she could gather around the house without drawing Father's notice.

In the end, she chose a small rucksack for herself and packed a change of underthings, a dress, nightgown, comb and hair pins, and extra stockings. It could hold nothing more, but she didn't dare bring a second bag.

Mother and Deputy O'Brien would have the benefit of a wagon. Liesl, on the other hand, would be departing on horseback. She could only take what could be hung on a saddle or worn on her own person.

After serving Father and the Charming Chaps their daily lunch, she returned to the house and grabbed the small carpetbag she'd filled with things for her mother, hiding it in the pony cart. She told Mother she meant to check in on a family on the outskirts of town.

As she drove out toward the "Butler" house, she kept a wary eye on the road, looking for anyone coming or going, anyone watching her with undo curiosity. She'd always known Father had accomplices beyond the Charming Chaps, but never before had that reality left her so upended.

She arrived at her destination not having seen another soul. Her knock was answered by Deputy O'Brien, who motioned her inside and closed the door.

"I've brought my mother's carpetbag," Liesl said. "It's in the cart."

"Perfect," the deputy said. "I'll bring it in. Don't worry—I'll make certain it's with me when it's time to fetch your mother."

Liesl nodded.

Deputy O'Brien slipped outside just as Marshal Hawking entered the room. For some time now, seeing the man she'd thought of as "John Butler" had set her heart fluttering. That response had now been replaced with heart-deep pain. She had truly liked him. *More* than liked him. But he'd been lying to her. Lying and deceiving and probably laughing to himself to see her making sheep's eyes at him.

"Are you prepared to leave town?" he asked brusquely. The warm friendliness of John Butler was gone.

"I have. Your deputy is bringing in my mother's carpetbag. She'll have it when the time comes to run."

"You'll find a carpetbag cumbersome," he said. "We only have horses—"

"I know. I'm bringing a small rucksack."

"Pack light," he said.

Any lingering hope she had that he would return to the warm man she'd once known was disappearing like a mirage in the desert as the sun went down.

Marshal Hawking took a breath. "I've sorted a path for us to Savage Wells. It's roundabout, so we'll arrive a couple of days after your mother and Paisley. But anyone here looking for you won't stumble on our route. We'll have to pass through some other towns, which means we'll need to hide our identity. I suggested to Paisley—Deputy O'Brien—that you and I could pretend we're brother and sister. She insisted no one would believe it."

Liesl couldn't argue with that. Not only did she and Marshal Hawking look nothing alike, she suspected that even though she was frustrated with him, her expression might reveal the longing she still sometimes felt for "John Butler."

"What story *should* we tell everyone?" she asked, nervous about the answer.

Marshal Hawking hesitated. "We will pretend to be married. But we only have to play the part when we are around other people." He didn't look at all pleased at the idea.

"You have more experience than I do pretending to be someone you ain't. I'd be uncomfortable enough that I might give away the ruse."

"There's no other way around it," the marshal said. "We can't risk leaving a trail."

"Can't we avoid the towns and not have to lie about ourselves?"

"We will as much as we can," he said. "I don't think either of us wants to play those roles too long."

A new surge of disappointment tickled at her heart. She pushed it aside.

"How soon are we likely to be leaving?" she asked.

"My deputies should arrive soon. The morning after they do, Paisley will go to your house and fetch your ma. And you'll come here."

She nodded, familiar with this part of the plan.

"Our goal is to have all four of us away from town hours before you usually bring lunch to the jailhouse. When you are late, the Charming Chaps will begin to suspect something odd is going on. At that point, my deputies will step in and do what needs doing."

"Without you here to lead the charge?" That didn't seem wise. "They're dangerous men."

"And my team of deputies is legendary. They are known *by name* in Washington. There ain't a soul among 'em that can't face anything and everything tossed at 'em, and they can do it without needing any hand-holding. Paisley'll look after and protect your mother. You and I will get to Savage Wells safely. My men will handle everything here."

Deputy O'Brien stepped inside, a pile of blankets in her arms, which Liesl felt certain was disguising the carpetbag.

A man Liesl hadn't seen before followed directly behind the deputy. He was tall with hair the color of corn silk. He eyed the room with a sharp, evaluating gaze. Though he wore a long coat, she saw the telltale shape of gun holsters strapped to either side of his hips. Underneath that coat, she further suspected, was a deputy marshal's badge.

Marshal Hawking crossed to the newcomer and shook his hand firmly. "Ensio. Welcome to Sand Creek."

"Pleased to be here," Ensio said. "Things were getting dull in Sunrise."

"Who'd you bring with you?" the marshal asked.

Ensio stepped aside, and two men stepped in behind him.

The first was shorter than Ensio and Marshal Hawking, who were both unusually tall. He wore his black hair cropped short on the sides and hidden entirely on the top by his hat. He had a quiet but focused expression.

"Nick." Marshal Hawking shook his hand as well.

The last of the new arrivals was a tall Black man, solidly built. His outer coat was serviceable, but the vest beneath was made of a colorful and elegantly patterned silk. He hadn't the rough-and-tough look so common to people living in the West.

Marshal Hawking shook his hand. "Thad." To Ensio, he said, "You've assembled a cracking team."

"I thought so."

Deputy O'Brien, apparently having stashed the carpetbag, joined them. "This is Liesl Hodges," she told her fellow deputies. "She's our witness. Getting her and her mother safely out of Sand Creek is our first priority. No move can be made against the sheriff and his associates until these two women are safely away. Without Liesl's testimony, Sheriff Hodges will remain free—and he'll be looking for revenge."

Marshal Hawking didn't seem to object to one of his deputies offering instructions on his behalf, and a woman at that. Father never abided the women in his family offering him corrections or instructions or information of any kind.

The deputy marshals each greeted Liesl, and all three offered reassurances that they'd make certain she and her mother were safe. She nodded her acknowledgment but still felt a little unsettled. She knew better than to entirely trust the word of lawmen.

"Our plan goes into effect first thing in the morning," Deputy O'Brien said. "Tell your mother that I will be at your house at nine o'clock on the dot."

"She'll be ready," Liesl said. To Marshal Hawking, she added, "And I'll be here as soon after that as my horse can casually bring me."

And with that, she committed herself to what was certainly the most perilous act of rebellion she'd ever staged against her father.

Hawk carried two pistols and a knife on his person. He always hoped for the best but prepared for the worst. Paisley had left more than thirty minutes earlier; Liesl ought to be arriving soon.

Around him, Ensio, Nick, and Thad were solidifying their strategy for apprehending the sheriff and the Charming Chaps and seizing control of Sand Creek. Hawk and Paisley had warned the deputies of the Chaps' unidentified accomplices that still needed sniffing out, but he knew he was leaving Sand Creek in good hands. And with two fewer targets to protect, he was also leaving his deputies with a slightly less complicated task.

He was traveling to Savage Wells in prickly company. If he'd been able to think of any other way to accomplish Liesl's escape, he'd have snatched at it. He'd even considered having one of the newly arrived deputies make the journey, but he'd dismissed that quickly. Liesl didn't know them, which would make her anxious. And her survival was paramount. She needed the very best protection. While he trusted his deputies implicitly, there was a reason he was the marshal. He needed to be the one to act as protector.

He heard the faint approach of hooves. Most people would likely have missed the quiet crunching of the grass, but all three of his deputies turned toward the front window at the same time.

Ensio stepped away from the others and walked with Hawk through the front door.

Liesl had only just slipped off her horse. She stood with every indication of calm and poise, but he saw fear in her eyes and tension in her posture.

"Lead the animal into the barn," Hawk said.

She nodded, the movement tiny and strained. No one could

dispute her courage, but she was also too perceptive not to be keenly aware of how dangerous their next few minutes and days could prove to be.

Hawk wished he could reassure her, could promise it'd prove an easy thing. But she'd have seen that for the fib it was, and he'd lied to her plenty enough already.

Once inside the barn and away from any prying eyes, Ensio snatched up the bedroll waiting there and tied it to the back of Liesl's saddle. Hawk then tied an extra wool blanket around it. Ensio secured a saddlebag in which they'd put some foodstuffs.

Hawk's horse was saddled and ready to go. He mounted and motioned for Liesl to retake her seat.

To Ensio, he said, "Be careful today. These men are dangerous."

Ensio tossed him a wicked smile. "So are we."

"Send word once the dust settles. I'll get it when I reach Savage Wells." Hawk turned to Liesl. "We've three hours to get as far from Sand Creek as we can."

"I'm ready if you are." She spoke with unwavering determination. This was not a woman to be thrown off-kilter by even the stoniest ground.

That was good. Because as difficult as their journey to Savage Wells might be, the danger wouldn't end once they reached their destination.

Chapter 14

Hardly a word passed between Liesl and Marshal Hawking during the first three hours of their westward journey, and it wasn't a comfortable silence. For her part, Liesl didn't feel much like talking. She was fretting over her mother, fretting over Sand Creek, and, though he didn't deserve it, she was fretting over her father. The three deputy marshals who'd descended on Sand Creek didn't seem to be the sort to tiptoe around what needed to be done. Her father might get himself killed.

The day pressed on, and she watched the sun reach its midpoint in the sky. It would be lunchtime back in Sand Creek, and the Charming Chaps would be hungry—and angry. They'd search her out. Father would realize she and Mother were gone. And soon enough, the deputies would swoop in to seize control of the town.

Could it be done without gunfire? Likely not. Even if he survived the gunfight and was tossed in his own jail, her father might still manage to send people to sniff out her trail.

"Do you suppose your deputies have gone and done what needs doing yet?" she asked.

"If they ain't yet, they will any minute." He looked over at her. "Frettin'?"

"A little."

He didn't laugh at her or tell her to buck up, which she appreciated. "If you weren't, I'd wonder if you realized all we're trying to do."

"I can't like the idea of anyone getting hurt. My father and the Charming Chaps deserve it, I ain't gonna argue otherwise, but I still don't like it."

"That speaks well of you, Miss Hodges. Far too many who have been made to suffer become numb to it."

"Have you?"

Far from being offended, he answered with what sounded like sincerity. "In some ways, I suppose I have. I try to fight back against that, but sometimes it sneaks up on me."

A hint of compassion. She'd not ever seen that in a lawman.

"Do you need to rest a spell?" he asked. "We've been riding for hours."

She shook her head. "I ain't a two-dollar watch, made to run slow."

They needed to get as far from Sand Creek as they could, but they were confined to the back trails. Stopping didn't seem a good idea so soon.

"Cade O'Brien is really the sheriff of Savage Wells?" Liesl asked.

"He is."

Cade O'Brien was known for being a fearsome lawman, even a little terrifying. She and Mother were bound for another town with another frightening sheriff. She didn't overly like that.

"Are you worried about him?" Marshal Hawking, apparently, sensed her nervousness.

"He has a certain reputation," she said.

Without looking at her, Marshal Hawking said, "So do I."

"I know." Liesl took a mouthful of water from the canteen slung over the saddle horn.

"Cade O'Brien earned every ounce of his reputation. But he ain't a tyrant, and he doesn't revel in violence. He's most fierce in defending those who need it. I made my headquarters in Cade's town because it's run well and because he and I view the world a lot alike. I take my job seriously, but the lives in my keeping are my first priority. You'll be safe in Savage Wells. I swear to it."

No matter that he'd lied to her about his identity, she believed him in that moment. The tightness in her neck eased. They'd be safe in Savage Wells. But first, they had to get there.

"I don't know what I'm supposed to call you," she said. "We probably should sort that out before we get to Savage Wells."

"Sooner, actually. We both need false names while we're traveling in case anyone asks after us."

"Isn't 'John' a false name?"

"It's my real given name," he said, "but no one calls me that. It's common enough that we didn't worry about me using it in Sand Creek."

So something about John Butler hadn't been a lie. "I could call you John again."

He shook his head. "That's the only name they have for me in Sand Creek. My deputies are under strict instructions not to reveal who Paisley and I really are."

"What about 'Jack'?" Liesl suggested. "It's near enough to John that it shouldn't be terribly hard to remember or make a quick correction if I accidentally say 'John.'"

He nodded. "That'll do. What name should I use for you?"

"Lilly?" she suggested. "It has the same advantages as Jack."

He nodded again. "We'll need a surname."

Blast it all. This bit of misdirection was growing into a great many falsehoods. She understood the necessity, but she didn't like it at all. And to have John—Marshal Hawking—pretend a tenderness for her again would be more painful than she was quite ready to endure.

Focus on choosing a name, she told herself. She could do that much. If that had been all the marshal had done in Sand Creek, his deception wouldn't have hurt so much. But he'd acted like something was building between them, like there was hope for a future.

"An unmemorable name is likely best." She felt defeated, exhausted.

"Moore?" Marshal Hawking tossed back.

She nodded her agreement. They were discussing false names and identities with as much casualness as they might have discussed the weather. Meanwhile, back in her hometown, a gunfight might very well be happening.

"Once we're in Savage Wells, you'd do best to call me Hawk," he said. "That's how I'm known there. Paisley is generally just Paisley."

Liesl agreed. She would miss John Butler, but the sooner she admitted to herself that he'd never truly existed, the sooner she could find her feet again. The bit of her heart that he'd claimed, however, might prove more elusive.

An entire day in the saddle was taking its toll on Liesl. Stopping for the night would be more than welcome. As evening approached, she and Hawk came across two wagons and the two families traveling in them, stopped for the night. The adults in the group were busy with meal preparations and seeing to the needs of their animals. The little ones were running about, enjoying a bit of playtime.

"Halloo," Hawk said, waving to the group as they drew closer.

A man amongst the travelers walked over to them. "Horris Brown." He tugged at the brim of his hat.

"I'm Jack Moore. This is my wife, Lilly." Hawk rattled off the false names as easy as anything. "We've not seen anyone else on the trail today. Seems we've all picked a lonely road."

"We've room 'round our fire if you'd like a bit of company." Horris motioned back to their camp.

"That'd be welcome," Hawk said.

Liesl hadn't been at all certain if he meant to accept.

"See to your horses," Horris said. "Then join us."

While Hawk and Liesl got the saddles and bridles off their horses, Hawk spoke quick and quiet. "There's some risk interacting with people, but there's also safety in a crowd. This group'll keep traveling, which makes it less likely anyone looking for us will come across them."

"Sensible."

"We simply need to be convincing as an ordinary married couple making an ordinary journey. They'll not think twice."

Be convincing. She'd do her best, and she'd feel like a blasted hypocrite. Deceiving people wasn't something she undertook lightly.

As soon as the horses were free of their loads and rubbed down good, their front legs in hobbles so they'd not wander off too far, Liesl turned to face the families they'd be staying with. Hawk took hold of her hand. He held it softly, not grasping it like he meant to yank her about. They both knew this ruse was necessary, and she was glad that he didn't mean to strong-arm her.

"What can we do to help?" Liesl asked as they approached the families.

"We've most everything in hand," one of the women said. "We've had a bit to rest after journeying for the day. The two of you could likely stand to take a moment's rest, yourselves."

"We could, at that," Hawk said. He turned toward Liesl. "Come sit a spell, darlin'. I suspect you need it."

Darlin'. She would miss hearing him call her "lamb," but she didn't mind the way he said "darlin'." He sounded, in that moment, more like John Butler than Marshal Hawking.

He walked with her to a blanket spread out near the fire. One of the children was sitting on it, playing with a doll.

To the little girl, Hawk asked, "Mind if we plop ourselves down here?"

The little one shrugged and kept playing.

Hawk saw Liesl seated, then sat near enough to give the impression of being quite cozy together, quite comfortable. Liesl knew her part. She smiled and turned her attention to their surroundings, watching with a casual ease, hoping it would seem she hadn't a care in the world.

After a moment, the little girl scooted over to Liesl. She held up her doll, apparently wanting Liesl to see her treasure.

"What is your doll's name?" Liesl asked.

"Jenny."

"Pleased to meet you, Jenny."

The girl turned to Hawk, who, without any nudging, said, "A real pleasure, Jenny."

That seemed to satisfy their tiny companion. She turned away and once more gave her full attention to her doll.

Liesl's father had never shown any patience with children. Even when Liesl was little, her father had been unkind and frightening.

John Butler had been kind and thoughtful with the Harper children. Hawk was being kind with this newest child. Of course, it was just another act. She hadn't the first idea who he actually was, how much of the person she knew had been a ruse. Liesl had been lonely most of her life, utterly so since her brother, Otto, was killed. She felt *more* alone now than she had before the arrival of the lie that had been John Butler and his tender affection.

They'd not been sitting long before supper was ready. All their objections about eating the families' food were brushed aside, and Liesl and Hawk found themselves with bowls of hot soup. It was a far better meal than they'd've tossed together themselves.

"Where are you headed?" Horris asked between spoonfuls.

They hadn't discussed this part of their story. Liesl left Hawk to make the explanation.

"Laramie," he said.

Horris nodded, unsurprised by the answer. "You've quite a few days to travel yet."

"We do," Hawk said. "And we greatly appreciate having your company tonight. Who's to say how many more days'll pass before we find more fellow travelers."

"We're glad you joined us," one of the women said.

The conversation around the fire was light and friendly. As they sat together, Hawk occasionally set his hand over hers or offered a tender smile. She managed not to give away the ruse, though her heart thumped hard at every exchange. Her strategy was to pretend she was sitting with John Butler. Were he by her side, she wouldn't have needed to pretend to be pleased.

But he wasn't real. Just another lie she'd been told.

The families began gathering their little ones and settling them for the night in their canvas-covered wagons. Hawk and Liesl had no such accommodations, so Hawk fetched the bedrolls and length of canvas tied to their horses.

He spread the canvas on the ground near the fire, then flicked out their bedrolls. He then stepped up close to Liesl and set an arm around her middle, leaning in close. To anyone watching, they would look like a happy couple having an affectionate moment. She'd have believed it mere days ago. How naïve she'd been.

His voice at a whisper, he said, "Were we on our own, we could sleep with the fire between us and all the space you could hope for to be comfortable. But we need these people to believe we're married. They'd find it odd if we kept a distance."

Dadgummit, he was right.

"Fortunately, it's a bit of a chilly night. They'd not think twice to see us wrapped up in separate bedrolls."

"You'd still be right next to me, though?"

"No way around it."

She shrugged. "I can endure that for one night."

Liesl couldn't be certain, but she thought he laughed. The possibility lightened her heart.

They were soon situated, lying not far from the fire. She was wrapped up tight in her bedroll. He was wrapped up in his. The two families had grown quiet.

Liesl wondered if she'd be able to sleep with this man she barely trusted so close to her. But she was surprised to discover that she felt safe. Safe enough that she drifted almost immediately to sleep.

Chapter 15

The sound of movement woke Hawk, and he was instantly on the alert. With one eye cracked the tiniest bit, he scanned the area. Horris and his wife had climbed from their wagon, no doubt about to begin preparations for breakfast.

With that unthreatening mystery solved, he set his attention to sorting the rest of his surroundings. The fire had long since burned out. He was still wrapped in his bedroll. Liesl was sleeping beside him, rolled in her own blankets. And his arm, cold in the early morning air, was laid across her. When or why he'd done that, he couldn't say. More surprising still, he found himself reluctant to pull away.

But he did. Regardless of what was said about his cold, calculating heart, he wasn't a cad. She hadn't granted him permission to put his arm around her. Now that he was aware of what he was doing, he had no right to continue.

Careful not to wake her, he lifted his arm and sat upright in one quick, fluid motion. That caught the attention of the couple on the other side of the fire.

"Good morning," Horris said, quietly.

"Morning." Hawk shivered as his blanket fell away. "How can I help?"

"We're hoping to set off as soon as everyone's fed," Horris said. "Best get your horses ready."

Hawk nodded. He shook out his boots, making certain no critters had climbed inside during the night. After pulling his boots on, he stood, stretching out the stiffness in his muscles. He retrieved his hat and coat from the branches of a nearby tree. With no privacy for changing, he'd slept in the rest of his clothes. He looked quite a sight, wrinkled and rumpled.

But the state of his clothes wasn't the matter picking at his mind just then. It had been a cold night. Liesl had likely been shivering, so he'd reached out to offer warmth. That was likely all. And yet, it bothered him that he wasn't certain. He didn't remember setting his arm around her. Hawk never let his guard down. When sleeping in the open like that, he didn't sleep deeply. He noticed every sound, every movement. Including his own.

But he didn't remember that.

It was time he got his head on straight. Liesl Hodges had upended him, and he couldn't afford to let that keep happening.

Throughout the remainder of their time with the wagon-faring families, he managed the balance of pretending to be an affectionate husband and keeping the necessary emotional distance from the woman he was charged with protecting. If she noticed his restraint, she didn't say anything.

Truth be told, she *literally* didn't say anything. Not from the moment they parted ways with their temporary companions all the way to midday. And when she did break her silence, it wasn't to comment on the storm clouds gathering in the sky or the tension hanging between them.

"I think something's bothering my horse. She's favoring a back leg."

Yet another thing Hawk hadn't noticed. He was losing his edge.

Liesl dismounted and made a quick check. "Lost a shoe. That's what I was afraid of."

"We'd best go slow," he said. "Next town we come to, we'll look in on the blacksmith."

"Do you think anyone from Sand Creek is searching for us?" she asked as he retook his saddle.

"I guarantee it."

He could see the color fade from her cheeks, but she didn't shrink, didn't break down. Hers was the expression of someone who'd hoped to be wrong but already knew she wasn't.

"Stopping in a town increases our risk of being found," she said.

"A lame horse does as well. We'll keep quiet and won't stay long."

She looked over at him. "You seem put out with me, but I can't sort out why."

"I ain't put out with you."

"And *I* ain't stupid. Something's stuck in your craw."

"I'm a grumpy, unhappy, miserable, old curmudgeon, and it's got nothing to do with you."

"You're not old." She didn't argue against the rest of his assertion, but he thought he saw a hint of a smile tug at the corner of her mouth.

He didn't allow the same expression to pull at his lips. He needed to keep his focus.

Luck was with them. They reached Platteville a short time later. Hawk knew the place. It was a quiet town, one he checked on now and then but rarely needed to visit. It had been years, in fact.

By design, Hawk pinned his US Marshal's badge inside a pocket of his coat where it wouldn't be accidentally revealed. He kept his hat low on his head.

The blacksmith stepped out of his shop as they dismounted. "How can I help you folks?"

"Do you do the shoeing around here, or is there a farrier?"

"Blacksmith and farrier both—that's me."

"This gal lost her shoe," Liesl said, patting her horse's leg. "Had to walk a spell without it."

The man nodded. "Is the mare limping bad?"

"She ain't."

The blacksmith took a good look, cleaning out some of the muck picked up along the way, and pressing the hoof to check for bruising. "She seems to have come through it fine."

"Are you up to your eyes today, or do you have time to see to the poor thing?" Hawk kept his voice light. Drawing notice wouldn't help them at all.

"I've a bit to do first, but not much. Tie up your horses alongside the shop, then grab a bite to eat or drink—or at least find a place out of the weather." He glanced up at the cloud-laden sky. "I'll have her ready for you in an hour, most likely."

Hawk did as directed, then held his hand out to Liesl—they had an impression to give—and together they walked away from the smithy. Platteville wasn't as large as Savage Wells so it didn't have a restaurant, but the mercantile should have something they could fill their bellies with.

He'd have led his pretended wife directly there, but the heavens let loose with a torrent of rain.

"Boil and blast," he muttered.

They ducked under the nearest overhang and up against the building. So long as the wind didn't pick up, they'd not get much wetter. This being Wyoming, though, wind was a constant.

Hawk shielded Liesl as much as he could from the onslaught. He'd noticed the clouds as they'd ridden, but he hadn't expected the rain to be so heavy. It was a good thing they'd not been out on the trail when the storm had hit.

"For a grumpy, unhappy, miserable curmudgeon, you're being very thoughtful," she said from within his protective embrace.

The rain was making him grumpy. His lack of focus was rendering him unhappy. But, at the moment, holding her and hearing her say he was thoughtful . . . well, he wasn't the least bit miserable.

They'd been riding two days with no chance to bathe. Still,

somehow, she smelled good. He didn't even know how to describe the scent of her, only that he liked it.

Into the downpour, a voice called out to them from behind. "Step inside, you two. You'll catch your death out there."

He looked in the direction of the offer. Standing in the nearest doorway, the swinging doors leaning against her, was a woman in a revealing silk dress with a plume of feathers pinned into her upswept hair. Hawk had spent enough time out West to know at a glance the woman's profession. That realization brought his eyes to the nearby window. Sure enough, they'd taken refuge under the overhang of the town saloon.

"I can't take my wife inside a saloon," he said to the woman. "Though I thank you for the offer."

"Nonsense," the woman said, waving off his objection. "It ain't late enough in the day for this to be a rough place just now. Quiet as can be. And you'll only be inside long enough to dry off and wait for the heavens to stop their complaining."

Hawk looked to Liesl, wanting her thoughts.

"I *am* cold," she said. "A respite would be welcome."

If she wasn't felled by the location, he wouldn't be either. He kept an arm around her as he led her through the swinging doors and inside the dimly lit and all but empty interior.

Even quiet as it was, this was a dangerous place to linger. He didn't for a moment think Liesl was in danger, but the people he rounded up and tracked down tended to be the sort who found saloons quite to their liking. He was concerned he might be recognized.

Fortunately, having Liesl with him gave him a ready reason to tuck himself in a corner, away from any prying eyes that might turn their way. They'd think he was shielding her—which wasn't entirely wrong—without realizing he needed to not be noticed himself. He pulled his hat a bit lower.

The woman who'd invited them in crossed over to them. "Can I get you anything?"

Hawk shook his head.

Liesl, however, stepped away from him and pulled the saloon girl aside. It shouldn't have surprised him that Liesl took her situation firmly in hand. She had fire, this sheriff's daughter.

He couldn't hear what the women said to each other, but after a moment, Liesl returned and took hold of his hand. She tugged him toward her conversational companion. "We have to be quick."

He didn't argue, though he hadn't the first idea what was happening.

They were guided around the back of the staircase and through a narrow door. The bedroom beyond was furnished simply with a small but clean window.

"Thank you, Kat," Liesl said to the woman before she closed the door.

"You do realize this is a . . . working room, don't you?" Hawk asked.

"Of course I do. And Kat didn't bring us back here on account of the room's usual purpose." Liesl pulled off her sodden bonnet. "She's getting the two of us into a safe space. People'll start wandering into the saloon soon enough, and I got the impression you ain't particularly keen to be studied."

"You ain't wrong there." He took off his own hat and shook some of the water out of his hair. "What explanation did you give Kat?"

"I told her you were helping me escape a 'situation,'" she said. "And if the man in charge of that 'situation' caught us, we'd be done for."

"She thinks I snuck you out of a brothel?"

Liesl nodded. "I do believe she got that impression."

"Though you didn't outright lie."

She looked at him. "I prefer not to when I can avoid it."

"You might be surprised to hear, darlin', but I prefer that as well."

Liesl wrapped her arms around herself, bouncing a little on her toes. Poor woman was wet and likely chilled to her very bones.

Hawk pulled off his coat and hung it on a nail on the wall. His shirt underneath was mostly dry. "You'll want to hang up your coat, too, so it has a chance to dry."

She didn't argue.

"Wet clothes were a misery during the war." He rubbed his hands together to warm them. "Along with a great many other things."

"I didn't know you fought."

He nodded. "A Union regiment out of Indiana."

"You're from Indiana?" She seemed pleased with the discovery.

"Have you been there?"

She nodded. "When I was very little. I don't remember much about it."

She was bouncing again, hugging herself for warmth. "I feel like I'm getting colder."

He moved closer, wanting to help but not certain she would welcome his touch. He was even less certain he was ready to touch her again after the upending experience of waking with his arm around her that morning. He knew he would enjoy rubbing her arms or holding her in an embrace.

And that was precisely the problem. He had a job to do, and she loathed that about him.

But she was literally shivering. He couldn't let her suffer without at least trying to help.

"I can rub at your arms for a spell," he offered, watching her for any signs of disgust or objection. "Might warm you up."

To his surprise, she nodded. "Once I start shivering, I always struggle to grow warm again."

Hawk set his hands on her arms, telling himself to focus on the task at hand and not on the way his heart thudded to be touching her again, at how close she stood to him. *Focus on the business at hand.* "You should've told me you were chilled through."

"I didn't figure there was anything to be done about it, at least not while we were out in the downpour." She seemed to lean closer, which made focusing a bit more difficult. Still, he'd learned long ago how to rope in wandering thoughts, and he managed it once again.

There was a quick knock at the door, and then Kat stepped inside, a couple of blankets hung over her arm.

"They ain't anything fine, but they're clean." She set the blankets on the bed. "And there's a door next to this one. It leads out back of the saloon. You can leave out that way when the rain lets up. No one'll see you go."

"Oh, Kat, thank you." Liesl reached out a hand and squeezed one of Kat's.

"My pleasure." And with that, she slipped out.

Hawk dropped his arms away. He turned to the pile of blankets, firmly pushing aside his disappointment at losing the feel of Liesl being so close to him. With business-like precision, he wrapped the blanket around Liesl's shoulders. She clasped it in the front with her hand. He took up the other blanket and wrapped it around himself.

"There was a man who lived in Sand Creek before you came who also fought in the war. He didn't talk about it much."

"Neither do I," Hawk said. "I ain't ashamed of my service, but it wasn't a pleasant thing. It's nice to not think about it."

"I didn't mean to force you to." Color touched her cheeks. It might've been the lingering cold, might've been the warm blanket. Or she might've been blushing because she thought she ought to be embarrassed.

"I'd not've talked about it if I didn't want to."

"Why is it you go from kindly conversational to no friendlier than a rattler at the drop of a hat?" She pushed out a breath as she turned away.

"Because you throw me off balance."

She looked over her shoulder at him, brows pulled in confusion.

"I ain't an indecisive man, and unexpected things don't toss me about. But I haven't the first idea what to do with you."

Her eyes pulled wide, and her lips pressed together.

"Don't prickle up at me," he said.

"Don't you prickle up, then, when I tell you I haven't the first idea what to do with you, either." She advanced on him, looking equal parts frustrated and avenging. "John Butler was kind and considerate. But you're moody and gruff and impossible to sort out. One minute, I think you might even like my company. In the very next, you make it clear I'm little more than a parcel you're delivering against your will."

He stepped closer to her. "I may not be overly personable, but I care about the people I protect. I care about them *as people.*"

"Then why are you always snapping at me?" She was close enough that he could see the fire in her eyes, could nearly feel the heat from her body.

"Because it keeps me from doing what I'd actually like to be doing."

"And what's that?" she demanded.

His eyes dropped to her lips. Blast it all, that happened a lot. He pulled in a slow breath, trying to ignore the warmth of her nearby and the temptation to answer her question with a long, lingering kiss. His heart pounded in his neck.

Keep your head, you fool. One more breath settled his thoughts enough for him to speak.

"I'll try not to snap at you," he whispered. "It ain't fair."

"No, it ain't." Her whisper was even more broken than his.

They were playing with fire, the two of them. He forced himself to step away before they both got burned.

They waited out the storm in that tiny room, keeping to opposite sides of it. He'd not intended to confess to her the pull he felt. Now that he more or less had, nothing between them would be simple again.

Chapter 16

Hawk had never passed a more awkward two days in his entire life. The journey from Platteville to Savage Wells had consisted of only the necessary comments and near-silent work of cooking meals, tending the horses, laying out bedrolls—on opposite sides of the fire each night—and little else.

He'd told himself that he'd do best to keep a distance, to think of Liesl Hodges as simply another resident of the territory he'd sworn to protect. They'd managed that perfectly during the last two days of their trek; he'd hated it.

What in tarnation was wrong with him?

They rode into Savage Wells late in the afternoon of the day he'd planned to arrive. Even the stop to reshoe Liesl's horse hadn't slowed them overly much. At least that part was going according to plan.

All was quiet as they rode down the street. This was a town he didn't have to keep a constant eye on. Cade managed that perfectly well. That afforded Hawk a rare chance to breathe.

"This is bigger than Sand Creek." Liesl eyed the buildings as they passed.

"And still growing," Hawk said.

Their first stop was the jailhouse. Cade was inside, sitting in a chair with his booted feet crossed on his desk.

"Hard at work?" Hawk said.

"Always."

Cade slipped his feet from the desk and rose to his full height. His pistol, a particularly lethal variety the maker had named after him, hung at his hip. Everything about the man was intimidating. Hawk had heard it said that when he and Cade entered a room together, even the most unrepentant of sinners began praying for mercy.

"I see you've managed to not get yourself killed." Cade eyed him.

"That's always the goal." Hawk motioned over his shoulder to Liesl and lowered his voice so he'd not be overheard by anyone happening to pass by the door. "This is Miss Hodges."

Cade dipped his head to her. "Miss."

"Sheriff O'Brien." Her voice shook a little. Cade could be terrifying, even when he wasn't trying.

"You've nothing to fear from me," Cade said. "In fact, I'm about to be your favorite person." He turned toward his deputy, who was sitting in a corner, bent over a book. "Keep an eye on the place, Andrew."

"Will do, Sheriff."

Cade motioned Hawk and Liesl to follow him from the jailhouse. Hawk's eyes swept the street. He hadn't the least doubt Cade's did as well.

"We're for Dr. MacNamara's," Cade told them.

"Why are we seeing a doctor?" Liesl asked.

"He has something for you." Cade offered nothing more.

"For *me*?" Liesl gave the tiniest shake of her head, her forehead creased.

"You'll discover," Hawk said, "that the infamous Cade O'Brien likes being difficult."

She smiled a little. Hawk hadn't seen her smile since Platteville.

He was quick to squelch any emotional reaction to that. John Butler had the freedom to relish making her laugh; John Hawking couldn't afford to let his concentration slip.

Doc's sign telling arrivals to come in without knocking hung in the window by the door. They did as instructed.

Doc had a fine home, the largest in Savage Wells. He needed the space—not for his own family, but for patients needing attending. He was the only man of medicine in a hundred-mile radius.

Liesl's gaze swept over the entryway. It was an impressive place, Doc's house. She looked uncertain, a bit tossed about. She'd have some adjusting to do in Savage Wells.

"Miss Hodges." Cade stood on the threshold of the sitting room. "I think you'll be wanting to step in here."

She must have decided he was trustworthy; she followed his suggestion without hesitation.

Hawk entered the room after her and saw Paisley and Mrs. Hodges already talking with Mrs. MacNamara. Their path to Savage Wells had been a more direct one, allowing them to arrive faster. Liesl and her mother greeted each other with an embrace.

"That Miss Hodges is very fetching," Cade observed from his position beside Hawk. A laugh lay beneath the words.

"She's a citizen of this territory and in need of protecting. Nothing else."

Cade nodded, but not in a way that spoke of sincerity. He didn't believe Hawk was indifferent, which Hawk, of course, wasn't.

Changing the topic seemed like a good idea. "Any word from Sand Creek?"

"Ensio sent a telegram the day you and Pais spirited off our newest arrivals. The crooked sheriff and his Charming Chaps have been rounded up and tossed in cells with round-the-clock guards. He don't think it's a good idea, though, to hold them there. Seems they ain't been able to sort who else or how many in the area might be in cahoots with the criminals."

"Paisley," Hawk called out and waved her over.

She crossed the room confidently to join Hawk and Cade in the doorway. Cade snaked an arm around her but didn't interrupt Hawk's instructions.

"I'll be sending Manuel and Li to Sand Creek to assist Ensio, Thad, and Nick. There's the possibility they're outgunned in their effort to keep their prisoners locked up."

"I've been giving it thought," Paisley said, "and there's a complication to this we didn't fully think of."

With how distracted he'd been of late, he couldn't deny he might have missed something important. Blast it all. "What've you thought of?"

"The law says a person being tried for a crime has the right to be at that trial. If Sheriff Hodges and the Charming Chaps, and any of their conspirators our fellas manage to identify, are being tried by the circuit judge, they have to be moved from Sand Creek."

"And brought here," he muttered, knowing she was right. "Boil and blast."

Paisley narrowed her gaze on him. "We could have 'em dragged to Laramie."

"Getting the prisoners that far would require even more deputies than I'm already dedicatin' to this. I'll not leave the territory so unprotected as that. And we know the Charming Chaps and Sheriff Hodges have co-conspirators in the territorial prison. It wouldn't do to toss them in together and make things easier for them."

"And if Miss Hodges is to be the witness at their trial," Cade said, "she'd have to go to Laramie too. And it'd be harder to keep her safe there."

"Bringing her and her ma here might not've made them safer at all, not if the ones we're hiding them from are being brought here too." Hawk pushed out a breath. "Dagnabbit. Cain't believe I didn't see that. I ain't never this clodheaded."

"I didn't think of it either," Paisley admitted. "We were focusing on getting those women out of harm's way. Which, I'll point out, we did manage."

And Liesl wasn't exactly praising his name for that. "I suppose I'll have to tell Liesl about this hitch in the plans."

"Promise I can be there when you tell her?" Paisley grinned. To Cade, she explained, "Liesl's near about the only woman I know who'd not hesitate to hand Hawk his head on a plate."

"One of two, love," Cade said, tossing his wife a look of amused affection.

Hawk ignored both the show of tenderness and the unexpected twinge of jealousy he felt. He'd long ago accepted that love wasn't going to be part of his life, and it hardly ever bothered him, let alone chipped away at him as it was doing in that moment. Best to move on past that reaction and back into safer territory. "I'm assigning you to see to the protection of the Hodges women, Paisley."

"Are you expecting trouble?"

Hawk hooked a thumb through his gun belt. "Always."

Cade and Paisley nodded in unison. Trouble was always on the horizon in Wyoming Territory. The arrival of four men known to have destroyed lives, planned an assassination, and murdered the son of one of their own only added to it.

Hawk met Liesl's eye from across the room. He waved her over. She said something to her mother before crossing to where he and Paisley and Cade stood. She watched Hawk, a mixture of uncertainty and wariness in her expression.

He'd certainly complicated things for them, hinting at all he felt, likely making it clear he'd wanted to kiss her. There was a reason he'd learned to be cold. It was safer. And far easier.

"My deputies successfully took control of Sand Creek."

She paled a little. "My father?"

"Is in jail, along with the other Charming Chaps."

She released a quiet breath full of relief.

"They'll be transferred as soon as more of my deputies arrive there."

"Where are they being transferred to?"

He didn't answer immediately, unsure if he ought to ease into the explanation or simply break the news quickly.

Liesl looked at all three of them in turn before settling her gaze on Hawk once more. "Where?"

"A jail where their trial is held. The law requires it."

Tension pulled at her mouth. "You said their trial was going to be held *here*."

"The only other option is Laramie, and we know two of the prisoners there have been working with them. We can't take that risk."

Liesl squared her shoulders and folded her arms across her chest. "You told me my mother and I were getting away from them."

"They'll be in the jailhouse. You won't be."

She eyed him dryly. "And 'Liesl Hodges' is such a common name that no one lookin' for me will ever guess I'm in town."

"You'll need a false name while you're here. At least until the trial is complete, and there's no one trying to stop it from happening."

"And why is this a better option than my mother and I staying in Sand Creek if my father was going to be brought here?"

"I hadn't planned on him being brought here. I should have thought of it, should have realized, but I didn't." He could understand her frustration, but there was no avoiding it. "They can't be tried if they aren't present. There's not a choice."

"I trusted you," she said tightly.

"And I don't know how to convince you that you still should after I failed to realize something so crucial."

"Are you certain these Chaps have hidden allies?" Cade asked. "If they don't, the ladies could go back to Sand Creek until the judge gets here."

"Then make the journey *again*?" Paisley shook her head. "Mrs. Hodges was bravely determined on the trail here, but"—she looked to Liesl—"I don't think she'd fare well if forced to cover that much ground twice again. I don't know if she has it in her."

Liesl's mouth formed a slash of frustration. To Paisley, she said, "Her health and endurance have been fragile for years." To Cade, she said, "And I sure enough do know they have secret cohorts. I've heard them talk about them. And some of their schemes *require* help from people beyond themselves. They ain't alone in this. Problem is, we don't know who those conspirators might be, *where* they might be, or how violently loyal they are. I came here on the promise that I wasn't going to have to find out."

There was undeniable accusation in her final declaration. He deserved it. He'd be castigating himself over this failure for weeks to come, months maybe. Years. He couldn't remember a time he'd bungled something so badly.

But there *was* reason to believe the mistake could work to their favor.

"I told you before we'd be able to spot new arrivals. We can keep a weather eye out. And you'd have the protection of this town. I ain't wrong about that."

"This town don't even know me."

"They didn't know Mrs. MacNamara when she first arrived," Paisley said, "but they protected her."

She looked away, lips pinched. "How long would we have to use false names?"

"Depends on how soon we can have a judge here for a trial," Hawk said.

"You know I ain't one for lying if I don't have to."

He nodded. "But this is one of those times you likely have to."

That didn't appear to set her mind at ease. "And you *promise* my mother will be safe?" She rubbed at her neck.

"As safe as I can possibly make her."

Liesl turned to Cade. "These two have lied to me more than they've been truthful. I need to know from Cade O'Brien the sheriff, not Cade O'Brien the husband or Cade O'Brien the friend—can I trust the marshal?"

"You can." Cade punctuated the two words with a firm nod.

That brought Liesl's eyes back to Hawk. "And if anything happens to my mother, am I permitted to shoot you?"

He was too surprised to even respond.

Cade, however, laughed. In an echo of Paisley's earlier comment, he said, "Promise I can be there when she does?"

Liesl's unamused glare stayed on Hawk. "We'll sort out a name, but you'll have to help me find a place for us to hide."

"You mean a place to live?"

Her shoulders squared. "We'll have false names and no peace. My father, who'd kill us as soon as look at us, is being brought here. Men who killed my brother and were praised for it are coming too. Others who helped them hurt countless innocent people will likely be trailing them. I'll be looking over my shoulder even before the prisoners arrive, and certainly more so after they do. Does that sound like *living* to you?"

With that, she walked away, rejoining her mother in the sitting room, and she didn't so much as glance back at him.

He was doing his best, blast it all. But keeping people alive was seldom a simple thing.

Chapter 17

Liesl had never lived in a town with a hotel, let alone lived in a hotel herself. She might have felt she was living high off the hog if she'd not known the spot was chosen because it was easy to watch from the jailhouse while they waited for the judge to scoot into town.

In the meantime, Liesl needed a job.

The hotel sat above a restaurant, another unfamiliar luxury. She'd served food to the Charming Chaps every day for years in Sand Creek, and she couldn't imagine any of the customers at this restaurant being as difficult as those men. The fact that she could live and work in the same building seemed a safe arrangement, even if it meant she'd not go outside for who knew how long.

As soon as she and Mother were settled in their room, Liesl made her way down to the ground floor to have a chat with Mr. Cooper. He ran both the hotel and the restaurant.

"What can I do for you, Miss Moore?" His English accent fit him like a borrowed suit. It couldn't've been real.

"Are you hiring at the restaurant? I'm looking for work."

He looked interested. "Can you cook?"

She nodded.

"I could use help in the kitchen a few days a week."

Life had gone wrong so many times that Liesl was actually a bit blown back to have something go right so easily. Part of her didn't trust it. But she also didn't mean to toss it out like dishwater.

She and Mr. Cooper settled on a schedule that'd work for both of them.

Liesl had been given strict instructions to keep Paisley updated on any changes to her routine, so she trekked from the hotel to the jail. On the outside of the building, along the side closest to Dr. MacNamara's house, was a wooden staircase that led up to the second floor of the jailhouse. Up there, she'd been told, was the marshal's office at the front and Hawk's personal living quarters at the back.

Though Cade O'Brien spent his days in the jail itself, Paisley was a deputy marshal. More likely than not, she'd be upstairs.

Liesl climbed the weather-beaten stairs and stepped through the outside door. Just beyond was a short hallway. On either end was a door. The one to the front of the building was her destination.

It was open an inch or so, and she could hear Hawk's voice beyond.

"Liesl's taking a mighty risk testifying against her father. She doesn't deserve to feel like a prisoner while she's waiting on the judge. We have to find a balance. Keep her and her ma safe, but allow some normalcy."

"I don't know how possible that is," Paisley said.

"Find a way to make it possible."

Sometimes when Hawk spoke, she heard John Butler. John had, perhaps, not been quite as authoritative, but he'd been strong and determined and focused. He'd also been compassionate and kind. He was precisely the sort of person who would have wanted to keep someone safe while also wanting them to be happy.

She missed John Butler. If only he'd been real.

Liesl closed her eyes, hoping to reclaim her balance, but, without warning, her thoughts returned to Platteville. To Hawk trying to

shield her from the downpour. To that isolated room in the back of
the saloon, when they'd stood a breath apart. He'd watched her lips,
just as John had done when they'd sat on the creek.

For the length of a shaking breath, she'd thought he was going to
kiss her. A mighty battle had raged inside her. She'd wanted him to.
Even with the lies, even with her frustration with him, she'd actually
hoped he would. In the end, he pulled away, and she'd been disappointed and relieved and confused ever since.

She couldn't afford hesitation, though. She needed herself and
her mother settled before Father and the Charming Chaps arrived.
Scrambling to sort things out *after* the danger arrived would make
her about three pickles short of a barrel.

She rapped a quick knock against the door before pushing
it open. Paisley and Hawk stood on either side of the desk. Both
looked at Liesl as she stepped inside.

"Sorry to be interrupting," she said. "Paisley, you wanted me to
tell you if anything in my situation changed."

When Paisley nodded, Liesl continued, "Mother and I are settled in at the hotel. I've managed to get a job at the restaurant. In the
kitchen, in fact. It seemed the safest choice."

"I worked for Mr. Cooper for a time," Paisley said. "He'll treat
you fair. In return, you can pretend you don't know his accent ain't
real."

Liesl smiled a little. "I thought it might not've been." With her
next exhale, some of her tension eased. "I ain't yet sorted out the best
way to get what we need from the mercantile. I can't get there and
back without being out in the open."

"If you leave out the back of the hotel and walk down toward
the school," Hawk said, "then cross over the road down there, and
walk back up toward the mercantile, you won't ever pass the jailhouse. The cells don't have any street-facing windows, but an extra
bit of caution ain't a bad thing."

"Roundabout journeys seem to be the flavor of the day lately,"

Liesl said. "I've one other concern. My mother will be stuck in that one room at the hotel, day in and day out, with no one to talk to while I'm working. I wish she could have a spot of company. She ain't particular, likes most people, provided they aren't unkind or dangerous."

"How does she feel about moonshiners?" Paisley asked.

A look passed between Hawk and Paisley. It seemed they weren't speaking hypothetically.

"You have a local moonshiner?" Liesl asked.

"After a manner." Hawk shrugged. "Tansy lives just outside of town. She comes from a long line of proud moonshiners. Her contribution happens to be nothing stronger than sweet tea, but she sells it after the manner she grew up seeing."

Liesl frowned. "Sometimes the moonshining 'manner' is a bit violent."

"Tansy has a good heart," Paisley said. "She's also very protective of people who are vulnerable. She's been vulnerable often enough in her life to know how that feels. She has a lot of interesting stories to tell, but also doesn't mind listening, or even sitting in silence. She'll not pose a danger to you or your mother."

"Do you think this Tansy'd be willing to come gab with Mother sometimes?"

Paisley shrugged. "I'll make the introduction at the town social tomorrow night."

"There's a social tomorrow?" Liesl looked at them both. Her mother needed a bit of lightness and frivolity. Heavens, Liesl needed a bit of it herself. "Would it be safe for us to attend?"

"The prisoners won't arrive for another two or three days," Paisley said. "There'll not be a risk until then. It'd be a good thing for you to get to know some of the townsfolk and for the town to get to know you."

"I think you mean, get to know 'Florence and Lilly Moore.'" Those were the names she and Mother would be pretending were theirs. Liesl was growing quite tired of false names and didn't like that she was required to use one. She knew the pain that particular sort of lie could cause.

"You'll still be yourselves," Paisley said. "And they'll like getting to know you."

Liesl nodded, trying to hold herself together and doing her best to give every impression of being entirely sure of her decisions and the danger she was wading through. But, truth be told, she was drowning.

"Where's the town social held?" she asked.

"Conveniently enough, at the restaurant."

That did make things easier.

Paisley offered a quick farewell and left, saying she meant to head downstairs and into the jail. Liesl assumed she ought to leave also, but Hawk spoke before she could move.

"Even with the restaurant being in the same building, there's something of a risk taking on a job."

"My mother and I have to eat."

He met her gaze, and for just a moment John Butler was looking back at her. "I wouldn't have left you to starve," he said softly.

"I ain't overly fond of charity," she said.

"It wouldn't've been charity."

She watched him. Studied him. "What would it have been, then?"

He held her gaze. There was something pleading in his eyes, something that made her want to cry. And she never cried.

"I don't like that you don't trust me, Liesl."

"You know who I was raised by," she said. "I don't trust anyone."

A flash of regret passed over his features. "John Butler likely didn't help that."

In a quieter voice than she would've preferred, she said, "John Butler was the first person I've had faith in for years. And, in the end, he wasn't even real."

They stood there a moment in silence. She held out an unspoken hope that he'd say those weeks he'd been John had meant something to him, too. Then at least that part wouldn't have been a lie. She thought at least he might apologize for having misled her and disappointed her. But he didn't. He just kept watching her with that same look that made her want to cry. But now, it also made her want to hug him.

Confused and tired and heavyhearted, she turned and left the room. She took the exterior stairs one slow step at a time, trying to sort her thoughts. By the time her feet reached the street out front, she'd restored some of her equilibrium.

She'd come to Savage Wells to testify at trial. She'd come here to save the lives of her friends in Sand Creek and to protect her mother. That was what she'd focus on. No amount of heartbreak or frustration would be permitted to distract her.

Chapter 18

One never knew what Andrew Gilbert was going to feel equal to undertaking from one day to the next. He'd served in the Civil War at far too young an age, sent up into the trees to watch for the approach of enemy battalions. It had taken a toll on his young mind.

Before Cade's arrival in town, Andrew had spent all day, every day, up in the trees surrounding Savage Wells. Now, he spent most of his days in the jailhouse, Cade having deputized him. He and Paisley's father, Mr. Bell, had been the very best of friends, despite the differences in their ages. But Mr. Bell was in what Dr. Gideon MacNamara had told Paisley was the final stages of senility. He no longer remembered his friend or how to play checkers, the game they had bonded over.

Andrew, Hawk suspected, was lonely. He knew precisely how that felt.

Until recently, he'd dismissed the moments of loneliness as a bit of human frailty, getting in the way of what needed doing. Sand Creek had changed that. And it worried him.

He'd sworn to protect lives in this territory. If he let his guard down, people died. Losing focus was the reason they were scrambling to keep Liesl and her mother safe in a town *he* had insisted would be a haven for them. So much could go wrong if the marshal safeguarding the territory let himself get distracted, even for a moment. A weight that heavy on a fella's conscience could sink him in an instant.

But he missed having people in his life who weren't there only as his deputies or the people he protected. He missed having friends. He missed family.

And, though he would never have admitted it out loud, he missed Liesl. And, blast it all, he missed being John Butler. It had been a false front, sure enough, but there'd been a shocking amount of him there, the man he'd been before fighting and marshaling and carrying the weight of a territory had hardened every soft part of his soul.

As John Butler, he'd had a taste of what life might've been. Losing it was proving more painful than he'd have guessed.

The night of the town social arrived, and Andrew had cried off at the last minute. People sometimes were too much for him. Cade and Hawk both had fought in the war, so they knew the toll it took on some former soldiers.

Andrew remained behind at the jailhouse, though their prisoners had not yet arrived, and Cade and Paisley, along with Dr. and Mrs. MacNamara, made their way to the social. Hawk was the resident hanger-on.

As he stepped into the restaurant, its dining room emptied of tables and chairs, Hawk told himself that he wasn't looking for anyone in particular, but he knew that was about as accurate as a sundial at night.

Liesl stood near her mother in a corner of the room watching the comings and goings. Neither looked overjoyed, but Mrs. Hodges looked worried. And Liesl looked exhausted.

Was she being worked too hard at the restaurant? Had she given herself enough time after her arrival in town to rest?

There he went again, fretting over a woman he'd do best to put out of his thoughts entirely.

"Do you mean to stand about glaring at everyone all night?" Paisley asked out of the side of her mouth. "Because if you do, I plan to keep to the other side of the room. Tonight is meant to be enjoyable."

"And I'm meant to be keeping this place safe. That don't allow for much enjoyment."

"Nonsense," Miriam MacNamara said. "I remember one particular town social at which you enjoyed yourself quite a lot."

Hawk glanced at Gideon, who smiled, not the least concerned that his wife was reminiscing about a social she'd attended with another man before they were courting. Hawk didn't have a lot of friends, but he counted these four among them. They were good for him. But they didn't always fully appreciate the weight on his shoulders.

Tansy stood across the way. With a word of excuse to his companions, Hawk crossed to her.

"Hawk," she said with a quick dip of her head. Tansy was not overly talkative.

"Have you met the Moores?" Hawk felt it best to get straight to the heart of the matter. Tansy preferred it that way. So did he.

"I ain't met 'em."

Hawk motioned her toward the women in question. "I think you ought to. They're new to town, and a touch lonely. Could benefit from someone who knows the lay of the land."

Tansy walked with him. She was wearing what he knew was her best dress, but with the mud-crusted bowler hat he'd never seen her without. And, though her shotgun was her weapon of choice, tonight she wore a six-shooter in a holster, likely because it was less cumbersome.

"Lilly, Mrs. Moore," he said by way of introduction. "This here's Tansy."

"Pleasure," Tansy said, dipping her head to each of them in turn.

"I've heard you keep the town supplied with moonshine," Liesl said.

Tansy's gaze narrowed on her. "Might be."

No matter that Tansy's concoctions weren't actually alcoholic or illegal in any way, she always acted as if she were doing something truly nefarious. No one was quite sure if she didn't actually know that her enterprise was an honest one or if she merely liked to pretend. Didn't really matter. Being a risk-taking moonshiner gave her a sense of purpose and identity, and no one in town intended to snatch that away from her.

"I've heard good things about your moonshine," Liesl said. "It's a real honor to meet you."

Whether she realized it or not, Liesl had struck upon the exact right way to earn Tansy's trust and respect.

Hawk eyed Mrs. Hodges, unsure if she knew the game that was being played. Her gaze continually swept the room, as if she expected to be tossed out at any minute. Her husband's doing, no doubt.

"Tansy, here, is from Alabama," Hawk said to them.

"Are you, really?" Mrs. Hodges said, speaking for the first time. "My mother was from Alabama."

"No fooling?" Tansy sat in the empty chair next to Mrs. Hodges. "Which bit of it?"

And just like that, Mrs. Hodges—known to everyone here as Mrs. Moore—had a friend. Hawk didn't doubt Tansy would sit by her and talk of Alabama all night long.

He offered Liesl a quick smile, hoping to communicate that he'd done what he came to do and didn't mean to cause her trouble. She smiled fleetingly. She shifted her weight from one leg to the other, sometimes looking at him, sometimes looking away. He searched about for something to say.

Behind him, the musicians struck up the start of the tune. It was a familiar waltz, one played at nearly every town social.

For the briefest of moments, Liesl looked at him, hope in her eyes. But she swept it out immediately. He'd disappointed her. Again. *John Butler wouldn't have.*

"I'd ask you to dance, Miss Moore, but . . ."

"If you tell me you're a horrible dancer, I'll have to warn you I've been told that before by someone I discovered wasn't always honest. I'm not sure I'll believe you."

He'd forgotten that part of the ruse. *Curse you, John Butler.*

"I'm not entirely cow-footed, but I ain't exactly graceful, either. I do know how to waltz, but I've not done it often. And, while I'm being so blasted forthright, I'll add that as often as not when I join in the dancing at a social, I get tugged out of the dance by someone or another needing something from the marshal."

A hint of a smile touched her lips. "That's a refreshing string of honesty there, Marshal Hawking."

"I told someone recently that I prefer not to lie when I can avoid it. I hope eventually she'll believe me."

Liesl watched him for a moment, not answering and not giving anything away. Life had given her ample reason not to trust people, and he'd reinforced that. He couldn't really blame her if she couldn't think well of him again with that chasm between them.

To his shock, she set her hand in his. His lungs hitched a bit, heat stealing up from his hand, along his arm, straight to his heart.

"This ain't me believing you," Liesl said. "This is just me wanting to dance."

A needed splash of cold water. "Fair enough." And he led her out to the open space where others had gathered to waltz.

The tune was played at a decent clip, though the musicians sometimes erred on the side of too fast. Hawk was grateful they'd manage the correct tempo this time. He set his arm around Liesl's waist and held her other hand in his. Her arm was set along his with her hand resting at his shoulder. With steps he wouldn't exactly describe as graceful, he took them through the rhythm of the tune.

She smiled a bit at him now and then, but for the first minute or so, nothing was said between them. Hawk couldn't be certain it wasn't a sign that she was miserable.

"Thank you for introducing Tansy to my mother," she said after a bit. "It's good for her to have someone to talk to."

"Happy to do it."

"I worry that she'll clam up entirely in another day or two." Then, her voice dropping lower, she added, "Considering everything."

Hawk tightened his arm around her just enough to pull her closer. "I don't doubt she's worried. I suspect, though, she ain't the only one who needs to be reassured."

Liesl sighed. "I've been trying to hide how worried I am. Doing a poor job of it, apparently."

"Nonsense," Hawk said. "You hide it very well. But I've spent a good amount of time with you. I've learned to read your face better than I might've otherwise."

"John Butler could see right through me," she whispered.

"Not as much as you might think," he said dryly. He'd always found her incredibly confusing.

"You likely think me ridiculous for being so afraid. The famous John Hawking is afraid of nothing and no one, and his deputies aren't either. He never shirks, and he endures no cowardliness."

That was likely his exact reputation. Had he been told that even a month ago, he probably would have nodded proudly, even crowed a bit at how accurate the list was. Seeing how it had convinced Liesl that he would have no compassion for her, he found himself not nearly as pleased as he might have been.

"There's a heap of difference between being afraid of something that warrants fear and being a coward."

"But if I fall to pieces, so will my mother. I've hid every bit of fear I've felt for years. She couldn't have gone on otherwise. But I don't know how much longer I can do it."

For two people who were constantly picking at each other, it was a remarkably personal conversation. He wasn't certain if she was confessing so much because she was tired and had no one else to talk to, or if she was starting to trust him a tiny bit.

He'd told her in Platteville that she confused him. That hadn't changed.

The tune came to a close and he, of necessity, dropped his arms and joined the crowd in applauding the musicians. He looked back to Liesl, prepared to offer her a glass of punch or walk her back to her mother, but she wasn't there anymore. He spotted her the instant before she disappeared through the door of the dining room.

Without hardly realizing he was doing it, he followed her.

She wasn't moving overly quick, and he caught up to her as she stepped inside the kitchen. The room was empty, the restaurant closed for the day, and lit by nothing beyond the moonlight slipping in the windows and the spill of candlelight from the dining room.

She stood with her back to him. Her posture was hunched, her head bent. Though Hawk couldn't be certain, he thought she might be crying.

"Saints, if I've upset you—"

She spun around, apparently surprised to hear his voice. "You didn't upset me."

"But you look upset, and I was the last person you talked to."

She shook her head. "I'm exhausted. I'm worn to a thread. And I ain't sure I have the strength to face what's coming here. It's pitiful and cowardly."

Until that moment, he hadn't realized how much of a toll this was taking on her. Liesl did such a good job of pretending to be unaffected and unshaken.

He stepped over to her and took her hands in his. "In the time I've known you, you've shown yourself one of the bravest people I've ever encountered. You don't have to be strong every moment of every day."

"When the threat is in your very house you do."

"But, this time, that threat'll be held in *my* house." He brushed his thumb over a tear glistening on her cheek.

"And you guard your house well?"

The smile he felt spreading over his face was likely as cocky as the King of Spades. "Oh, lamb. I guard it better than *anyone*."

Her smile was tremulous, but her eyes weren't as heavy. "Promise I can watch while you do?"

An echo of what Paisley and Cade had both said to him on the day he'd returned to Savage Wells. A bit of humor. A bit of lightness. A hint of friendship.

"Do you promise you'll let yourself rest, even for a moment now and then?"

She took a breath so deep her shoulders rose and fell with it. "I'll try."

He twitched his head back in the direction of the town social. "Go enjoy yourself. Sometimes, that's the best rest of all."

Liesl snatched up the suggestion and left with a bit more bounce in her step. Hawk remained behind, standing in the moonlight, torn between wanting to spend the rest of the evening with her and keeping enough of a distance to not start whispers. All the while knowing it wasn't the whispers he was most worried about.

Chapter 19

Two days had passed since the town social, and Liesl hadn't stopped thinking about it. Mother'd found a friend in Tansy, who'd proven herself a good listener and seemed to like talking with Mother.

Liesl had met a number of people from the town, some of whom looked in on her in the kitchen at the restaurant when she was working. She'd come to know Dr. MacNamara and his wife better. She'd grown less intimidated by Cade O'Brien, though she knew he was as dangerous as she'd heard he was.

Even with all that, Hawk was the person most often on her mind.

He'd been kind at the social. He'd spoken to her without dismissal or anger. When she'd been sinking, he'd buoyed her. And he'd promised her she wouldn't be facing the coming trouble alone. She'd felt safe, or as close to safe as she ever had.

He had been her John Butler again. Almost.

Almost.

A knock echoed at their hotel room door mere moments before she would be headed down the stairs to the kitchen.

She cracked opened the door to see Paisley and Tansy on the other side.

She motioned them inside, closing the door behind them.

"Everything all right?" Worry nibbled at her mind.

"Prisoners are set to arrive today," Paisley said. Her eyes darted to the door, likely checking to make certain it was closed all the way. "We thought you ought to know."

Liesl was grateful for the warning but surprised it was offered with Tansy there.

"I've been deputized before," Tansy said. "They trusted me with this so I can help look out for the two of you."

Mother, who was sitting in a chair nearby, sighed in relief. "Oh, I'm so glad. I did not enjoy telling you falsehoods, especially when most everything we talked about was true. Only my name was a lie."

Only my name was a lie. That was the balance Liesl was trying to strike as well, being as honest as she possibly could. And, in the back of her mind, was the possibility that Hawk had done the same in Sand Creek. He'd woven a lot of tales, but maybe there'd not been so many falsehoods in it as she thought. Maybe the lies that had hurt the most weren't *complete* lies.

Tansy dipped her head in acknowledgment. "Once Paisley explained, it all made sense. You gabbed about everything, except where you came from before here. You'd do best to keep your name to the false one. No point inviting more risks."

Mother nodded. She looked calm. That never happened.

"For today," Paisley said, "I'd suggest you stay inside and keep the curtains pulled. We can't risk any of the prisoners spotting and recognizing you. Once they're locked in the jailhouse, they'll have no chance of seeing you as long as you stay away."

"They all know you as Mary Butler," Liesl said.

"Hawk and I won't be part of the group bringing them in or locking them up. We'll stay in the marshal's office while that's happening. And for as long as they're here, Cade, Andrew, and Ensio will take shifts watching them."

It all made sense, though it sounded terribly complicated.

"I'm meant to work in the kitchen today," Liesl said. "Is it still safe to do that?"

Paisley nodded.

Tansy smiled at Mother. "I invited a couple of women to come by here today. I think they'll enjoy getting to know you, though they'll know you as Florence Moore instead of Mildred Hodges."

"Visitors?" Mother's eyes pulled wide with excitement. In Sand Creek they'd kept to themselves, not daring to have people over to the house with Father's unpredictable temper. And protecting everyone from the Charming Chaps had occupied all of Liesl's time away from home. Days could pass, weeks even, without her mother seeing anyone outside their family.

"I'll stop in at the restaurant later today," Paisley said to Liesl. "Once the prisoners are safely locked away, I'll let you know."

"I thank you, kindly," Liesl said.

Tansy remained behind, already gabbing with Mother. Knowing there'd be someone looking after her and keeping her safe set Liesl's mind at ease.

Liesl and Paisley parted ways on the ground floor of the building, with Liesl heading back to the kitchens and Paisley out to place herself in the marshal's office for the day.

Work in the kitchen wasn't quite the distraction Liesl hoped for. Any moment now, her father and the Charming Chaps would be in this town that she'd worked so hard to reach, that she'd promised her mother would be safe. Having Father anywhere nearby snatched that safety clean away.

This time, that threat'll be held in my *house.* The memory of Hawk's words calmed her. Recalling how he'd called her "lamb" again made her smile.

As the day wore on, she grew more jumpy. With every flicker of shadow, every hint of movement she could hear in the dining room, every slight crunch of wagon wheels, her heart seized. She'd not be surprised if she'd turned blue from how often she'd held her breath.

"Appears someone is expected at the jailhouse." Mr. Cooper dropped that gold nugget as easy as anything when he stepped into the kitchen to snatch up a plate.

"How do you know?" Her voice emerged calmer than she felt.

"Sheriff O'Brien has been stationed out under the front overhang, watching the road. And Andrew Gilbert is up in the tree on the outskirts of town."

Liesl focused her eyes on the pie she was making. "Does that not happen much?"

"Only when someone important is expected."

"Important how?" She knew the answer, of course.

"I can't be certain," Mr. Cooper said, taking up a second plate, "but if someone is headed for the jail, it probably isn't for a friendly visit."

He stepped back out again, leaving Liesl with her thoughts and the breaths that didn't come easily. This was the day. The four people in the world she was most terrified of would be in town today. But, she reminded herself, as soon as the judge arrived and Liesl gave her testimony regarding the Chaps' crimes, she'd never need be terrified of them again. Sand Creek would be free from their tyranny. Mother would be safe. That would make these few days of overlap in Savage Wells worth it.

A half hour passed. She worked without her mind noting much of what she was doing. Only when Hawk and Paisley stepped inside the kitchen did she pull herself into the present.

"We can't linger," Paisley said. "We're just hoping to discover what's on the menu."

Odd.

"A bowl of stew would be just charming," Hawk said. His slight emphasis on the last word caught her ear.

Behind them, the door to the kitchen was open. People were in the dining room. There was a risk of being overheard. *Charming*. He was giving her a clue.

"We ought to offer that with a thick-cut slice of bread," Liesl said. "My father always liked that with his stew."

"Yes." While Hawk made the word sound casual, there was something in the back of his eyes that told her it was anything but.

The Charming Chaps *and* her father had arrived.

"Don't make any changes, though, if it'd be any trouble," Paisley said.

"Is it likely to be much trouble?"

"None at all," Paisley said.

Liesl kept her relief silent but let it show in her expression. The prisoners had arrived, and Hawk and Paisley weren't expecting any trouble from that quarter.

"Any chance people passing by on the street might spy the charming stew?"

Hawk nodded at her coded message. "There ain't a chance of the stew being anywhere near a front-facing window."

"You're keeping an eye on things, are you?"

"Always." He was every bit the fearless and focused US Marshal who'd brought peace to this territory.

Seeing him, seeing how calm and sure he was, Liesl felt a little less burdened and a little less worried. The arrival of the four prisoners was, by all accounts, the riskiest day they'd had since arriving. There was still a chance the Chaps would be followed to Savage Wells by one or more of their unnamed accomplices. So long as she and Mother were careful when going about, and Andrew and Cade proved as skilled at spotting strangers in town as she'd been promised, they could survive even that.

Just until I can testify. That was her goal, her aim. And it felt possible. Liesl was not well acquainted with hope, but she felt a bubble of it in that moment. "Thank you," she told them.

Paisley offered a quick, "You're welcome." Hawk tipped his head.

Safe, she told herself. For the first time in years, she felt almost safe.

Chapter 20

The town of Savage Wells boasted a great many unusual people, and perhaps the most mysterious of all was Thomas Larsen, attorney and rumored ghost. Larsen had lived in the area for years but was seldom seen. It was generally understood that he spent at least part of his time somewhere else. Where that "somewhere" might've been was anyone's guess.

The town had even less idea *why* he spent any time at all in such an isolated area of the world. A man with his education and skills could've made quite a name for himself in a large city, or even a middling-sized one. Instead, he floated around this tiny watering hole, helping a great many local people out of sticky situations. And the town was grateful.

Hawk was hoping for another of the man's miracles.

Paisley brought Liesl by the marshal's office a couple days after the arrival of the Charming Chaps. Paisley didn't remain but returned to her home to look after her ailing father.

Larsen had sat, waiting calmly for her arrival. Hawk, uncharacteristically, had been pacing. He was usually more self-assured, but the matter of the four prisoners and the trial looming on the horizon had him on edge.

"Paisley said there was something you were needing from me," Liesl said, eyeing them both in turn.

"This here's Mr. Larsen," Hawk said. "An attorney who lives hereabouts. He's going to assess what we're up against with this case and help us decide the best means of moving forward."

Her brow pulled sharply. "I thought testifying *was* the best means of moving forward."

Hawk nodded. "I'm still certain it is. But it ain't a bad idea to get an expert opinion."

"You know, you've changed your tune about a whole lot of things." Liesl's posture had grown stiff. "We were fleeing to Savage Wells to get away from my father, and now he's here. Locking up the Charming Chaps was going to keep my mother and me safe, but now we're tiptoeing around this town, still in hiding. Testifying against them was going to be enough, but now you ain't sure of that anymore. I'm running out of excuses to trust you, Marshal."

Few people had so quickly and efficiently dressed him down. He had to admit he deserved it.

"I only want to make certain. I didn't ask him here because I have mountains of doubts," Hawk assured her.

"Well, I'm having a few doubts of my own." And yet she sat at the table with Mr. Larsen, giving every impression she didn't mean to argue further.

"Marshal Hawking has given me a basic understanding of the charges brought against the four prisoners below us. What I need to know from you is which of their crimes you can testify to."

"I brought them their lunch every day. They didn't stop discussing their plans and plots while I was there. They likely didn't do much of anything that I didn't hear about in one way or another."

Larsen jotted down notes. "You can, certainly, testify to anything you heard them discuss that relates to crimes." He looked at her. "But how many of those things can you prove? Do you have anything they wrote down or records they kept of the things they did?"

That was the heart of Hawk's worry. Liesl could testify to overhearing a lot of things, but a hard-nosed judge might not think that ironclad enough.

"I did grab a few things from the jailhouse and from our home before we left Sand Creek," Liesl said. "I put them in my mother's carpetbag."

"Why didn't you carry them yourself?" Hawk asked.

"Because if something happened to me, I wanted her to have some chance of escaping my father's wrath."

She'd given the impression of being quite confident during their journey. It seemed she hadn't been as sure as she'd appeared.

"And what is the nature of these papers?" Larsen asked.

"Most are ledgers. Accountings of things they seized and money they took. Among them are notes of the violence they rained down when someone couldn't pay."

Mr. Larsen nodded; apparently, that would be helpful. "Do you have any proof that *they* are the ones who carried out the violence?"

Uncertainty entered her eyes. "Everyone in Sand Creek knows they did it."

"Would any of them testify?"

Liesl shrugged. "I don't know. They're rightly terrified of the Charming Chaps. If they testify, and the trial don't go their way, they'd be done for."

Mr. Larsen held her gaze. "You do realize the same is true of you? Especially in the matter of crimes you can't testify to *seeing* them carry out."

"I'm becoming more and more aware of that."

Hawk paced away, feeling the weight of that realization himself. He'd encouraged others to testify in trials with uncertain outcomes. He'd acknowledged to himself and them that there was a risk, but he'd always hoped the outcome was worth the gamble. In that moment, simply *hoping* didn't feel like enough. Liesl was in very real danger, and he had encouraged her to be. If something happened to her, it'd be on his head.

"I'd be interested in seeing the papers you've brought from Sand Creek," Mr. Larsen said.

Liesl nodded.

"Embezzling and doing harm to people is certainly against the law," Mr. Larsen said, "but they aren't the sort of charges likely to see these men locked up for long. Marshal Hawking said they were planning an assassination."

"I overheard them discussing it," Liesl said. "That's why I sent a telegram here. I was hoping to warn him, since Marshal Hawking was the target."

"Can you prove *that*?" Mr. Larsen asked.

"I can't. I heard what I heard, but I can't prove it."

Hawk looked at Mr. Larsen, asking an unspoken question. The attorney's tense and downturned mouth wasn't reassuring.

The confident John Hawking who had planned the flight to Savage Wells and the takeover of Sand Creek was disappearing with each new setback. He wasn't at all accustomed to the experience. He didn't consider himself arrogant, but he had reason to have faith in himself.

Where was that faith now?

"Assuming we can even get a conviction," Mr. Larsen said, "charges of a false tax scheme and beating people won't see these men held anywhere overly secure. And they won't be there for long."

"Likely not even as long as they're supposed to be," Liesl said. "They'll escape sure as we're sitting here. They have a lot of friends who'd help them."

"Can you prove that?"

Hawk chimed in. "Deputy O'Brien and I took a few things out of the telegraph office in Sand Creek. A few of the telegrams sent by Mr. Yarrow, one of the group downstairs, mention cohorts of theirs helping out with things. They aren't all named, but the ones that are have criminal histories long as your arm."

"That might be enough for something," Mr. Larsen said.

They needed something stronger to ensure that Hodges and the Chaps would be sent away for good. "You told me you could testify that they killed your brother," Hawk said to Liesl.

She grew pale, something that happened whenever the subject of her brother's death arose. "I can. My mother and I both witnessed it."

Mrs. Hodges had seen her son murdered, at the behest of her husband—or at least with his approval. Little wonder the woman struggled to get through each day.

"Would your mother testify?" Mr. Larsen asked. "*Two* testimonies to the same crime would make a difference."

"She'd never get through it," Liesl said. "And I doubt she'd manage a single word if required to talk about Otto's death. Doing so if my father is present? That would be impossible."

"Will *you* be able to?" Mr. Larsen asked.

"I don't see what choice I have. I promised my mother that she'd be safe, that we could finally escape my father's iron fist. If I can't keep that promise . . ." Liesl shook her head, apparently too overwhelmed to finish the thought.

"Murder is a significant charge." Mr. Larsen spoke with authority. "If the men are found guilty, you'll not need to worry about them again."

"I ain't overly fond of you using the word 'if' so much," Liesl said.

"I wish I could give you more of a guarantee," Mr. Larsen said.

So do I. Hawk paced away. Never before had he felt so personally responsible for the outcome of a plan or a trial. This was why sensible lawmen refused to become emotionally involved with anyone. It added too many complications.

"If I testify against my father, and he goes free or escapes, he won't merely be angry. He will kill me. And he'll kill my mother too for good measure."

Mr. Larsen's expression was utterly serious. "Has he killed other people in addition to your brother?"

"He has." She held up her hand, cutting off any reply from Mr. Larsen. "And, no, I can't prove those murders. But I can tell you who can."

That brought both of their attention to her fully and completely.

"The same man who meant to help them assassinate Marshal Hawking. His name is Rod Carlisle, and he's currently in the territorial prison in Laramie awaiting trial."

Mr. Larsen looked back at Hawk. "Do you think he could be convinced to turn?"

"Can't say," Hawk said. "He's a tough one."

"Might be he's your best chance."

Their best chance was a man who'd fully intended to help the Charming Chaps kill Hawk. If that didn't sum up the situation, nothing would.

He moved to the window, cursing himself for not realizing these complications sooner. He ought to have. He usually did. But he'd been distracted by the tug he felt to Liesl Hodges. He'd wanted her to be safe and nearby so much that he'd not stopped to really think it through.

It was really a shame the saloon owner in Cheyenne hadn't been right about Hawk not having a heart. That heart was sure making a mess of things at the moment.

Mr. Larsen rose, picking up his lead pencil and notebook. "Get those papers to Paisley or Hawk," he said to Liesl. "I'll look through them and see what will be the most helpful for our cause. The more we can prove against them, the better our chances will be."

"Thank you," Liesl said.

"And," he said, hovering near the door, "a bit of non-legal

advice: confide in Mrs. MacNamara. She went through something shockingly similar to this not long ago."

Liesl looked to Hawk.

He nodded. "Testified in a trial where her word wasn't guaranteed to be enough, and there'd be hell to pay if things didn't go her way."

"Did they? Go her way, I mean?"

The knot in his stomach grew tighter. "Not exactly."

Mr. Larsen dipped his head to both of them before leaving the office. It was hard to say when exactly they'd see him again. He wasn't overly predictable, and yet he was as reliable as a sunrise.

Liesl stood. Hawk thought she might start pacing; he'd certainly done enough of that himself. She didn't. She stood rooted to the spot, looking worn down again.

"When we left Sand Creek, this seemed such a sure thing."

"I wish it had stayed that way," Hawk said.

"So do I."

His hand twitched as though instinctively reaching out to touch her. "I'll walk you back to the hotel."

"You don't need to. I'll go back the way I came, passing behind the jailhouse to make extra sure I'm not seen."

"I know I don't need to, but I'd like to."

She met him in the doorway. "Why's that?"

"For your protection. For my peace of mind. To avoid spending even more time in this room or my living quarters entirely alone. Again."

"Loneliness eats away at a person, don't it?" She spoke as one who knew.

"It surely does."

They made their way down the exterior stairs and around the back of the jailhouse and mercantile. They were likely being more careful than they needed to be, but her life was on the line. Hawk found that more than ample reason to be overly cautious.

He'd never before let his personal feelings color his decisions. But the strength of these feelings had snuck up on him. He didn't yet know if giving way to them would make him more motivated or prove his undoing.

Almost without meaning to, Hawk slipped his hand around hers. He'd thought about that often—more often than he'd like to admit—and about that fleeting moment in the rain, when he'd held her in his arms.

They walked to the back entrance of the restaurant. She smiled up at him as they approached. It was a soft and friendly smile, one filled with gratitude and contentment. Ordinary in every way. And, yet, it did something odd to his heart. Heat spread from that usually undisruptive organ through every inch of him.

He'd do just about anything to see her smile at him that way again.

That, he thought, as she disappeared inside the restaurant, might prove a dangerous thing indeed.

Chapter 21

Despite her worries over her father and the coming trial, Liesl was finding life in Savage Wells enjoyable. The people she interacted with at the restaurant were kind and friendly. Her mother had three bosom friends, something Liesl had never known her to have. And the two of them had been invited to a dinner party at the home of Dr. and Mrs. MacNamara.

Mother dressed with care. Liesl had included Mother's best dress in her carpetbag, but she had only packed one change of clothes for herself, and neither of her options were particularly fine. Still, no one in Savage Wells had treated her unkindly, and she didn't anticipate that they would start doing so over a simple dress.

And so they arrived at the MacNamaras' home, both overflowing with excitement.

"I couldn't imagine doing anything like this in Sand Creek," Mother said as they waited for the door to be answered.

"No one would have wanted Father at their home," Liesl said. "And he wouldn't have let us go anywhere without him."

Mrs. MacNamara opened the door, and they were eagerly welcomed in. Liesl knew everyone present. Mother's new friends— Mrs. Wilhite, who sold ribbons, and Mrs. Carol, who was the local milliner, and Tansy—were in the sitting room, which doubled as the doctor's examination room. The mayor, Mr. Brimble, and his wife were there as well.

So was Hawk.

Liesl couldn't help the smile that spread across her face when she saw him. He'd looked in on her and her mother a few times in the days since the meeting with Mr. Larsen, and he had more than once held her hand when they had been together. It wasn't the heated gaze from their brief stop on the journey to Savage Wells, and it wasn't the tender brush of his thumb across her tear-streaked face from the night of the town social, but it was a connection, a reassurance. Her heart had tugged with each touch of his hand.

She had a hard time trusting people, and Hawk had most certainly misled her. But she was beginning to understand *why* he had, and it eased the pain of it enough that she truly liked having him nearby.

Conversation was light and general. A few minutes passed before the doctor invited everyone into the dining room for supper.

Hawk walked near enough to Liesl for her to ask him, "Are Cade and Paisley not joining us?" She would have guessed they'd be invited.

"Paisley's father's ailing. They're home with him."

Liesl had heard Mr. Bell wasn't well. "That leaves the jail down one guard."

"Ensio and Andrew are both there tonight. Cade'll spell one of them come morning."

"What about the other deputy marshals who accompanied the prisoners here?"

"They needed to return to their other posts. Savage Wells has lawmen enough even without them here, and even with such dangerous prisoners."

They had the situation sorted, it seemed. "Do the O'Briens usually come to the MacNamaras' suppers?"

"Cade and Gideon are good friends, as are Paisley and Miriam. And Paisley and Gideon are cousins."

Liesl smiled. "In other words, the O'Briens and the MacNamaras are inseparable."

"As whiskers on a pig."

She laughed. "I don't think you're supposed to call your hostess a pig ahead of dinner. She might poison you."

"If she does, I fully expect you to send me a telegram warning me."

"Consider yourself warned."

He nodded solemnly. "I will."

He sat next to her at the table. Mother sat on her other side. How much had changed in a few short weeks. Before they'd escaped from Sand Creek, the whole world had seemed to be crashing in around her. Now, she was in a town of new friends, her mother safe for the moment, and bits of John Butler were peeking through the stony facade of the battle-hardened marshal.

"The hat you designed looks gorgeous in our shop window," Mrs. Carol said to Mother. "We'll sell loads of bonnets and ribbons and hats with you helping."

"I quite enjoyed it," Mother said. "I had no idea I had a talent for millinery."

"You must help us make our ribbon corsages for the next formal town dance," Mrs. Wilhite said. "It is a Savage Wells tradition."

"I would love that."

"As much as you love my moonshine?" Tansy asked, her expression genuinely curious.

"My parents loved sweet tea," Mother said. "They'd have been delighted with your moonshine. Best I ever tasted."

Liesl listened to the conversations with relief. Mother was so happy here.

"It's a shame the O'Briens couldn't be here tonight," Mr. Brimble said. "A shame."

"A relief, really," Dr. MacNamara said. "Deputy O'Brien and Marshal Hawking might toss the lot of us into the river."

Hawk's shoulders shook a little, as if holding in a laugh.

"Would you do something so shocking?" Mrs. MacNamara asked, a little too innocently. "Throwing people into rivers?"

"Sometimes people need a little cooling off." Hawk shrugged like it was an ordinary topic of conversation, but amusement showed in his eyes.

"What might lead a person to need that particular cooling off?" Liesl asked.

"Could be a fella was running his mouth after a certain marshal and deputy marshal told him to shut his yammer while they sorted out the ins and outs of a brawl that'd erupted. And it could be that fella didn't listen."

"And it follows that the marshal and deputy marshal tossed that loudmouthed fellow into the river?"

Hawk shrugged. "Could be."

The table laughed. Hawk smiled genuinely. She liked this side of him. Liesl was terribly fond of an entertaining story.

"Have you ever tossed anyone into a river, Miss Moore?" Dr. MacNamara asked.

"No, but I did once thoroughly best a man in a rock-skipping competition."

She saw the corner of Hawk's mouth twitch.

"There was this brother and sister who moved to town. They seemed very lonely, a bit awkward around people."

The twitch grew more pronounced.

"The brother had the slowest reflexes." She recounted the story with enough humor in her voice that she doubted anyone thought it anything but a silly memory. "I thought about taking pity on him and letting him win with his hard-fought, double-skip toss. But, in the end, I couldn't resist the chance to outshine him with a four-skip effort of my own. I am certain he was absolutely devastated."

Chuckles sounded around the table.

Hawk leaned closer to her and whispered, "You are trouble."

"I am also the champion rock skipper."

In the next instant, Andrew Gilbert rushed inside, his attention immediately focused on Hawk. He didn't say a word, but he didn't appear to need to.

Hawk offered a quick word of apology to the group and rose, walking with Andrew out of the dining room.

"I wonder if this is to do with those newly arrived prisoners," Mrs. Brimble said. "Everyone is curious about them, but no one at the jail will say a word about who they are or why they are here."

"Seems to me that's proof enough we'd best keep our noses in our own business," Tansy said. The town must've been used to her abruptness. No one in the room batted an eye.

Liesl glanced at her mother and was relieved to see she wasn't entirely upended by the reference to a man not everyone at this table knew was her notorious husband.

The MacNamaras knew, and they kindly turned the topic to the possibility of another town social. That set Mrs. Wilhite and Mrs. Carol abuzz at the need for corsages and adornments. Mother joined in the discussion, and Tansy smiled after being assured her moonshine would be missed if she didn't provide it.

Through it all, Liesl's mind spun with the possible reasons for Andrew's arrival. He was stationed at the jail tonight. Had there been trouble? Had someone escaped? Did she need to snatch up her mother and run?

She had far more questions than answers by the time Hawk returned to the room. He didn't offer any explanation, but instead returned to his seat and took up his utensils again.

"Anything amiss?" Mr. Brimble asked.

"No, simply a report of some information."

Liesl watched him, searching for signs of what he wasn't saying.

Too much was at stake for her to be appeased by such a quick response.

He looked over at her. With a little smile, he said, "Everything really is fine."

She didn't believe it. Nothing involving her father was ever "fine."

Hawk set his hand on hers. "Trust me," he whispered.

She took a deep breath. "I'm learning to."

He raised her hand to his lips and kissed it gently. He'd never done that before. It helped more than she could possibly have guessed.

And then she remembered they weren't alone. A quick glance around the table told her Hawk's tender gesture hadn't gone unnoticed. Smiles, some held back, others blooming fully, appeared on every face. Dr. MacNamara even raised an eyebrow at the US Marshal.

Would he be embarrassed to have been caught out being tender? He had a reputation, after all.

But Hawk merely chuckled quietly and returned to his meal.

Liesl found him endlessly confusing and increasingly fascinating. And she liked it very much indeed.

Chapter 22

Hawk didn't at all like being forced to spend his days in the marshal's office waiting. Waiting on telegrams. Waiting on information. Waiting on Mr. Larsen. He wasn't the *waiting* type. He'd rather be downstairs *doing*.

Andrew's interruption of the dinner party the night before had been a welcome bit of involvement, but it had also made Liesl worry, and he hadn't at all cared for that. He felt like he was balancing on a blade and the slightest thing would upset his precarious equilibrium.

He paced the marshal's office, something he'd done almost constantly these past two weeks. The matter of the Charming Chaps was hardly the stickiest he'd ever faced, yet he could think of hardly anything else. It even kept him up at night.

A quick knock sounded at the door before Liesl slipped inside. She smiled when her gaze settled on him. His heart responded by pounding and jumping and tying itself in admittedly enjoyable knots. He'd never known a woman to have that effect on him.

"You'll never guess," she said, crossing to him.

Why that greeting made him want to laugh, he couldn't say. "You'll have to tell me then."

"I've been invited to join the women's auxiliary organization here in town."

"Ah." He nodded. "Mrs. Holmes tracked you down, did she?"

Liesl's eyes scrunched with her smile. "At the restaurant. And I'm glad she did. I get to help plan the next town social. The organization also helps people in and around town. I've missed feeling useful and helpful."

This was the Liesl he'd come to know in Sand Creek. He truly admired how driven she was to help others.

"Mrs. Holmes said she means to ask Mother to join as well. Mrs. Wilhite, Mrs. Clark, Mother, and Tansy will become quite the foursome here in town." Liesl stood near him, talking as easily and casually as if they visited with each other every day.

Interruptions usually frustrated him. He'd been known to lock the door in order to be left alone long enough to finish his work. Her arrival was proving entirely welcome. Having her there brought a sense of tranquility to the office. He'd spent the evening before in her company at the MacNamaras', yet he'd missed her in the short time that had passed since.

"Did Mrs. Holmes say when there's likely to be another social?" he asked.

Spots of color touched her cheeks. "Are you hoping there'll be one soon?"

"I rather enjoyed the last one. Didn't you?" He sat on the edge of the table, facing her.

A smile played lightly across her lips, but a different one than she'd entered with. There was something warmer in it. He might've only been seeing what he hoped to, but there was a hint of flirting there.

"When you have your planning meeting"—Hawk moved his hand enough for his fingers to brush against hers—"make certain they allow time for dancing on the schedule."

She came the tiniest bit closer. "I thought you didn't like danc-ing."

He lightly ran his thumb over the back of her hand. "I said I wasn't good at it, not that I didn't like it."

"I don't think you're a bad dancer at all." She made the declara-tion softly but with authority.

"Maybe it's a matter of having the right partner." He threaded his fingers through hers.

"I can't say I have ever been considered anyone's 'right partner.'"

Hawk stood and slipped his free arm a bit around her waist. "You've been dancing with the wrong people, lamb."

Her eyes met his. He watched, fascinated, as her pupils dilated. This was, indeed, the best kind of interruption. What would it be like to have her visit him every day? It was an idea he could spend hours lost in.

Paisley knocked at the door and stepped inside. She was a good deputy, but she had a terrible sense of timing.

Liesl slipped away, placing herself a step away from him. He didn't doubt Paisley had noticed their cozy arrangement. Paisley didn't miss anything. Ensio passed through the door behind her.

"We received a telegram," Paisley said.

It couldn't have been good news; she'd gone directly to the matter at hand without so much as raising an eyebrow. And Ensio looked unusually somber.

"Where from?" Hawk asked.

Paisley closed the door behind them and moved further into the room. The light from the window glinted off her hip holster. "Sand Creek."

That caught Liesl's attention.

"From Nick?" Hawk asked.

Paisley nodded.

"Good news?" he pressed.

She shrugged, giving the impression she wasn't certain how to categorize what she'd learned.

Liesl crossed back to him. Her worried brow struck him deeply. He didn't like that he couldn't give her a measure of peace here. He didn't like that she continued to live in fear.

"What did Nick have to say?" Hawk asked Paisley.

"He's been digging about, seeing if he can find more information about the land-repossessing scheme and who might be changing names on the deeds for the farms and homes. He's found something, but he doesn't know what to make of it."

"Something that could *prove* the Charming Chaps are involved in that scheme? The judge won't necessarily believe my word on it." Liesl's voice was too heavy for the question to be a casual one.

Mr. Larsen's warning that more proof was needed to move forward with true confidence hadn't left her thoughts any more than it had left his, apparently.

"Not proof in the direct sense," Paisley said, "but something that might lead us to some."

Liesl stood beside Hawk once more, though she was watching Paisley. He suspected she didn't want to feel so alone as they faced the enormity of this difficulty. He set his arm around her again, holding her to his side.

"Nick found papers referencing another man connected with the scheme," Paisley said.

"Harry Bendtkirk?" Hawk figured it must be. That was the name he'd discovered on his own land deed.

Paisley shook her head.

"Mr. Dressen?" Liesl clearly hoped the land clerk was not involved.

Again, Paisley shook her head. "Everett Reynolds."

"Mr. Reynolds?" Liesl glanced at Hawk. "He owned the farm before you bought it."

That didn't make sense. "You told me he was run out of Sand Creek by the Charming Chaps."

"I thought he was."

"It's the perfect cover." Paisley popped her hands casually on her hips. "Give the impression he's a victim of the very scheme he's helping to run. People will think he's disappeared to seek safety, but he now has anonymity enough to step up his efforts."

"He's not been seen in Sand Creek since?" Hawk asked Liesl.

"Not even a hint. Some people—me included—were afraid he might've been killed instead of running off."

Ensio nodded slowly and deliberately. "It's possible he *was* killed. Maybe the Charming Chaps turned on him."

"We keep pulling at threads, but none of 'em loosens this knot at all." And it was blasted frustrating. "Did Nick have anything about the Bendtkirk fella the land's all been claimed by?"

"Only that he can't find any record of anyone with that name."

"This town's got a lawyer," Ensio said. "Could that fella look into Bendtkirk, see if he's even real?"

Ensio was thinking the same thing Hawk was, it seemed. "I'm more convinced with all we're learning that Harry Bendtkirk is a false name. One of the Charming Chaps or their accomplices is using that name to hide what they're doing."

"Everett Reynolds, maybe?" Ensio suggested.

"Mr. Reynolds lived in your house in Sand Creek," Liesl said to Hawk and Paisley. "Could be he left behind some kind of clue. Especially if he was being double-crossed."

"Hadn't thought of that," Hawk said.

Reluctantly, he stepped away from Liesl and crossed to Paisley. He gave quick and detailed instructions for a telegram to be sent back to Nick. If there was any chance Reynolds had left behind evidence, they needed to find it. Paisley nodded, then she and Ensio left.

"I'll tell the judge all I know," Liesl said quietly, "but Mr. Larsen

couldn't promise it'd be enough. If me testifying to a murder I saw
ain't a guarantee the murderers'd be found guilty, I cain't imagine
telling the judge I heard them talk about stealing land but never saw
them do it, and don't know how or who all is part of it, would do a
lick of good. Might make him believe me less on *all* the things I tell
him."

She wasn't wrong. Liesl needed as much proof as possible. They
couldn't move forward with confidence otherwise. And if her testimony wasn't enough and the Chaps and her father went free, she'd
never truly be safe again. He couldn't doggedly pursue this if it continued to be so risky to Liesl. Never before had he hesitated so much.

Never before had he cared about someone so deeply.

"Is this what Andrew talked to you about at the dinner party last
night?" Liesl asked.

Hawk shook his head without turning back to look at her. He
needed to get his feet back under him again. "He was delivering a
report from Laramie."

"About the prisoner we're hoping will testify?" she pressed.

He nodded. "He's proving a tough nut to crack."

"You thought he would be."

"I can't promise you this is going to go well," he said. "We might
not be able to bring down the Charming Chaps after all."

She stepped around in front of him, facing him. "I meant what I
said last night. I'm trying to trust you more. But I need you to be as
honest with me as you can be."

"There'll be things I cain't tell you," he said.

She gently touched his face. "I know."

"And me not being John Butler was one of those things."

She smiled a little. "That hasn't proven to be as much of a lie as I
once thought it was." Her hand slipped down his neck to rest on his
chest. "There's more of him in you than I think you know."

"We do share a first name."

"That ain't at all what I meant." She leaned toward him and

pressed the lightest of kisses to his cheek, the scent of her, somehow the indescribable aroma of sunshine on a warm day, encircling him once more. "I will make certain the next social includes dancing, John." With a quick smile, she stepped away and slipped out of the room.

John. It was his actual given name, and he knew she knew that. Hearing her call him John worried him more than he liked.

John Butler was the version of himself he might have been without the weight of this territory on his shoulders. But John *Hawking*, US Marshal, war veteran, and oft-declared possessor of a stone heart, was also an integral part of who he was.

He was falling for Liesl; there was no point denying it. And he felt certain she was starting to love him in return.

But could she ever learn to love *all* of him?

Chapter 23

Liesl had every reason in the world to be worried about her situation. Mr. Larsen hadn't responded since she'd handed over the papers he'd requested to see. They'd found no further proof. Nick's telegram from Sand Creek had given them a hint, but nothing solid. Her father and the Charming Chaps were in the jailhouse nearby, but if the judge wasn't convinced during their trial, the criminals would be free to exact what revenge they chose. Everything was topsy-turvy.

And yet, she felt more anchored than she had in ages.

She and her mother had quickly found their place in this new town, and so much of the weight that had worn down her mother all of Liesl's life was gone. Vanished. If it took every effort she had, Liesl would make certain her mother could stay in Savage Wells.

And if that meant Liesl herself could stay . . .

A warm prickle of hope flitted over her heart. She would very much like to stay.

She'd come to know the people of this town, and they'd welcomed her. Yes, they called her by a false name, but that was the only thing about their interactions that wasn't truthful. She and Mother were every bit themselves. She only hoped that after the matter of her father's trial had passed—successfully, heaven willing—the people of Savage Wells would understand her reasons for the false-hood.

She'd been so angry when she'd learned that John Butler wasn't real. That frustration had turned to amazement as she'd spent more time with Marshal Hawking here where he was at home. He was far more like John Butler than she would have believed when she'd first learned of the ruse. John *Hawking* likely didn't realize how much of John *Butler* he truly was. The kindness, compassion, and the care she had seen in him in Sand Creek was still there. Yes, it was tempered by his work keeping the territory running and the need to strike fear into the hearts of criminals and would-be troublemakers. But John Butler was still there.

And she'd kissed him.

A simple peck on the cheek, yes. But a kiss. At that moment, she couldn't help herself. He had been wearing the same look of concern that had been there in Sand Creek, and she'd been lost in the warmth and reassurance of that familiar, caring expression.

Two days had passed since that tender moment, and it continued to lay softly on her mind. Perhaps someday, he'd sit with her on a creek bank and skip rocks. Or perhaps hold her in the rain. She wanted to believe that the tenderness he'd shown her, the impression he'd given while he was John Butler that he'd been losing his heart to her, hadn't been feigned. She had reason to trust he had a growing and deep fondness for her, but hearts were fragile things, and hers was more than most.

"We've a crowd today." Mr. Cooper disrupted her thoughts.

Liesl had grown accustomed to his assumed English accent. She'd come to like him very much, and working for him was enjoyable. "I'm between preparations just now. Do you need me to carry a few plates out?"

"You'd be the hero of the dining room."

"Are we truly in such a state?"

He shrugged. "I exaggerate a bit."

She brushed her hands together and then reached for two plates. "I'll carry these out. Which table?"

"Four."

She'd memorized which number went with which table, no matter that she was almost never in the dining room. It proved helpful in moments like this.

The room truly was busy, with nearly every table being used. Liesl set the plates at table four. She snatched the water pitcher from the sideboard and filled the cups at table one as she passed. She took a quick look around the room to see if anyone else was in need of anything.

Her gaze stopped at a table under the far window. And then her heart stopped.

She knew them.

Mr. Reynolds and Mr. Kersey.

For a moment, her mind refused to accept what she was seeing. Mr. Reynolds was the very person Ensio and Hawk were attempting to find. The man whose name had been tied to the schemes in Sand Creek. His presence here, where the Charming Chaps were being held, was no coincidence. And having Mr. Kersey, who was also from Sand Creek, with him made her more certain still.

Had they come to break out her father and his accomplices? Come to lay a trap for the circuit judge when he arrived? If they spotted Liesl, recognized her—

Moving as swiftly as her shaking legs would carry her, she left the dining room and straight out the front door. She didn't dare walk past the restaurant windows; the men were sitting directly beside them. She set her steps in the opposite direction, down the street toward the schoolhouse. She'd double back once she knew she was out of sight, then make her way back to the jailhouse from behind, away from the street.

What was she going to do? What was her best course of action? She didn't think the two men had seen her, but she couldn't be certain. She had just walked away from the restaurant without so much as a word to Mr. Cooper. How would she explain that without confessing to everything? She was likely going to lose her job.

She shook that off. It was hardly her biggest concern.

Mr. Reynolds and Mr. Kersey knew her mother by sight. And Mother didn't know she was in danger.

That made up Liesl's mind on her first stop.

She crossed the street from the far side of the schoolhouse, then made her way around the back of the mercantile and slipped inside. She gave a hasty wave to Mr. Holmes and headed directly for the stairs at the side of the shop that led up to the family's residence. That was where the women's auxiliary meeting was being held.

The sitting room beyond the door at the top of the stairs was neat and comfortable. The women gathered there could be described in precisely the same way.

"Why, Lilly," Mrs. Carol said. "We weren't expecting you to be able to join us. Please, sit."

"Do," Mrs. Wilhite added with an encouraging smile.

"I'm sorry; I can't. I have only a moment." She hoped she was managing to hide her panic. "Tansy, could I ask you a question? It will be quick, I promise."

She didn't know who else to turn to with this difficulty. Tansy had shown herself a good friend and a reliable associate. And she had been deputized in the past.

Tansy walked with her to the other side of the room, far enough away to not be overheard if they kept their voices low.

"Can't thank you enough for the interruption," Tansy said. "Planning a sociable ain't exactly my cup of tea."

"What about hiding someone who's in danger?" Liesl asked in a whisper. "Is that your cup of tea?"

Tansy's attention sharpened. "Done it before. Who's needing hiding now?"

"My mother."

Tansy nodded firmly. "I'll see to it Mildred makes it to my house. She'll be safe there. I'll keep an eye on everything."

"You have to get her out of town without being seen by anyone. There's two men at the restaurant who know her. I can't say where they might be when you leave here."

"You done right, Liesl. I'll get her out safely; I swear to it."

Liesl felt a small surge of relief, though her mind was far from at ease.

"Do Hawk and Paisley know?" Tansy asked.

Liesl shook her head. "I only just spotted the two men. I came directly here, by way of the schoolyard."

"Wise. Wouldn't do to have them men see you come over."

"My thoughts exactly."

"And it speaks well of you that you didn't simply crumble in a heap of panic."

Liesl smiled. "You're going to discover, Tansy, that I don't crumble easily."

"Then we have that in common, you and I."

"Thank you for looking after my mother. For being her friend. She ain't had that for years."

Tansy's expression softened. "I ain't either."

Liesl gave a swift and quick goodbye to the other ladies, trusting Tansy to invent some reason for her quick arrival and even quicker departure. And she left it to Tansy's judgment to determine how much to tell Mother.

She hurried back down the stairs and out the mercantile door, circling back behind the buildings once more. There weren't likely many people in Savage Wells who were as familiar with the spaces behind the buildings as she was. How she hoped someday she could live in this town without needing to hide, but that day was not to-day.

Worry sped up her steps. She'd told Tansy right: she wasn't one to panic. But she also knew a grave situation when she was in it. Up the exterior stairs, she went directly to the door of the marshal's office and knocked.

Hawk opened it a moment later.

"Standing on ceremony now, are you?" he asked with a smile and a laugh in his eyes. But his ease vanished on the instant. Her expression must've warned him that something was wrong.

"Mr. Reynolds is here. At the restaurant. And he's here with Mr. Kersey from Sand Creek."

Hawk muttered a word Liesl recognized but never actually said herself. Rather than pulling her into the marshal's office, he led her to the other door in the tiny hallway and motioned her inside his personal quarters.

"Stay here. I'll get someone to keep an eye on them, see if we can figure out why they're here and what they know," he said.

"Hawk, they know you—at least Mr. Kersey does. He knows you as *John Butler*. Seeing you here will tell him everything he needs to know. You're in danger too."

"I know. Paisley's in the same boat. But there are others who can be our eyes and ears."

"Not Tansy. She's taking my mother out to her place."

Hawk nodded in approval. "No safer place for her to be."

"Then that wasn't a mistake?"

"Not at all."

She pushed out a tense breath.

"Stay here until I get back," Hawk said again. "You'll be safer here than you would be in the marshal's office. Safer than you would be in your room at the hotel. Don't open the door to anyone. I have a key, and I'll let myself back in the room."

"You intend to leave me here to twiddle my thumbs?"

"No. I'm gonna leave you here to wait until we have more information. It ain't that I don't trust you, Liesl. It's that it don't do to go rushing into trouble until you know the shape of it."

He didn't mean to shut her out. He didn't lack confidence in her. He was being wise, and he was keeping her safe until they knew what to do next.

Trouble was, she wasn't sure there were any good options ahead of them.

Chapter 24

The curtains were drawn in Hawk's room. Liesl hadn't left since her arrival earlier that day, but she was no longer alone.

Ensio, Paisley, and Hawk had arrived separately, but all within a few minutes of each other. Watching them interact and talk and plot, it was clear they'd worked together before and often.

They were capable and smart.

They were also ignoring her.

"While we don't know what Reynolds looks like," Hawk said, "all of us would recognize Kersey. Of course, he'd recognize us too. But we have the advantage; *we* know that we're looking for him."

"He'll know I'm here," Ensio said. "Everyone in Sand Creek knows who I am and that I accompanied the prisoners to Savage Wells."

"That could probably be turned to our advantage," Paisley said. "Ensio doesn't have to hide. He'd be able to move about more freely."

Ensio nodded. "I can go out to Tansy's place and check on Mrs. Hodges."

"Tansy'll have everything well in hand," Hawk said. "Until all's secure here, I'll not have us risk Mrs. Hodges being sniffed out."

For so long, Liesl had been the only one trying to keep herself and her mother safe. It was good to have someone shoulder a bit of that load.

She opened her mouth to add her agreement, but the plotting continued without her.

"Part of our difficulty," Paisley said, "is, even if we round these two up, we don't have anything to hold them on."

"Reynolds is connected to the land stealing somehow," Hawk said.

"But the only thing about that scheme we can prove is that Dressen, the Sand Creek land agent, isn't part of it." Paisley set her hands on her hips, a posture she often struck when frustrated by something. "He sent the telegrams he said he did, trying to sort out the changed land deeds."

"It's a miracle the clods behind the scheme haven't killed him," Ensio said.

"We don't have anything to hold Reynolds on." Paisley shook her head. "And there ain't even a whisper of anything around Kersey."

That was always the difficulty; they couldn't prove hardly anything against the Charming Chaps or their associates.

"But if we can at least keep 'em where we can watch 'em," Hawk continued, "then we can make certain they don't hurt Liesl or her ma."

"Liesl would appreciate that," Liesl said dryly.

All three of them turned to look at her with near identical expressions of surprise. She'd wondered if they'd forgotten she was there. It seemed they had.

"I'm happy to let you know anything else Liesl would like," she said. "She and I are very close."

Ensio laughed, something she suspected he did often. She hadn't interacted with him much, but she found she liked what she knew of him.

Hawk looked less amused. "We ain't excluding you on account

of not trusting you. The three of us work together on this sort of thing all the time. We know how each other thinks."

"And you and I made a long journey to Savage Wells together. I think I know pretty well how *you* think."

"Do you now?" Hawk had been oddly prickly ever since joining them in his personal rooms.

"I ain't trying to break up your trio," Liesl said. "You might be shocked to discover that I have a mind too, and it's done some fine thinking now and then."

"Don't twist this around," Hawk said, "trying to make it sound like I'm calling you thickheaded or sapskulled."

"Then quit being thickheaded and sapskulled yourself," Paisley said. "It don't make a lick of sense leaving her out of this. She knows both men, which none of us can say. And she strategized well enough to protect the people in Sand Creek for years before any of us sauntered into her town."

"But her life wasn't in danger then," Hawk said. "You can't argue it isn't now."

"Leaving her out of these plans won't change that," Ensio said. "I, for one, would like to hear what she has to say."

Hawk's expression was somehow both begrudging and intrigued. He motioned for her to proceed.

Liesl pushed on. "You keep talking about strategies for apprehending these two men. It seems to me our time'd be better served trying to get *information* from them. We cain't prove anything against them. We cain't entirely prove most things against the Charming Chaps either. Even me testifying that I saw them kill my brother isn't guaranteed to be enough as most judges don't always trust a woman's word. Proof is the tallest mountain we're trying to climb right now. Your prisoner in Laramie ain't cooperating, and Nick ain't written back to say he's found anything. Mr. Reynolds and Mr. Kersey arriving ain't a happy thing, but it also might be a spot of luck. And we'd be wasting it simply rounding them up and tossing them in a cell."

"The cells are pretty crowded as it is," Ensio said out of the side of his mouth.

"I doubt these men are going to go around blabbing about crimes they committed and laws they're planning to break." Hawk, thankfully, didn't make the observation sarcastically, but as if he was thinking about what she was saying. That was encouraging.

"They might be willing to talk to people who're involved in what they're doing," Liesl said.

"Other than each other," Paisley said, "the only other people involved are the Charming Chaps."

Liesl nodded.

Ensio shook his head. "They don't have any opportunity to talk to them. Can't exactly waltz right into the jailhouse and ask for a private conference with our prisoners. Even if they came in under the guise of simply being curious, they wouldn't shoot the breeze if that breeze was criminal and the famous Sheriff O'Brien was listening."

That was true. But there had to be a way around that. They needed to get confessions.

"Each of the cells has a barred window facing the side alley," Paisley said. "An enterprising person could have a conversation that way."

Those windows were the reason Liesl had been warned to avoid the western side of the jailhouse. It was unlikely she would be seen walking past, but they weren't willing to take the risk.

"Could be they'd whisper across to each other if they had reason enough." Ensio looked from each of them to the other, including Liesl. "The window of the marshal's office sits right above those windows. If someone were paying enough attention, that someone might be able to overhear what was being said."

Hawk nodded, his brow pulled. Perhaps they were stumbling upon a good method.

"What's to stop them from simply passing a note?" Paisley asked. "It could be read without anyone wiser."

True. "And whoever amongst the Charming Chaps snatched it up could simply tear it to bits before anyone had a chance to take it from them."

"Andrew's always angling for some task to do," Ensio said. "He could install something around those windows that could make it harder to toss a bit of paper between them. I can't think what, but he has a good mind for such things."

"Good idea," Hawk said, rising from his seat and beginning to pace. He did that when he was thinking over something that worried him. Their plan, it seemed, wasn't good enough yet.

"We've a marshal, two deputy marshals, and Cade all in town," Paisley said. "I suspect the new arrivals aren't likely to risk chatting with prisoners unless the need outweighs the consequences."

"And since we don't know what their reasons are for being in Savage Wells, it's hard to say what might motivate them to take that extra step." Ensio leaned back in his chair. "I've my suspicions they've come with the intention of helping the prisoners escape. They'll find that harder than they expected."

"We need to force their hands," Liesl said. "Give 'em an irresistible reason."

Ensio shrugged. "If you've any ideas, I'd love to hear them."

Liesl swallowed and took a reassuring breath. She could hardly believe the suggestion she was about to make. "They might be willing to break their silence to tell my father that his daughter is in town."

Hawk spun about, staring at her. Paisley's mouth opened with surprise and worry. Ensio whistled low.

"Absolutely not," Hawk said.

"Hear me out," Liesl said. "I know it's a risk. I know it's dangerous. But without proof, my testimony ain't guaranteed to be enough. The danger I'd be courting by letting word reach my father and the

Charming Chaps that I'm in town ain't nothing compared to the danger I'd face the rest of my life if I open my mouth in front of a judge and my father walks free."

Hawk shook his head mechanically.

"You'd be risking your mother, too," Paisley said.

"No," Liesl said. "We'd keep her where she is, safe at Tansy's house. The only person we let these two know is in town—or at least *might be* in town—is me. They might wonder if my mother's here. That'd give 'em reason to talk instead of tossing in a note. They'd likely stand beneath the jail windows and discuss it. We need that to happen."

"Once they know you're here," Hawk said, "they'll be looking for you. Even this hiding place might not be enough."

"If we don't stop the Charming Chaps," Liesl said, "someone will *always* be looking for me, and no hiding place will ever be enough."

To Hawk, Paisley said, "You need to look at this as Marshal Hawking. This is a strategic decision, a calculated risk. You make them all the time. This is just another one."

"You make me sound heartless," Hawk muttered.

"You know as well as I do that sometimes you have to be," Paisley said.

Hawk's gaze settled on Liesl. His eyes were filled with uncertainty and hesitation. This was not the decisive US Marshal who had overseen this territory and brought down criminal rings and bands of thieves and corrupt sheriffs.

"We need Hawk right now," Liesl said.

He started pacing again, his posture rigid. He turned back toward them all, and the change in him was almost startling. There was a hardness to his mouth and a sharpness in his eyes that made her take a step back. This was a man who shouldn't be trifled with.

"I'll find out precisely when we can expect the judge to arrive for trial. That'll tell us what our timeline is. Meanwhile, sort out a strategy for dangling Liesl in front of these men, and if we're lucky, we can do it without getting anyone killed."

"Avoiding death is always good," Ensio said dryly.

"But not always possible." He was Marshal Hawking again, utterly and completely without remorse or regret. "Ensio, you keep an eye on the jailhouse downstairs. Paisley, drop in at the restaurant— give Cooper some reason for Liesl's absence." He looked to Liesl, and she thought she saw the tiniest bit of tenderness flicker through his eyes before they sharpened once more. "You'll need to stay in here until we know how we're moving forward. This is the only place we know we can keep safe from the two blokes we're chasing."

She nodded, but a swirl of conflicting emotions kept her silent. She was grateful Hawk was looking out for her and her mother, and she was impressed at how formidable he was in the doing of it. But she also had very real reason to be afraid. Even with her father and the Charming Chaps in Savage Wells, she'd started to feel safe and at home. That had changed in a heartbeat, and she felt worryingly unsteady.

"I'll remain in the marshal's office and keep the window above the cells open." Hawk looked at the group. "You have your assignments. No arguments. No complaining." On that clipped instruction, he left the room without a backward glance.

Following his departure, Liesl let the air out of her lungs. "Is he always this harsh when he's focused on his marshaling?"

In near perfect unison, Paisley and Ensio said, "Yes."

Then Paisley added, "But he gets things done, and that's important."

"He don't seem happy, though," Liesl said. "That's important too."

Paisley's studying gaze settled on her. "He had seemed happier of late."

Liesl had seen that herself. He'd been lighter, more tender. The weight that usually seemed to press on him had lessened. Fully stepping into his marshaling role had brought that easiness to an end.

"So, he can either be Marshal Hawking, or he can be happy?"

Ensio nodded. "So far."

Liesl's heart broke at the thought.

The other two exited the room, presumably to fulfill their assignments, and Liesl was left in Hawk's living quarters by herself. Alone with her thoughts and the pain in her chest.

Marshal Hawking and John Butler were at war.

She had to find a way of brokering a cease-fire.

Chapter 25

Andrew dropped into the marshal's office the next day. "Thought you could use a break from listening at that window."

"I could, at that." Absolutely nothing had happened during Hawk's hours of listening. Nothing outside, at least. In his own mind, however, a whirlwind had blown ceaselessly. "Think you could do the listening for an hour or two?"

"Surely could." Andrew had grown a lot in the time since Cade had taken him under his wing. He'd begun to heal.

With Andrew in position, Hawk slipped from the office, closing the door behind him. But rather than stepping out onto the exterior stairs, he stood in the short hallway, eyeing the door to his personal room. The room where Liesl was hiding out.

He needed to talk with her, but he'd been dreading it. He missed her, and he missed the easy interactions they'd had. He'd been softening, and she'd been warming up to him. In his foolishness, he'd let himself imagine being John Butler in ways he'd never dreamed of before.

All that had evaporated.

The situation called for Marshal Hawking. That's who he needed to be. And Marshal Hawking had a plan, one John Butler would never approve of.

They had to move forward, and he couldn't afford to let his heart overrule his head.

He planted himself at Liesl's door and gave a quick knock. He paused, then he said, "It's Hawk. Just warning you, since I said I'd let myself in and you ought not to open the door."

Again, he paused, then he unlocked and slowly opened the door.

When he peered inside, she was standing near his table. She didn't hide her relief when their eyes met.

"Being in here, alone and unarmed, might not be our wisest decision," she said.

"Do you shoot?" he asked.

"I do."

That was good to know.

He closed the door behind him. "If you have a weapon in here, how do I know you won't simply shoot me the next time I come in?"

She raised one shoulder. "That's a risk you'll simply have to take."

As much as he'd like to stand there and banter with her, he had business to see to. "I have an idea for letting Reynolds and Kersey discover that you're in town."

"What is it?" Not even a hesitation. She'd know soon enough that she ought to be wavering a little. The plan had its risks.

"The town social," he said. "Everyone will be there. That'd lure out our crooks, I'm certain of it."

"You think they would attend a social?" she asked.

"No, I don't." He crossed to the small wood stove, warming himself. "But with most everyone else distracted, I'm guessing they'll take advantage and study the jailhouse. Cade and Andrew, of course, will be there so none of the Chaps will escape, but it'd be their best chance to talk with their comrades."

"Where do I come into it?" She moved closer. Her mouth was tense and her brow creased.

"You'd attend the social, but you'd leave from near the jailhouse so they can spot you."

"*Spot* me?" Her eyes pulled wide. "What's to keep them from simply snatching me up? Or worse?"

"Ensio. He'll be accompanying you. And Paisley will be stationed on the street within sight of you at all times."

She pressed her fingers against her temple. "It's some protection, at least."

"There ain't no way to undertake this without risk," he acknowledged. "But giving them a glimpse of you when they're in a position to whisper what they've seen to the Charming Chaps is our best chance."

"They won't, though, if Andrew and Cade are inside."

He nodded; he'd thought of that. "Cade will wander out under the front overhang at one point, while Andrew tucks himself into the backroom of the jailhouse. That'll afford them some opportunity to talk."

"But we'd have no opportunity to overhear," she pointed out.

He'd thought of that too. "I'll be at my window above them."

She rubbed her fingers over her lips, eyes darting as she thought. "And my mother?"

"She could attend the town social, if she and Tansy think it could be managed safely."

"You trust Tansy that much?"

Hawk nodded. "If I thought she'd be at all interested, I'd ask her to join the marshals. But her history with lawmen ain't a pretty one. I can't blame her for not wanting to be officially connected to us."

"That's another thing she and my mother have in common." A fleeting smile pulled at her lips. Just as quickly, her ponderous expression returned. "I'd have to walk past the jailhouse, where my father is, out in the open, knowing two men who are chums with him will see me, recognize me, and tell him they've found me."

"That's the ins and outs of it."

"And if they don't take the bait? They know I'm here but don't blab anything?"

"There are never guarantees. We do the best we can and take the risks we must. They might not blab that night, but I'd wager they will eventually. And someone'll always be listening."

She turned back to him. "Can you promise me that . . . Ensio will dance with me?" A glint of humor sparkled in her eyes.

He clamped down both his urge to join in her teasing and the temptation to track down Ensio and belt him. John Butler had him all upended.

"Ensio will keep you safe."

She crossed closer to him. "But dancing was my favorite part of the last social."

"I'm certain plenty of people would be willing to dance with you."

Her hand brushed lightly along his arm. "But who will dance with you if you're here all alone?"

She couldn't demand he be the hardened marshal then insist he be maudlin and sentimental.

"I have a job to do, Liesl. Dancing don't factor into it."

"Does Marshal Hawking never allow himself a moment's frivolity?" She stood so close. How was he to keep his head if she wouldn't keep her distance?

"Marshal Hawking doesn't rest, and John Butler doesn't save people. You get one or the other."

Liesl stretched and kissed his cheek. "You *are* both, whether or not you know it," she whispered. She kissed the corner of his mouth. "Somewhere, there's a balance between the two."

He took a step back. Then he took a breath. "If you're ever in

Cheyenne, there's a saloon owner there who can tell you what that balance is."

She paled a little but with bright pops of red on her cheeks. He knew that look. She'd worn it when he'd first told her he wasn't John Butler. She was hurt and embarrassed. Again. And he was the reason. Again.

"What would this saloon owner tell me the balance is?" she asked quietly.

"Marshal Hawking has a heart of stone. That's the only way any of this works."

Chapter 26

Liesl stood outside Dr. and Mrs. MacNamara's house, Ensio at her side. It was the night of the town social. The night Hawk's risky plan was to be put in place. They'd discussed it with all involved, and everyone had agreed that, though not guaranteed to work, it was the best idea they had to get the Chaps or their newly arrived accomplices to say something incriminating.

"I've accompanied ladies to socials before," Ensio said, "and I can honestly say they weren't always enthusiastic—they often had better choices than this old bag of bones of mine—but this is the first time my companion's displeasure ain't felt insulting."

He offered the observation so dryly, she couldn't resist matching his tone. "You ain't taking it personally?"

Ensio looked at her with theatrically drawn brows. "Should I?"

Liesl laughed lightly and shook her head. Ensio was funny and always quick with a quip. She appreciated that more than he likely knew, and not merely because she was quaking like a cloud in a thunderstorm. Hawk had been cold. Distant. She'd have understood if he'd just been focusing on pushing things forward. But it was more than that. Sometimes she found herself wondering if he'd actually decided that he hated her.

"I ain't never lived in a place where corsages made of ribbon were part of town socials." She motioned to the one made of purple ribbon Ensio had pinned to her dress.

"Neither have I," he said. "But Mrs. Carol told me I'd be a regular hangdog if I didn't give you one. Figured I'd do best not to argue with her."

"Well, I appreciate it." And she did. It was a little kindness in the midst of a lot of worry.

"You should know," Ensio said, "I'm a daisy of a companion at a social. I dance when asked, sit when requested, and I ain't at all opposed to sneaking about and snatching bits to eat as often as the evening requires."

She could actually smile, something she'd not thought she'd do that night. "I'll certainly not starve."

"That is my goal for the evening."

"Mine is getting to the social in one piece."

He nodded. "I suspect your goal's gotta be met before mine."

"Has to."

The night was beautiful. The usual Wyoming wind was little more than a breeze. The air was cool and light. The distant sound of happy voices and the hint of music being played spoke of a town social already underway. She wanted to enjoy the evening, but her mind couldn't be at ease, so her heart couldn't be at peace.

Ensio's gun was worn in full view, as was his deputy marshal's badge. He wasn't hiding who he was. For the first time since arriving in Savage Wells, neither was Liesl. She'd imagined revealing her true identity would come *after* her father was twiddlin' his thumbs on the other side of iron bars somewhere far away, never to come back. She'd have far rather it had happened that way.

Across the street and down a spell, not quite as far as the restaurant, but a bit past the jailhouse, a light quickly flashed four times from a lantern. That was the sign. It wasn't entirely dark yet, so a person'd have to be looking directly at the lantern light to notice it.

"You ready?" Ensio asked her in a low voice.

"Does it matter?"

"'Course it does. You're taking the risk. How you're feeling about it matters."

A kindness, that. "I ain't sure your boss'd agree with you."

"Hawk?" Ensio sounded surprised. "He don't take these things lightly. And he don't force danger on people. He'd let you cry off even now, if you wanted."

She believed it. And, even with Hawk's coldness these past days, she trusted him. "I'm nervous, but I'm ready." She took a breath. "Let's head to the social."

Ensio walked at her side, but he didn't slip her arm through his or hold her hand or any of the things a courting couple might do. They weren't meant to look like they were courting, and Ensio needed to be able to move quickly should the entire thing go wrong.

They deliberately strolled in front of the jailhouse, then stepped off the boardwalk onto the dirt road. Anyone looking in her direction would see her quite clearly. She and Ensio walked more slowly than they might've otherwise.

She thought she heard a bit of shuffling somewhere behind them.

"Steady on," Ensio whispered.

They'd not yet reached the other side of the road when someone called out, "Is that you, Liesl?" It sounded like Mr. Kersey.

They'd planned what to do if she was hollered after: keep walking. The new arrivals didn't have to *know* she was Liesl; they just needed to wonder. Liesl and Ensio paused for a second, as if startled by what they'd heard, but they didn't look back.

Ensio stepped back up onto the boardwalk. Liesl did as well. He was the tiniest bit ahead of her, his strides being longer. Only the length of the two buildings, and they'd be clear. Only a few moments more.

Then the night exploded with a gunshot.

Liesl ducked, shielding her face with her arms on instinct. When she looked up again, Ensio wasn't standing next to her. Had he chased down the shooter? Ducked out of danger?

No.

He was slumped against the side of the building.

"Ensio?" She slid up next to him.

He was breathing heavily, wincing. Blood had already begun soaking his shirt and jacket just below the shoulder. "Cain't be out in the open." His words were tight and rushed.

She tucked her arms under his and began tugging him toward the dark shadows alongside the building.

"Leave me," Ensio said.

"Ain't gonna happen."

Another gunshot rang out. Wood splintered off the building beside them. In the next instant, she had Ensio tucked in the shadows. Her left hand was wet with his blood. With her right, she pulled his six-shooter from its holster.

"Before you ask," she said, "yes, I've shot before."

"Shot a *person?*" That he was talking and making sense seemed a good sign.

"Not yet." She watched the side of the jail, alert for any movement.

A shot rang out from their side of the street. Something thumped in the dim alley across the way. In the same instant, more gunfire sounded, followed by the sharp shattering of glass. People were pouring from the restaurant where the town social was being held, shouts of confusion adding to the terror of the night.

Paisley darted to Liesl's side.

"Ensio's shot," Liesl said.

"So's one of those doing the shooting." Paisley looked back toward the distant crowd and waved someone over.

Dr. and Mrs. MacNamara were there in the next moment. Paisley offered clipped instructions. Her authority couldn't be questioned, and neither of them bothered. The doctor took possession of Ensio's gun. Mrs. MacNamara—a nurse in her own right—immediately tended to the deputy's injuries. Paisley slipped stealthily across the street.

"They're after—Liesl—" Ensio was struggling to talk. "Get her—out of—view."

Without taking his eyes off the street, Dr. MacNamara spoke to Liesl. "Tuck yourself back a bit—enough that you can't be seen. We'll get you inside once we know which building we can get you to safely."

Safely? Liesl wasn't certain she'd ever feel safe again.

She wouldn't let herself think about it. Wouldn't let herself feel the fear flooding over her. Or look at Ensio's ashen face. Or listen to him struggling to breathe. She didn't dare glance toward the jailhouse, not knowing the casualties she might find there.

She crouched down, hunched low, and slipped back into the narrow and dusty darkness between the buildings.

People ran along the street. Voices shouted.

And from the back of the alley, someone grabbed her.

Chapter 27

Kersey was dead, his gun still in his hand. Reynolds was nowhere to be seen.

Paisley arrived on the scene the moment after Hawk did. She held her rifle at the ready, eyes scanning the area. "They fired at Ensio and Liesl."

He'd been afraid of that. "Where are they?"

"Ensio's hit. Gideon and Miriam are with him now."

"And Liesl?"

"Looked unhurt when I saw her. She's with 'em."

He allowed himself only half a breath to be relieved. The danger hadn't passed.

"Did you see which way Reynolds went?" Paisley looked up and down the narrow passage between the jail and the mercantile.

Hawk shook his head. "I couldn't get out of the marshal's office quickly enough. One of them shot out the windows. I don't know if they knew I was in there or were just hoping I was. By the time it was safe to slip out, Reynolds was gone."

Townspeople were scattered about on the road, voices raised in worry and confusion. They'd never find Reynolds now. He'd had too much time to escape, and there were too many people milling about. He could be anywhere.

Hawk muttered a few choice words.

"My thoughts as well," Paisley said. "I'll look around back."

"I'll check on Ensio."

Paisley paused, catching Hawk's eyes. "He was in a bad way."

He nodded. Hawk knew how to maintain his composure under pressure, but a warning helped.

He ignored the questions thrown at him as he rushed across the street. Miriam was bent over Ensio, tying a makeshift bandage around his chest. It was already red with blood. That wasn't ever good.

"What does he need?" Hawk asked.

Miriam looked up at him. "To get to the house, but I can't get him there alone."

"Why can't Gideon help?"

"He's looking." She adjusted Ensio's bandaging.

"For what?"

The doctor emerged from the side of the building. "Is Liesl with you?"

Hawk's chest went cold. "She ain't here?"

"She got Ensio out of sight and guarded him with his gun, then when we arrived, she tucked herself in the shadows so she'd stop getting shot at." Gideon looked around, brows pulled together and eyes a bit frantic. "Now I can't find her anywhere."

"Could she be hiding?" Miriam asked.

"Maybe." Gideon's attention was fully on Ensio. "We need to get him to the house. It's our best chance to stop the bleeding."

They were entirely engrossed in their doctoring; they slung Ensio's arms over their shoulders and lugged him toward their home.

Hawk, his gun still drawn, made his way down the dark alley. He didn't dare call out her name. Reynolds might be looking for her, and Hawk wasn't going to give him any clues.

There was nothing in the alleyway to hide behind. Hawk walked the length of it—slowly—without encountering anything but the walls on either side and the dirt beneath his feet. The back of the buildings offered no answers. The nearest building behind these was a good distance off.

Where was she?

Hawk turned back. She had to be somewhere. Had to be. Her being gone didn't make a lick of sense. Something wasn't right.

He slowly retraced his steps. This was where she was last. But where was she now?

Something in the dirt caught his eye. Careful not to let his guard down, Hawk hunched and picked up the odd-shaped lump. He stood and shook the dirt off.

A purple ribbon corsage.

Liesl would've had one. Every man who accompanied a woman to a town social gave her a ribbon corsage. It was tradition. He'd told Ensio that himself.

Paisley had been here, not at the social, so she didn't have a corsage.

Miriam had been at the social, but—he tossed his mind back— she still had hers pinned to her dress.

This corsage was Liesl's. He was certain of it. And, he looked closer, there was blood on it.

He swallowed down a sudden surge of panic. He needed to keep his head. Had to.

Hawk moved swiftly to the marshal's office. The interior was strewn with broken glass, and no one was inside. He crossed to his personal quarters. Empty as well, and, he realized, its windows had also been shot. Someone had sorted out where he would be. Liesl hadn't been the only target that night.

Boil and blast.

She wouldn't be in the jailhouse, not with her father and the Charming Chaps there. She could be holed up at the MacNamaras' or the hotel. She might've headed to Tansy's, but she'd have had to go on foot, and that would take half the night. If she were hurt or in danger, he didn't have half the night.

Hawk stepped out into the street and searched the faces around him. He pulled aside Mr. Clark. "Have you seen Lilly Moore?"

Clark shook his head. "What's going on? We heard gunshots."

The entire town had heard them, no doubt.

"Go to the hotel and ask if Cooper has seen her."

"Surely will."

"Report back to Sheriff O'Brien."

Clark nodded and headed for the restaurant.

Hawk spotted Mrs. Holmes just outside the mercantile. He moved to her. "Was Tansy at the social tonight?"

She shook her head.

"Have you seen Lilly Moore?"

Another head shake. *Blast it.*

"I need you and your husband to drive out to Tansy's. See if Lilly's there with her ma."

"The gunshots—" Mrs. Holmes abruptly stopped. "We'll go check."

"Report back to Sheriff O'Brien." Hawk turned away, moving swiftly to the MacNamaras' home.

He stepped inside and headed for the sitting room and surgery. Doc and Miriam were bent over Ensio, digging for a bullet. He wanted to ask if he could help, but there wasn't time.

"Did Liesl come here?"

"No." Doc spoke without looking up.

Hawk didn't need more than that. He stormed back out again.

Clark was approaching from the direction of the restaurant. "No one's seen her."

He wasn't surprised. But he *was* worried.

The Holmeses wouldn't be back with their report for some time, but his gut told him Liesl hadn't fled to Tansy's house.

She was gone, in danger, because his plan had failed. *He* had failed. And she was paying the price.

Chapter 28

Liesl could hear the chaos on the street below. Mr. Larsen had provided a hiding spot for her, and she didn't dare give it away. During the firefight, he'd taken hold of her arm in the alley, urging her to slip further into the shadows where she wouldn't be seen. She'd wanted to stay, to find a way to help, but then Mr. Larsen said something that changed her mind.

"The odds aren't in your favor with three accomplices outside of jail."

Three.

They only knew about two.

Her heart beating fast, she'd slipped down the alley with Mr. Larsen to the back of the land office. He had a key and let them both inside before locking the door. In the pitch-black, with voices shouting outside, they'd carefully climbed the stairs into yet another room.

"No one is ever in here," Mr. Larsen had said. "Especially not in the second-floor room. Once the chaos dies down, we can get word to Hawk or Cade or Paisley that you're safe."

And so they'd sat in darkness, waiting. Liesl tried not to think about Hawk searching for her, worried.

"We know about two of the Charming Chaps' comrades," Liesl whispered. "But you said there are three."

"The telegram log Ensio brought from Sand Creek mentioned a message from Laramie that referenced Hawk. Though it didn't specify details—Mr. Yarrow was too careful for that—I suspect it had to do with their planned assassination. That means they have someone in Laramie."

"Them two blokes in prison in Laramie are working with the Chaps," Liesl said. "My father mentioned them specifically."

"Can't be." They were still talking in whispers, still sitting in the dark. "Some of the telegrams were sent after they were imprisoned. Prisoners don't get to send telegrams."

That was true. Who, then, *had* sent them? Who was this other co-conspirator?

"You must have reason to believe this fella would come all the way to Savage Wells and risk giving away his part in all the charges facing his partners," Liesl said.

"There was a paper in the pile that looked like a scrawled-out transcript of a telegram. It read, 'You're talking too much. I'm warning you to keep your mouths shut.' That got me thinking about honor among thieves and how everyone in this criminal circle could rat on the others. This fellow in Laramie warned them not to. I think there's a good chance he'd come here to make certain his partners in crime were doing what he demanded."

The voices outside had grown quieter.

"If this person was supposed to help with the assassination plot, he'd have to know about Hawk's comings and goings. Or at least be keeping a close eye on those two prisoners, since it was their trial Hawk would be arriving to attend."

"Another convincing argument for our third accomplice being someone who's not behind bars," Mr. Larsen said.

Liesl rubbed at her face. "It's also someone who can send threatening telegrams to a sheriff and not raise eyebrows."

"Lawyers and judges often warn lawmen to take care what they discuss, even over telegrams. I daresay Cade and Hawk send their share of unusual messages."

Cade and Hawk. "Could be we're looking for a lawman." Liesl had known her fair share of corruption among those in that profession. "Another sheriff Hawk has brought down, maybe? Or maybe someone who wanted to be a deputy marshal but wasn't accepted."

"Or someone who got in but is looking to make a little money on the side."

That stopped Liesl mid-thought. "Could one of Hawk's deputies be our third man?"

Mr. Larsen was silent for the length of a breath. "Could be."

"I'd wager my eyeteeth it ain't Paisley," Liesl said.

"I'd wager more than that." Mr. Larsen's shoes scraped against the floor, the sound of him walking. "And though it could be an elaborate ruse, I suspect it's not Ensio either, considering he may very well have been killed in the firefight."

Liesl swallowed the lump growing in her throat. She'd been fretting over Ensio, unsure how life-threatening his injuries had been. He'd been charged with keeping her safe as they lured the threat out of hiding. What if *he* was part of that threat all along?

She didn't want to believe it.

"Two other deputies were at Sand Creek to arrest the Charming Chaps," she said. "Another two helped lug the prisoners here. If the turncoat was any of those four, the plan would've fallen to pieces. They could've undermined him. They could have *killed* him during any of that."

Mr. Larsen nodded. "I don't know how many deputies Hawk has, but it'd be worth asking."

There was a traitor in Hawk's midst; she was sure of it. And he had no idea. All this time, they'd been scrambling to protect *her*. How could they have forgotten that all this began because of a target on *his* back?

"He trusts his deputies," Liesl said. "Trusts them implicitly."

"The street sounds calmer," Mr. Larsen said. "I think we'd be safe to slip out."

"We need to find Hawk," Liesl said. "We have to warn him."

They made their roundabout way toward the marshal's office, lingering behind buildings until they could pass between them without being seen. The streets weren't entirely empty, and while the danger was less, it was certainly not over.

As they approached the jailhouse, the windows above were entirely dark. The tiniest bit of moonlight shimmered off the shattered remains of the glass panes.

Liesl's heart dropped to her boots. Were they too late? Had someone already come for Hawk?

"There are lights inside Dr. MacNamara's house," Mr. Larsen whispered. "We'll go there."

Light glowed beneath a back door, one that likely led to a kitchen.

Liesl moved swiftly but as quietly as she could manage. Hawk was in more danger than he realized, but that didn't change the fact that she was still in danger as well.

Hawk and Paisley were likely on edge; if they were inside and Liesl barged in, she might get herself shot. She knocked lightly.

Footsteps sounded inside, growing louder. From just on the other side of the door, came a voice.

"Who's there?" *Hawk.*

His voice. She forced down the lump that formed in her throat. Hearing him, knowing he was there, made her want to cry with relief and exhaustion.

"It's Liesl," she said.

The door flew open, and, before she could even think, Hawk had pulled her into his arms. She melted into him, clinging to him.

"Liesl." She felt his chest shake with his next breath. "I couldn't find you."

From inside the room, Paisley said, "If you don't let her inside, everyone and his dog'll 'find' her."

Hawk pulled her inside. Mr. Larsen followed, closing the door behind him. Hawk didn't let her go, didn't loosen his embrace. Liesl felt both the tenderness of John Butler and the solid strength of Marshal Hawking.

"Where've you been?" he whispered.

"Mr. Larsen helped me escape the gunfire. We've been hidin' above the land office."

"Your ribbons were in the alley. Blood on 'em." Hawk set her back enough to look at her. "There's blood on your dress."

She glanced down in surprise. Mr. Larsen's hiding place had been too dark, and she'd been too preoccupied with other concerns to pay herself much attention.

There was blood on the front of her dress. She wasn't soaked in it, but it couldn't be missed. And she knew on the instant where it had come from. "Ensio's," she said.

Hawk shifted his hands to her face, cupping her cheeks. "You're sure you ain't hurt?"

"Certain." Liesl studied his face. A long gash marred his cheek, and a series of small cuts peppered his jaw and forehead. "You're hurt, though." Worried, she eyed him up and down. He had cuts on his hands too. Dots of blood on his sleeves.

"Put away the panic, Liesl. I ain't been shot or roughed up. It's glass from the windows."

"In the marshal's office?" She'd been afraid he might've been hurt in whatever happened there.

"You weren't the only target tonight," Paisley said to Liesl. "If Hawk had been standing by any of those windows when they were shot through, he'd likely be dead."

Dead.

Hawk didn't look shaken. Angry, yes. But firm and resolved. "What I can't sort out is how Reynolds and Kersey managed to shoot

Ensio, fire off another shot, and shoot out the windows on two different sides of the jailhouse all in the same instant."

Liesl knew the answer to that. "Mr. Larsen's been going through the papers we gave him and discovered the Charming Chaps have *three* accomplices, not just the two we've been watching."

"Three?" His gaze flicked to Mr. Larsen.

Mr. Larsen nodded. "The telegrams received by the Charming Chaps included information from the prisoners in Laramie, but prisoners aren't permitted to send telegrams."

"*From* the prisoners?" Liesl hadn't realized that bit. "Not just *about* them?"

Mr. Larsen nodded.

"Criminey," Paisley muttered. "Reynolds ain't the only one we're looking for."

"Whoever this third person is," Mr. Larsen said, "he can visit the prisoners often without drawing too much notice. He must feel sure he can send threatening messages to a sheriff without raising eyebrows." He looked at Hawk. "*And* he knows your movements. There's really only one group of people who can do all those things."

Hawk muttered under his breath, his expression darkening like a storm cloud.

Paisley wasn't so tight-lipped. "You've got a Judas among your deputies, Hawk. One who tried to kill you tonight."

Hawk didn't argue with that stark evaluation.

Paisley pulled out a writing pad and a lead pencil from a pocket in her dress and began writing out what Liesl suspected was a list of Hawk's deputies.

"Can I assume I'm not a suspect since I haven't been to Laramie in months?" Paisley asked, not sounding the least offended that she might've been suspicious otherwise.

"It ain't you." Hawk began pacing the small office.

Paisley scratched an entry off her list.

"Mr. Larsen and I also don't think it's Ensio, seeing as he was shot," Liesl said. "Unless, of course, that was an accident or a ruse to make him seem above suspicion."

"Injured as much as he is," Paisley said, "I think we can safely say him being shot wasn't a strategy he agreed to."

"Ensio's alive, then?" Relief pressed sharply against her ribs. She'd wondered about Ensio but warning Hawk had been her priority.

Hawk looked back at her. "He ain't gonna be dancing at any socials for a while, but he's alive. And Doc says he'll stay that way. His life ain't in any danger."

Hawk's pacing took him past her once more. But he didn't continue on. Instead, he stopped and wrapped his arms around her. He lowered his head and pressed his forehead to hers. "You have no idea how panicked I've been since you disappeared."

She smiled. "You don't panic."

"Well, John Butler does."

She could feel her heart lighten despite the worries that still plagued them all. "*He* doesn't panic either. He worries. He cares. But he's as calm and cool as a mountain stream."

"Well, someone was panicking."

"That's a terrible thing to say about Paisley," she said, infusing her voice with as much teasing as she could.

Hawk laughed, and he pulled her even closer.

Liesl glanced at Paisley, wanting to make certain her jest hadn't given offense. Paisley only smiled. It was little wonder they'd been so believable as brother and sister. She and Hawk had a similar sense of humor and didn't mind teasing each other.

"As much as I'm enjoying holding you," Hawk said, "we need to figure out where this threat is coming from."

"Are you enjoying it?" she asked softly.

"How could I not be?"

"You ain't exactly been warm and loving lately."

"I'm navigating an unknown path, lamb. And I'm making a heap of wrong turns."

Lamb. She would never grow tired of hearing that endearment. Hawk brushed a kiss to her forehead, then stepped away once more. The deep cut on his cheek reminded Liesl to keep her focus, though she was sorely tempted to lose herself in the all-too-brief moment of tenderness.

"We don't need to be worried about Kersey," Paisley said. "And we know Reynolds is still around, but only Liesl and the Charming Chaps can identify him by sight."

"My mother can," Liesl said. "But I want her to stay at Tansy's and keep clear of all this."

Hawk nodded. "Tansy's as reliable as the day is long. No safer place."

And more than that, Mother was happy there.

"Why is it we don't need to worry about Mr. Kersey?" Liesl asked.

"He's dead." Hawk turned and began pacing across the room again.

Although the man had made every attempt to kill her and Ensio, Liesl still found herself shaken. "He was shot in the gunfire?"

Paisley's eyes remained on her writing pad. "Yes. And he had a gun in his hand. So either he's the one who shot Ensio, or he was part of shooting at Hawk through the windows."

Her heart seized painfully at the thought of Hawk being targeted, still being in danger.

Mr. Larsen pulled a chair out from the table. "You should sit," he whispered to her. "You look a little unsteady on your feet."

That was wise. She sat and tried to breathe.

"We gotta catch this traitor." Hawk's voice took on an edge of frustration. "Can't simply go by who seems above suspicion, because they all do. If they'd seemed at all suspicious, I'd never've hired them in the first place, and I certainly wouldn't keep 'em. But someone among them's a dirty scoundrel."

Mr. Larsen pulled a thick envelope from the inside pocket of his coat and began thumbing through the contents. "One of the telegrams with information from the prisoners arrived"—Mr. Larsen selected a piece of paper and looked it over before nodding—"four weeks ago. Were any of your deputies in Laramie then?"

"Any number of 'em could have been, except for Paisley and Ensio."

"You know Ensio wasn't there?" Liesl pressed.

Paisley nodded. "He was overseeing some difficulties in the town of Sunset."

Hawk looked relieved to have found a reason to take Ensio off the list. "I know for certain that Nick, Li, and Thad were in Laramie on official business. But any of the rest could've been there without me knowing it."

"We ain't narrowing this down much, are we?" Liesl said.

"Without a little more information, I don't see how we could be."

"I can send a telegram to a lawyer associate of mine in Laramie," Mr. Larsen said. "I could ask him which of your deputies has been in Laramie during the last month. Perhaps he can discover who has been visiting Rod Carlisle or Hepp Minor at the territorial prison."

"That could help." Paisley looked up from her list.

Hawk shook his head. "We can't afford to start any whispers. It's bad enough I ain't sure *I* can trust my deputies. If the people of this territory decide the same thing, we're sunk."

That was a complication Liesl hadn't considered. Finding out someone amongst the deputies was a dirty double-crosser would undermine the territory's faith in their marshal.

Hawk stopped his pacing and stood, his feet shoulder width apart, thumbs hooked on his gun belt. He was all marshal, except for the look in his eyes when he glanced her way. That was John Butler. How could she have ever thought John Butler had been a lie or an act? And how was it Hawk didn't see that he was *both* men?

"I can't promise my associate will have any useful information about prison visitors," Mr. Larsen warned.

"If not, we'll sort out a new strategy," Hawk said. "Maybe we dangle a deal in front of one of the Charming Chaps. Plenty of criminals will spill their secrets to avoid the noose."

"The dirty deputy warned them to keep mum," Liesl said. "Threatened them. Knowing he has some ability to skirt the law, they might be too terrified to turn on him no matter what you might promise them in return."

"In the meantime," Paisley said, "we don't know where the danger's coming from, but we *do* know that danger knows where to find you, Hawk. Made a fine mess of your home and office."

"As much as it will annoy you"—Liesl gave Hawk a significant look—"you need to keep hidden while this web is unraveled. You had too close a call tonight."

"So did you." Hawk pushed out a breath. "I ain't fond of hiding, but giving Reynolds and this dirty deputy fewer targets would simplify our search. But we'd need to find a place close enough to town for me to stay informed and act quickly."

Mr. Larsen pulled a ring of keys from his pocket, flipping through them. "I sometimes meet with people who need legal advice at the land office, but only ever on the ground floor. There's a room upstairs that no one's ever used but me. The building locks, but so does that room, and it locks with a different key. You're welcome to use it for as long as you need."

Hawk's forehead creased fiercely. "I don't like being forced into hiding."

"Neither did I," Liesl said, "but I ain't letting you grumble your way out of being safe any more than you'd let me."

Mr. Larsen handed Hawk two keys.

"Narrow that list down as quickly as you can," Hawk said to Paisley.

"I intend to." Paisley turned to Liesl. "When he gets antsy, remind him that getting himself killed won't help any of us."

Liesl squared her shoulders. "I intend to."

Chapter 29

Hawk slipped inside the back of the land office and up a narrow set of stairs, Paisley and Liesl close on his heels. At the top was a door that opened with the key that hadn't worked on the outer one. The interior room had a window covered in heavy fabric that blocked all light coming in or out. A lantern inside wouldn't be seen from the street. No wonder he'd not had any idea Liesl had been hiding there during the grueling and endless time he'd not been able to find her.

The room was completely empty, not a stick of furniture to be seen. All three of them sat on the floor, gathered around the only lantern they had and the only source of light.

"Larsen has a duplicate key to the outer door," Paisley said. "He'll report to you once he hears from his contact in Laramie."

Liesl scooted closer to him, settling herself directly beside him. No matter his heavy mind, no matter his frustration, he couldn't resist putting his arms around her again. Seeing her at the door of the MacNamaras' kitchen had broken what little resolve he had left to keep a distance from her.

She was alive. And she was there. And he needed her.

Hawk tucked her up against him, tightening his arms around her. He pressed a light kiss to her temple. It was fortunate Paisley was there instead of Cade, otherwise he'd have endured a heap of hassling for this.

"Did Dr. MacNamara take a look at all the cuts you got tonight?" Liesl asked.

"He did. The deep one on my face is the only one he looked twice at."

"That worries me a little too," she said quietly.

"It ain't as bad as it looks."

Leaning more fully against him, she said, "But it could have been worse."

She stayed there in his arms, and he took strength in it. He was certain she was nervous—she had every right to be—but she wasn't falling apart. She wasn't breaking under the strain. A man in his position couldn't hope for any kind of connection with a woman who didn't have steel in her backbone. Even then, it wasn't always enough. The far bigger risk was him losing his edge.

He'd already seen it starting. When she disappeared. When he'd feared she was dead. When she'd reappeared and he hadn't had the presence of mind to do anything but hold her and try not to fall apart.

But he wasn't willing to walk away from her. He loved her too much for that. But thawin' his heart of ice would be a liability, no two ways about it. And the Marshal Hawking this territory needed couldn't have any weaknesses. Of course, *that* Marshal Hawking oughtta be able to pick deputies who weren't slitherin' snakes. Everything he'd done as marshal, everything he was to Wyoming, was falling down around him.

"I can stay as long as you think it's helpful," Paisley said. "Cade's on patrol at the moment, so I don't have to go hunting for our runaway shooters. Beyond that, I can also run messages for you without being in the same danger you are."

Hawk nodded. "We'll wait until we have word from Larsen."

He rested more of his weight against the wall at his back. Liesl shifted her position to stay resting against him. He forced his mind to slow his spinning thoughts of outlaws and crooked deputies and mortal danger. Liesl was safe, which she hadn't been mere hours earlier, and she was with him. He wouldn't waste a minute thinking about anything but her and knowing she was safe for now.

He might have to give up marshaling to keep her with him. Might find a balance. Could be his turncoat deputy would catch up to him and end that future before it began.

But for this one moment, he was with Liesl. For this one moment, it was enough.

"We've checked the most obvious hiding places about town," Paisley said. "And Andrew has looked into the few abandoned farms and barns scattered around the area. I can't think where else they might be hiding out."

Hawk closed his eyes. "They must be in a place like this—a place where a person can hide in plain sight."

The three of them talked about places to check. Most of what they discussed were places already checked, or places that didn't make a lot of sense. They really couldn't do anything until they had more information.

"Hawk?" Paisley's voice had dropped to a whisper.

He opened an eye.

Paisley nodded toward Liesl. "She's asleep."

He looked down at her, tucked against him in his arms. "Flick my coat over her, will you? It's a bit of an icehouse in here."

Paisley managed it without making a sound. "I'll bring you blankets and such next time I'm here."

"Good idea." He watched her a moment as she slept. If they didn't both survive what was coming . . .

"How do you do it, Pais? You and Cade? Loving each other when everything's so dangerous?"

"Everything being dangerous just means we don't take our love for granted. And it means we're careful when we can be."

When we can be. "Sometimes it ain't an option."

"I know."

For the second time since meeting her, Hawk awoke with his arm around Liesl Hodges. This time, however, the realization was comforting rather than confusing. Paisley had kept watch for hours, and her vigilance had allowed Hawk to rest, rebuilding his strength for what likely lie ahead. And Liesl had slept soundly beneath the blanket of his coat, his arm resting around her shoulders.

A quiet knock at the door told him why he was suddenly alert. Even asleep, he'd been aware of approaching footsteps.

"Larsen?" Paisley, standing not far off, mouthed the name.

It likely was, but they had to be certain.

Paisley moved to the door, still quiet as the prairie before a storm.

"Periwinkle," was the quiet word from the other side, the one they'd chosen as a sign between them all.

Paisley let Mr. Larsen inside and then locked the door quickly behind him.

Hawk kept where he was, though Liesl had woken when Larsen entered.

"I have information from Laramie." His tone was serious. "The prisoners who've been getting information to the Charming Chaps escaped a week ago. And a few days back, my colleague read a report that they'd been found dead. Shot."

"Which of my deputies had been visiting him before his escape?" Hawk asked.

"He didn't know. All he could tell me was that Rod Carlisle and Hepp Minor escaped and are dead."

Blast it.

"As unexpected as that is," Larsen continued, "it isn't the worst of it."

Hawk met Paisley's eye and saw the same apprehension he felt.

"I had a chance to glance at the mayor's telegram records," Larsen said. "The report that you got a little while back about paperwork and discoveries in Sand Creek—"

Hawk nodded, urging him to get going.

"—those telegrams didn't come in on the line from Sand Creek. Mayor Brimble says they most likely came from Luthy."

Luthy? That town was in the wrong direction. And it was less than a day's journey from Savage Wells.

"Nick sent those telegrams," Paisley said. "But not, apparently, from Sand Creek like he said."

"Looks that way." Larsen wore a solemn expression.

Blast it. "Nick lied about where he was and what he was doing," Hawk said. "Why he implicated one of his co-conspirators, I don't know, but I think it's clear he's our traitor."

Liesl shifted, so he adjusted his arms, keeping her comfortably held against him.

"Could be he's eliminating witnesses," Paisley said. "Could be he helped Carlisle and Minor escape, intending all along to silence them permanently. The more people who are removed from the equation, the less likely he is to be revealed for who he is and what he's doing."

"He did warn the Charming Chaps to keep quiet about all they were doing," Larsen said. "They've made massive amounts of money with this deed-swapping scheme. Getting rid of the others involved means not having to share the profits with so many people."

"That don't explain why Nick's looking to kill me," Hawk said. "He'll get no money out of that."

"But he might get a job." Paisley met his eye. "I've never heard him say as much, but I'm beginning to wonder if he's planning to angle for your job and needs you out of the way. If he were running this territory on the right side of the law, he could get away with anything he wants on the wrong side of it."

A massive plot, an unrepentant traitor and murderer, and all of it right under his nose. He'd missed all of it.

"He must have suspected Rod and Hepp were going to squeal," Paisley said. "He wouldn't likely have taken such a risk otherwise."

"And he must think the Charming Chaps are likely to turn on him too, or he'd not risk coming here and giving himself away."

Even without the Chaps saying anything, Nick's involvement was being sorted out. He'd have been far smarter to scamper off and escape while the getting was good.

"Who's on patrol right now" Liesl asked.

"Cade," Paisley said. "I didn't dare draw attention by talking to him on account of I was coming back here. But I saw him."

Liesl sat up straighter. "He wouldn't be away from the jailhouse if Andrew wasn't there."

That was true.

"Ever since the Charming Chaps arrived, he's made certain there was always two people standing guard. I can't imagine he's changed that. But you two are here. So, who's the second person at the jail right now?"

He hadn't thought of that. It couldn't be Ensio; he was still recuperating at Gideon and Miriam's.

"Who would Cade trust to stand guard?" Hawk asked Paisley.

"Not many people."

Liesl leaned back from him, looking at him with worried eyes. "He'd trust a Deputy US Marshal, especially one he thought you trusted."

Nick.

Paisley must have pieced that together at the exact moment he did. They shot to their feet in unison.

"Nick is planning to kill you, Hawk." Liesl scrambled to her feet as well, Hawk's coat in her hands. "You leave here, and you'll be in danger."

"Now that I know Nick is our rat, I have to try to stop him." He gently took his coat from Liesl. "And I need you to stay safe."

He tucked his hand behind her neck, pulling her near enough to kiss her, a fervent and desperate kiss, one of longing and worry, but one he refused to think of as a farewell.

Her fingers brushed his face, the tenderness of the gesture contrasted by the twinge of pain from the gash on his cheek. One more quick kiss, then he pulled back. He couldn't delay, couldn't remain. He didn't dare allow himself to be tempted into doing just that.

"Keep away from the window." He gave her one last look before forcing himself away.

He and Paisley rushed down the stairs and out the back door, closing and locking it behind them. Weapons drawn and at the ready, they moved toward the jailhouse.

The door was hanging on a hinge. The front window was broken.

They rushed inside to find the table overturned, the doors of the cells flung open, the cells themselves empty. Mr. Kirkpatrick lay on the floor in a pool of blood. Slumped on the floor against the desk was Andrew.

Paisley rushed over to him while Hawk searched the back room. When he stepped outside again, Paisley said, "He's alive, but he's taken a mighty blow to the head."

Hawk checked on Kirkpatrick. That man was not so fortunate as Andrew.

"Do you suppose Andrew fired the shot that took him down?" Paisley asked.

"I'd bet my badge it was Nick taking out witnesses."

They had three prisoners on the loose, as well as Reynolds, and a murderous deputy marshal. It was impossible to say how many of the Charming Chaps would survive the culling their lawman executioner meant to enact.

But one thing was certain: once Nick realized the marshal he worked for knew he was part of this criminal ring, his next target would likely be Hawk.

Chapter 30

Savage Wells was eerily quiet. Everyone in town had been warned to stay inside, away from windows, and not answer their doors. Liesl had kept to the upper room of the land office, waiting alone in the disconcerting silence.

Hawk had chosen not to hide the reality of their situation from the townspeople. They had a murderer lurking nearby, one who'd not hesitate to kill again. He'd pleaded with Liesl to remain hidden and safe but hadn't returned to hiding himself, though he'd promised he'd be as careful as he could be.

Footsteps sounded on the stairs beyond the door. Liesl quietly placed herself to the side of the door, out of range of any bullets that might splinter the wood.

"Periwinkle," a voice whispered from the other side.

She carefully opened the door to see Ensio on the other side, one arm in a sling. He stepped inside, and she closed and locked the door behind him.

"I'm a rough-looking guard, but here I am." Ensio eyed the curtained windows.

"Are you healed enough for this?" Liesl asked, nodding to his sling.

Ensio smiled. "My shooting arm is just fine. Hawk figured that was enough to at least be helpful here if needed."

"Hawk sent you?" She couldn't help but smile at the reminder that the man she loved was thinking of her even in such a difficult situation.

"Cade and Paisley are guarding the jail." Ensio lowered himself to sit on the floor, back against the wall, facing the door. "Six more deputy marshals are on their way."

"How are you feeling?"

"Like I've been shot." He shook his head. "I'm hurting, but I don't feel like I'm gonna drop. It was tearing at me not being able to help bring down the lowlife that's been doing all this."

"Neither you nor I are the sort to sit back and do nothing."

"Hawk's fuming, I'll tell you that. He's been betrayed, and he's currently outgunned. He ain't used to that."

"I met Nick when the lot of you were in Sand Creek," Liesl said, sitting near him. "Nothing about him would've made me at all suspicious of him."

"Had you asked me a couple of weeks ago, I would've agreed with you." Ensio adjusted his position, his movements stiff. "Now that I'm looking back, though, I can see there were things that ought to've made us wonder."

"Like what?" she asked.

"Well, he never seemed upset at some of the things we discovered. All of us are a little hardened by the job, but we're still surprised sometimes. There've been things we've come across that'd turn stomachs of steel like ours. None of it seemed to bother him."

"Hawk gives that impression too," Liesl pointed out.

Ensio shook his head. "With Hawk, you could see he was holding himself together so he could keep going—so *we* could. With Nick, it just didn't seem to bother him at all."

Nick, then, was the cold, heartless, unfeeling person Hawk had been told *he* was.

"And there's something Nick said now and then that, looking back, makes me wonder." Ensio's brow creased heavily. "A couple times we were chasing down some no-good fella and were frustrated at not being able to catch up to him or figure out where he was hiding. Nick would say, 'You gotta figure out what a person's willing to risk getting captured for. Lure him with something that matters enough.'" Ensio's mouth twisted in a tight knot of frustration. "It was also a good strategy, so I didn't think much of it. But I remember once he mentioned that even varmints have families." He slowly shook his head again. "What kind of person goes after a person's family?"

"The kind who forces his accomplices out of hiding and kills 'em one by one?" Liesl suggested.

"I know one of those accomplices is your father." Ensio turned concerned eyes on her. "No matter that he's guilty of a lot of things, he's still kin to you. That cain't be an easy thing."

He'd struck at the heart of something she hardly let herself think about. Though she was fully prepared to testify against her father and have him face justice, she didn't relish the consequences of that. But she didn't want to see him murdered in cold blood. No one deserved that.

"Nick has to be shrewd," Liesl said. "Keeping his double-cross secret for as long as he did wouldn't have been a simple thing. So I can't sort out why he would risk being found out by murdering his accomplices and traveling to the very town where the marshal works."

"He either thinks Hawk ain't too bright, or he thinks his own accomplices are going to turn on him, save their own necks by handing over his, and he's desperate to prevent that."

"But Hawk already knows what the Chaps or those prisoners in Laramie would have told him about Nick," Liesl said. "Killing people would make Hawk *more* likely to go after Nick. He's making things worse for himself."

"Or"—Ensio's eyes narrowed—"he's dangling a lure Hawk cain't resist. Maybe he's been hunting Hawk all along. Someone that heartless and calculating likely thinks murdering someone he hates would be worth the risk, especially if he could torture him a little in the lead-up."

There was something in that. "So, what's the lure Nick can't resist?"

Ensio eyed her sidelong. "You thinking of turning Hawk over?"

She shook her head immediately, firmly. "Not a chance of it. I'm only thinking this is the first insight into a weakness of Nick's. There has to be a way to use it to our advantage."

"I wish Hawk was here. He's got the best mind for strategizing I've ever known. You've a mind for it yourself, Miss Hodges."

"Maybe he's a good influence on me."

"Or a bad one." Ensio started to laugh, but stopped himself with a look of pain. "You have yourself a pathetic guard, Liesl."

She stood up and began pacing.

"Another way he's had an influence on you," Ensio said. "He paces when he's sorting things out."

"Helps a person think," Liesl said. "You should try it."

"Sure thing, just as soon as moving about don't make my shoulder hurt." Another laugh ended in a wince.

"Do yourself a favor, Ensio. Quit tryin' to entertain yourself."

He smiled. She continued her pacing and thinking.

If they could find a way to dangle Hawk safely—more safely than they'd dangled her the day before—they might lure Nick into the open. She shook her head. Nick's goal was to kill Hawk. He'd likely just shoot him from a distance.

Think, Liesl.

The lure had to be something Nick wanted but couldn't afford to kill. It had to be something that only had value if unharmed.

What he needed wasn't Hawk, but something he could use to

lure Hawk. He'd likely risk his safety to snatch up whatever that was but wouldn't want to damage it.

Something to lure Hawk with. Or someone.

Someone.

She turned slowly back to face Ensio. "I know what we can use to lure Nick out of hiding."

He watched her without answering, without moving, but his already pale face lost even more color. After a breath, he said, "What's that?"

"Me."

Chapter 31

Hawk was holding his breath.

A letter had been posted around town, nailed to various pillars and fences, informing the fugitives that Sheriff Hodges's daughter wished to know if he was still alive. She requested to see him in person and know his condition. It was a double back on the strategy they were using with Nick. The dirty deputy would dangle in front of Liesl something he felt she thought was worth risking her safety for in order to dangle her in front of Hawk as something he was willing to risk his safety for. They'd gone from playing checkers to chess.

Hawk replayed their plan in his head over and over again as he stood in the shadows. Their earlier plot to let Liesl be seen by Reynolds and Kersey had carried some risk. But, then, she'd only been passing by on the off chance that she'd be noticed in the distance. Today, she was literally stepping out into the empty road to face down a murderer.

He hated it.

They'd gone through every scenario, tried to anticipate every complication. Cade and Paisley would be positioned on either side of the street, weapons at the ready. Hawk's six deputies had arrived in town the night before, and they were spread out on rooftops and behind windows and buildings, all ready to do what needed to be done. Ensio was stationed at a window as well, ready to help as much as his injuries would allow.

Even if Nick had let the remaining three Charming Chaps live and had connected with Reynolds, he would be outnumbered and outgunned.

Hawk only hoped his own preparations were enough.

He was positioned in a room above the bank, window open, and curtains parted a crack. He could see the street, but he couldn't be seen *from* the street. They had regularly checked this place when trying to locate Reynolds, Nick, and the Chaps.

Li stood next to him, hidden as well. He wasn't the crack shot Paisley was, but he was a quick thinker and could run like the devil was chasing him. A fast response was crucial in deadly situations.

The hour had arrived. Nothing could be heard in Savage Wells beyond the constant whirl of the wind. The townspeople were safely holed up with friends on farms out in all directions. The only people left in the place were Hawk, Paisley and his other deputies, Cade, Andrew, and Liesl.

His Liesl.

She stepped out of the MacNamaras' home and onto the deserted street. She knew how many guns there were, how many people were looking out for her safety. But she was standing alone and unarmed, prepared to meet not only one murderer but potentially a whole heap of 'em.

"This better work," Hawk muttered.

"It will," Li whispered. He couldn't be certain of that, but Hawk appreciated the sentiment, just the same

He'd been dead wrong about Nick. He'd blasted better not've been wrong about any of the others.

"Made of steel." Li tipped his chin toward Liesl, standing on the street below.

Few people had backbone enough to do what she was doing.

And she'd done it twice now. This time, though, she was standing there on her own.

She didn't speak, didn't look around. Nothing in her posture or glances gave away the location of her protectors. Nick would know there'd be people looking out for her, but where and how many needed to be a surprise.

Dust spun about in whirls and twists. A dry tangle of weeds blew across the road. Still, Liesl didn't move, didn't flinch. She simply waited. Hawk swore he could feel all of his deputies holding their breaths.

We're guarding you, lamb. You're not alone.

A moment later, Sheriff Hodges emerged from the other side of the hotel and began walking down the center of the dirt road, directly toward his daughter.

Hawk glanced up at his lookouts on the roof. They were holding steady. He couldn't see Cade and Paisley from where he was, but he trusted them to have their wits about them. Andrew was in a tree on the other side of town, watching for any arrivals who might decide to make a surprise appearance.

"Are you hurt?" Liesl asked her father. Her voice was steady, but there was concern in it, concern that didn't sound feigned.

"Not everyone's expendable." A cold answer. Fitting.

Deputies still holding steady. Town still quiet. Out on the streets, the family reunion continued.

"You shouldn't've come here, Liesl," Sheriff Hodges said. "You should've stayed in Sand Creek where you belong."

"Mr. Kirkpatrick is dead," she said. "I don't know if you've heard."

Nothing in Hodges's expression changed. No flash of regret or mourning. No relief or gladness. Nothing.

"And Mr. Kersey from Sand Creek," Liesl said. "He's dead too."

Keep him talking, Liesl. She was giving them all time to spot Nick.

"People die," Sheriff Hodges said. "Not much to be done about that."

"And people lie," Liesl said. "You taught me that."

"Too bad you ain't never had much skill for it," Mr. Hodges said. "You're weak. Like your mother."

Hawk breathed through a surge of anger. Too much was at stake for even a single misstep.

"Are Mr. Dana and Mr. Yarrow still alive?" she asked. "I've been worried you all were dead."

Sheriff Hodges shrugged. "Some people are more useful than others."

Liesl was too persistent to leave it at that. "They weren't useful?"

"Not any longer."

Facing her father's inhuman indifference, Liesl remained firm. "Are you?"

A shot rang out. On instinct, Hawk crouched but kept his eyes on the street. Liesl was still standing, thank the heavens.

Her father, however, was not.

Hawk couldn't tell if he was breathing, if he was alive.

Liesl took a step toward her father, but a voice stopped her.

"Stay where you are." Coming up behind where the sheriff had stood, sauntering casually as if he were out for a leisurely stroll, was Nick, his gun drawn.

He stopped closer to Liesl than her father had, but he didn't look at her. His eyes darted around the surrounding buildings and windows. "I know you're out there, Hawk. I know how your mind works. And *you* know I can outshoot all but one of your deputies."

Paisley. She could outshoot everyone in the territory, likely most everyone in the world.

"I want both O'Briens out here, hands up where I can see 'em, no weapons in sight." Nick raised his weapon and pointed it directly at Liesl. "If someone tries to shoot, I'm fast enough that she'll be dead before I am."

Hawk knew better than to take the bait and reveal his location. He also knew not to call Nick's bluff. Thankfully, Cade and Paisley understood that as well. They emerged a moment later from their respective hiding places exactly as Nick had requested.

"How long was Reynolds useful to you?" Liesl asked Nick.

"Long enough."

With that, Liesl had managed to find out how many accomplices Nick had, how many guns he still had on his side. The fact that he was alone actually made him more dangerous. He had nothing to gain from this standoff other than seeing Hawk dead and anyone else he thought necessary. He had to have known there was no way out of this for him, no escape. A man with nothing to lose and a heart as cold as ice wasn't likely to be merciful or logical.

"And did you hear that six other deputy marshals have arrived in Savage Wells? Don't those odds seem uneven to you?" Liesl said.

"I'm getting impatient, Marshal," Nick shouted as he stepped right up beside Liesl, the barrel of his gun nearly touching her head. "Are you gonna show your face? Or are you letting a woman do your heavy lifting?"

Liesl didn't flinch.

"Killing her won't get me what I want," Nick shouted, looking up at each of the buildings in turn, his six-shooter unwavering. "But taking this prize with me . . . Well, that could be fun." His sinister smile sent shivers down Hawk's spine.

His deputies were at the ready, but his sharpest shooter still stood in full view with her hands up, unable to take a shot.

"We need a distraction," Hawk whispered to Li.

Nick needed to lower his weapon for just a moment. Look away for just an instant. Someone might be able to take the shot. But Liesl was right there. So close. There was risk, but there was no avoiding it.

Hawk met Li's eye. Neither said anything. Li nodded.

Hawk slipped out of the room, down the stairs, and into the

shadows on the side of the building. He took a deep breath, then he stepped out into the street.

"You say you know me, Nick. So what am I thinking now?"

Nick whirled in his direction. It changed the angle of Nick's weapon enough that if he pulled the trigger, he'd miss Liesl, but barely. But shooting *him* without hitting *her* would take a steady hand and a sure aim that no one short of Paisley had.

A shot pierced the air.

Nick's gun dropped from his hand. Another shot, and his right leg gave out under him. A third, and his left crumbled.

Liesl, still standing in the same place, kicked Nick's gun far away from him.

Hawk didn't waste a moment. He rushed toward Liesl, all the while searching for the source of the gunfire. Paisley didn't have a weapon in her hands. None of his deputies could've made those shots.

Hawk stopped directly beside Liesl, his gun trained on the traitor.

"Are you whole?" he asked Liesl.

"Entirely."

Who'd made the shot? Who but Paisley could have? Cade, maybe, but he was unarmed as well.

Tansy stepped from the millinery and ribbon shop and out onto the street. Her gun was in her hand as she moved to where Nick lay moaning, his hand and legs bleeding.

She looked down at him in disgust. "Women have *always* done more than our fair share of heavy lifting. Never forget that."

With that, Tansy put her six-shooter in her holster and walked away.

Chapter 32

Liesl's heart beat a terrified rhythm in her chest. Somewhere, hovering just out of reach in her mind, she knew Hawk was there, Nick was down, and she was safe. But she didn't *feel* safe. The street, which had been still as a lake on a windless day, was now filled with movement as Hawk's deputies moved from their positions and Cade and Paisley rushed over.

Breathing was about all Liesl could manage for the moment. That and pushing out of her memory the sounds of gunfire: the three that had brought down Nick, hitting their marks so close to where she'd stood, and the one she'd feared was coming for her but had taken down her father.

That pulled her gaze to where he lay in the street. Almost like they were moving without her participation, her feet took her toward him. As near she could tell, he'd not moved. But she needed to know. Someone might've called out to her, might've suggested she stay back, but all the sounds in the street were jumbling and swirling together like a dust devil in the desert.

Her father was lying on his side, his back toward the boardwalk, his front facing the street. As she drew nearer, she saw him move. Just a little, but enough to know he wasn't dead. He'd been shot from behind, so she couldn't see where the bullet had hit him, but the thick, blood-colored mud around him told her it weren't a minor injury. But life had taught her not to trust anything to do with him. His six-shooter was on the ground nearby. There was a chance he could've reached it. Before even saying a word, before checking to see how near to death he might be, she kicked it away.

"You dead?" She knelt down on the ground beside him.

"You'd like that," he rasped out.

"I ain't never liked people dying. I ain't like you."

He coughed. The sound was too wet for his lungs to be clear of the blood spilling from him. "You ain't like me. You're weak. Like your ma."

Even with his dying breaths, he couldn't think of a kind thing to say about her or her mother.

She turned back toward the gathering of lawmen not far away. Hawk was walking toward her. She called out to him. "He ain't dead. Send for Doc."

"Where's my gun?" Father's words were slurred and garbled.

"It ain't here."

"Afraid I'd shoot you?"

Why lie to him now by pretending he wasn't the monster he was? "I figured you might."

His eyes opened wider, looking right at her with a glare of hatred so deep, so piercing, it would've been shocking if it had come from anyone other than him. "I would've."

"I know. You celebrated Otto bein' murdered."

"Deserved it," her father rasped. "He tried to stop me."

Footsteps sounded behind her, too slow and measured to be Gideon rushing to give aid. These steps belonged to Hawk; she knew they did without even looking.

Father's eyes shifted, looking just past her. "We should've killed you first."

Hawk hunched down next to him. He set a hand on Liesl's back, but his gaze was on the man lying in front of him. "I'm certain you would've tried, but better men than you have failed at it."

"What do you . . . mean to do with me?" Father was talking quieter now, though Liesl doubted it was on account of being humbled. The man was filled with hate, and she knew how horrible a person he was, but it still hurt watching him suffer, watching him die.

"What I mean to do is see to it Mrs. Hodges has the life she deserves, now that she's free of you. I mean to build a life with her daughter. You will be easily forgotten, nothing but a two-bit criminal everyone hated, even the people you thought respected you. You'll be forgotten, and they will be loved."

Father didn't say anything. Maybe he was out of strength. Maybe he was just mad.

Liesl's mind didn't know what to focus on: the blood pooling on the ground around him, the anger pouring from him, or the fact that Hawk had just casually said he meant to marry her. Without warning. She hadn't often imagined being proposed to, but she'd never thought it'd be in front of a dying criminal.

Just then, Gideon and Miriam arrived and dropped down beside the unrepentant Sheriff Hodges, ignoring his muttered curses and angry words, and Cade called Hawk away.

Though she'd like to think he did so reluctantly, he went back to work, issuing orders to his deputies. He was the marshal of this territory, with responsibilities. And in this moment, after a shoot-out in the street and having learned that somewhere on the outskirts of town were at least three more victims of a double-crossing murderer, he had quite a mess to address.

She stood and took a few steps back from the scene of frantic doctoring. She didn't ask if her father was going to live. In her heart, she already knew. There'd be no trial. When he was buried, there'd be no real grief either. The grief her heart would feel would not be the sorrow of losing him in particular, but from the pain he'd caused.

And she knew she'd never be able to entirely free her mind of the terrifying moments she'd spent standing alone on the street in Savage Wells.

The marshal's office was chaotic, with people coming and going. Hawk was gathering all the information he could from everyone who'd been part of that day's troubles. Paisley had assured Liesl she didn't have to be there, that she could rest in Hawk's room for the rest of the day, but, though she was exhausted to her bones, she didn't want to be alone.

So she sat in a chair in the corner, watching the goings-on, hearing what people were saying but not always listening. Father had been carried back to the MacNamaras' house, where Gideon and Miriam had sewed him up as best they could. Word had come only a few minutes earlier that, while he was still on this side of the ground, he wouldn't be for long.

Nick had been next on their operating table. His wounds weren't life-threatening, but Gideon wasn't keen on leaving lead inside anyone. So he'd sewn up the hole Tansy had shot clear through Nick's hand, then dug out a bullet from each leg.

Liesl listened as Hawk strategized which of his deputies to place where and how to rotate them so he could get the reports he needed without leaving Nick unguarded or the streets unpatrolled. The people who lived in town would be trickling back in. The danger had passed, but it'd do their courage good to see they hadn't been left alone.

At some point—Liesl's mind was spinning so much she couldn't remember precisely when—Hawk had laid his coat around her shoulders. She was wearing it still, its arms too long for her and the coat itself big enough to wrap around her and half again. He likely did it to make certain she wasn't cold, but it did more than that. Though in the same room, he was busy and out of reach. Being engulfed in a coat that smelled like him and felt like him made her feel less alone.

Tansy stepped into the room and walked directly to Hawk.

"Deputy Marshal Li said you needed to gab with me, Marshal?"

"I do," Hawk said. "I wanted to thank you. The shot had to be taken, and the only person I knew of who could make it was unarmed. If you hadn't been there . . . Well, I'd hate to think what would've happened."

"Liesl's important," Tansy said. "All people are important, but she's Mildred's daughter. And Mildred's the only friend I ever had. I wasn't about to let any of them horned toads hurt her."

"Thank you," Hawk said.

"And I know a judge is coming around, but whenever he gets here, you tell him that I ain't sitting through any trial. I won't deny I shot a man, but I didn't kill him. Shot him on account of he'd murdered a lot of people and was about to murder more."

Hawk smiled and dipped his head. "Between myself and Cade and Mr. Larsen, I doubt you'll have reason to ever even tip your hat to the judge."

Tansy's eyes darted about the lawmen gathered there. "Anything else you need from me?"

"You wouldn't consider joining the marshals, would you?" Paisley asked with a smile.

"Being a lawman would be a terrible step down for a moonshiner." Tansy spun around and made her way toward the door, passing Liesl's chair as she did.

"Thank you, Tansy," Liesl said. "For saving me today. But, more than that, for saving my mother. You're the first friend she's ever had too."

Again, Tansy tipped her hat. She left without another word.

Liesl's own dying father had snarled at her that he'd've killed her if he'd been given the chance. Tansy, who had known her no more than a few weeks, had saved her life and declared that she was important. Until she'd left Sand Creek, Liesl'd fought hard to believe that there was value in her at all.

Though she was enjoying Hawk's coat, it wasn't enough. She needed *him*. Maybe he'd finally reached the end of his interviews and report-taking. Just as she was about to rise from her chair, Mr. Larsen arrived. She slumped back, telling herself to be patient.

"I just received a telegram from the circuit judge. He's in Laramie now, but he's coming here directly and should arrive in two or three days."

"Glad to hear it," Hawk said. "Little point stretching this out for weeks, when we can take care of it now."

Mr. Larsen pulled a piece of paper from his inside pocket and unfolded it. "I made what accounting I could for each member of Nick's gang and what their fate was, what we know they were involved in. I thought it might help with your report."

Hawk nodded. "It will, thank you. And it'll help the judge speed things up when he arrives."

Mr. Larsen set the paper on the table. Liesl could make out the words, but only just. Only a couple weeks ago, she would have thought such a list would be shorter than it proved to be.

"I know how complicated all this is likely to be," Mr. Larsen said. "I'll stay at the hotel until the judge leaves so I'll be on hand if I can help."

How different this town was to Sand Creek. Frightening things happened. There was danger and uncertainty. But the people helped each other, even when the difficulties didn't impact them personally. Liesl was glad she and her mother had come here. It'd be a new start for them in so many ways.

Just as Tansy had done, Mr. Larsen paused as he passed her chair.

"Thank you for all you've done," Liesl said. "I'd likely not be alive if not for you."

"You're welcome." His smile was quick and fleeting but also

friendly. That was another thing she liked about Savage Wells. The people were kind and welcoming.

He slipped out.

Liesl stood, thinking maybe now was her chance to finally have a moment of Hawk's time. But he was quickly in deep conversation with his deputies. Liesl sat back at the table and took up the paper Mr. Larsen had left. He'd listed the gang members by their initials. After each were the things they knew each of them had been involved in or plotted to do.

NT—assassinate the marshal, organize criminals, forgery, land theft, murders

That was Nick Tobin.

Her eyes ran past *AK, RD, BY.* The Charming Chaps. At the end of each of their list of crimes, in capital letters, was the word "DEAD." *ER* and *RK.* Everett Reynolds. Rip Kersey. Both marked as dead. The only two who weren't marked dead were Nick and *IH,* her father. But he would be soon enough.

Into her heavy thoughts came Hawk's beloved voice. "Difficult seein' it laid out like that, isn't it?" He stood next to her.

She nodded.

"How are you holding up?" he asked. "It ain't been an easy day."

"Especially since you ain't even held me yet."

His arms enfolded her immediately. "I've wanted to. There are many times I don't like being a marshal. Having to gather all these reports instead of putting my arms around you has proven one of them."

She leaned into him. "Do you often have days like this?"

"Like this? No. All my deputies've said the same thing. They ain't never seen someone like you, Liesl. I suspect that a lot of them'll be spending the weeks to come wondering if they'd have had the courage you showed today. *I'll* be spending a lot of time wondering if I was wrong to go along with the plan that put you in so much danger."

She reached up and gently touched his stubbled cheek, careful of the deep cut there. "It was the only way for us to be safe. That's what I kept thinking. We would be together, and we would be safe. That made it worth doing, even though I was terrified."

Hawk leaned closer and pressed a kiss to her lips. It was soft and tender, not a kiss of passion and heated hearts, but one of gratitude and reassurance, and the promise that what they'd gone through that day would be worth it.

A throat cleared from somewhere behind them. "Were you hoping for a round of applause or an evaluation of your technique?" Thad asked.

Liesl probably should've been embarrassed, but all she could do was laugh. And, heavens, it felt good to laugh.

Hawk met her eyes, looking both amused and annoyed by the interruption. In a voice that was sharp, but somehow still laughing, he answered the question. "If the three of you don't make yourselves scarce in the next three seconds, I'll have a few criticisms of my own."

With chuckles and joking decrees that Hawk was being unfair, his deputies left.

"You realize, Liesl," Hawk said, still holding her, "if you toss your lot in with me, my deputies will likely tease you mercilessly the rest of your life."

"Did you mean what you said to my father?" she asked. "Do you really want to marry me?"

He slipped his arms under the coat and wrapped them around her waist, a closer touch and more tender embrace. "I'm thinking about it."

"Tansy did say I was very important." As much as his deputies liked to tease her, she loved to tease him. His smile never failed to send her heart swirling about.

"I've wanted to marry you for some time now, but the life of a marshal ain't simple or safe. And I certainly couldn't ask you while the Charming Chaps and all they were doing hung over our heads. But that ain't a worry now."

"I have Mr. Larsen's list to prove that."

"What did he put with the initials *HB*?" His expression changed quickly. She knew he wasn't unhappy about their current close arrangement; his marshal's mind was just spinning again.

"Those initials ain't on the list."

"Do me a favor, lamb. Let me keep one arm around you while I look at that list."

"I'll suffer," she said, "but I'll do it."

With an all too quick kiss on her lips, he made the adjustment. And, with the arm that wasn't still snaked around her, he took the list she'd been holding.

"Wonder why Larsen didn't put Harry Bendtkirk on here. It's his name on all the stolen land deeds."

"I thought we assumed that was a false name."

"I still think it is. But we haven't yet sorted out who that false name belongs to. I can't rest knowing the folks in Sand Creek don't have the deeds to their land."

That was her John Hawking, always thinking about the vulnerable people and wanting to do right by them.

She studied the list again. Nowhere had Mr. Larsen indicated which of the members of the gang he thought was actually Harry Bendtkirk.

"What if we can't ever figure it out?" she asked. "Will the people in Sand Creek never get their land back?"

"They will," Hawk said, "but it'd happen faster if we knew that bit of it."

Each man represented by the initials on the page had been capable of playing a dirty trick on people. Some were smarter than others, but they were all clever enough to piece together a scheme like this. And all of them benefited from it except the two blokes in the Laramie prison.

All the others.

All.

"Wait a minute."

"You think of something?" Hawk asked.

She ran her fingers down the line of initials. "If you take out the two prisoners in Laramie—Mr. Larsen didn't put 'stealing land' or 'forgery' by their names—all the letters left—" She double-checked in her mind, but she was certain she was right. "Harry Bendtkirk." She looked up at him. "Their initials, rearranged, spell 'Harry Bendtkirk.'"

"I'll be dognabbed." His eyes widened. "This gives us a trail. I'd wager with this information, Mr. Larsen, his colleague in Laramie, and Mr. Dressen in Sand Creek could sort it out."

"Everything'll be better in Sand Creek," she whispered.

"They owe it to you, lamb. And not merely because you sorted this latest mystery."

She stepped back a little, just enough to look at him straight on. "Will you think me terribly selfish if I don't want to go back there? I could help them through all this, and I likely should, seeing as their difficulties are due to my family, but I don't want to leave Savage Wells. I don't want to go back to that place where everything was so terrible."

Hawk set down Mr. Larsen's list and took both her hands with his. He raised them, one at a time, to his lips. "I'd like you to stay here too, Liesl. Not because I'm a coward or think you are—you ain't, in case that thought enters your mind again. Savage Wells is my home, and I cain't imagine it without you here."

"Neither can I," she said. "John Hawking, you are home to me."

She hooked her arms around his neck, just as he set his around her once more.

"I love you," she said.

"And I love you more than I thought I could. You taught me that love ain't weakness."

"Promise that after you finish each new marshaling trip, you'll always come back here, back home to me?"

"Always," he whispered in the breath before he kissed her once more. This time, it was the fervent heart-pounding kiss of a man who'd found love and a woman who meant to claim it.

Chapter 33

It took weeks for Savage Wells to recover from the enormity of all that had happened. They'd known violence before—few Western towns hadn't—but the trail of destruction Nick had left was vast. But, as the town had always done, they'd seen each other through and emerged stronger than ever.

It was against this backdrop of relief and happiness that Hawk arrived at the Savage Wells chapel and schoolhouse on a bright, sunny morning. He wore his best trousers and vest, along with the only jacket he had that wasn't worn at the seams. He'd shined up his badge and pinned it in place, taken extra care with his hair, given his teeth the twice-over with powder. He stood at the front of the chapel, wondering why so many men were unsure on their wedding day.

Hawk had never been more sure of anything in his life.

Cade stood beside him. The church was full, the walls echoing with conversations. Liesl and her mother had endeared themselves to the entire town, and then had solidified that admiration through Liesl's unflinching bravery and Mrs. Hodges's immediate acceptance and friendship with Tansy, who was cared about by all and sundry.

Hawk didn't for a moment think the town was as happy for

him as they were for Liesl. He liked her too much to think anyone wouldn't be entirely partial to her.

"You nervous, old man?" Cade asked.

"Not at all," he said.

"Likely because you figured this day would never come. You're too relieved to be nervous."

Hawk chuckled. "I won her over as John Butler. By the time she discovered I'm actually a grumpy, miserable wretch she was too in love with me to change her mind."

"I think she likes that you're a grumpy, miserable wretch sometimes."

Hawk smiled to himself. He thought so too. And that was nothing short of a miracle. He'd not for a moment believed he'd find someone who would love him as entirely as she did.

Everyone turned toward the door. While the conversations didn't entirely stop, they did grow quieter. The bride had arrived.

She wore a simple calico gown and carried a bouquet of wildflowers. He'd never seen anyone look as radiant as she did in that moment. He smiled as she approached, and she smiled back.

No, there were no nerves today. Only joy.

The ceremony was simple, without any extra frills or distractions. The preacher declared them married, and the town cheered. Hawk didn't have to be told twice to kiss his bride, and she certainly didn't object.

They made their way through the chapel to the well-wishes of their neighbors. As he passed Ensio and Li, they exchanged knowing looks. He'd placed them in charge of the territory for the next three weeks. Paisley had been his first choice, but she'd turned him down flat.

"Get someone else to fill in," she said. "You ain't the only person wanting to spend a little time with a loved one."

Her work as a deputy marshal kept her apart from Cade. He was beginning to understand what a sacrifice that really was.

Hawk stepped out into the sun with his bride. The warm light brought a glow to her cheeks. He pressed a kiss to her temple, still struggling to believe his good fortune. They climbed up onto the wagon and waved farewell to those gathered around to see them off.

Liesl leaned against him as they rode from town. She'd done that in Sand Creek when they'd driven back together. For so long he'd worried that only John Butler would ever receive that kind of affection and tenderness. He'd told himself then that he'd have to learn to live without it.

He'd never been so glad to be wrong.

"Three whole weeks away from marshaling," Liesl said. "You're going to be miserable." A laugh lay in her words.

How easily he smiled when he was with her. "You're facing three whole weeks *with* a marshal. You're going to be miserable."

She threaded her arm through his. "At least we'll be miserable together."

His grin still firmly in place, he said, "I am beginning to suspect you like me, Liesl Hawking."

She stretched up and kissed his jaw. "I love you, John Hawking. Every single thing about you."

Acknowledgments

Jolene Perry, for invaluable information on horses, tack, wagons, and a million other related things I know far too little about.

Annette, Traci, Sian, Jo, and Sammie for writing sprints, accountability, encouragement, and venting sessions.

Thanks to the countless readers who kept hoping Hawk would finally get his happy ending.

Discussion Questions

Discussion Questions

1. Hawk feels torn between the cold-hearted marshal he feels he has to be and the more tender-hearted farmer he temporarily pretended to be. Do you think he'll struggle with that balance in the future? In what ways do we sometimes struggle with our own contradictory views of ourselves?

2. Liesl has spent years trying to save people against an undefeatable threat and hasn't always been successful. What do you think kept her trying? What do you think would have happened to her and her mother and the people of Sand Creek if she had given up?

3. Why do you think Tansy and Mrs. Hodges became such fast friends when neither of them had truly had friends before?

4. Why do you think Tansy kept her sharpshooting ability a secret for so long?

5. Killing the Charming Chaps was Nick's way of keeping them from testifying against him. But his murderous spree is what revealed him to be part of the criminal ring. Why do you think he took such a risk going after his partners in crime when he could have simply fled the territory and kept a step ahead of the

law? Do you think Nick always planned to kill his accomplices? If not, what do you think triggered his destructive spree?

6. What do you imagine lies in the future for Liesl and Hawk, Cade and Paisley, and the people of Savage Wells?

About the Author

Sarah M. Eden is a *USA Today* best-selling author of witty and charming historical romances, including 2019's Foreword Reviews INDIE Awards Gold Winner for Romance, *The Lady and the Highwayman*, and 2020 Holt Medallion finalist, *Healing Hearts*. She is a two-time "Best of State" Gold Medal winner for fiction and a three-time Whitney Award winner.

Combining her obsession with history and her affinity for tender love stories, Sarah loves crafting deep characters and heartfelt romances set against rich historical backdrops. She holds a bachelor's degree in research and happily spends hours perusing the reference shelves of her local library.